Inspector Ravenscroft Detective Mysteries Book 1

THE MALVERN MURDERS

A captivating Victorian historical murder mystery

KERRY TOMBS

JOFFE
BOOKS

Revised edition 2019
Joffe Books, London

First published in Great Britain 2006

Please join our mailing list for free Kindle books and new releases.

www.joffebooks.com

ISBN 978-1-78931-289-8

For Joan, who came to Malvern and stayed, and to Samuel, who joined us there.

PROLOGUE

LONDON, 1887

Ravenscroft looked down at the bundle of rags that lay at his feet, hoping to see some signs of life from within. The only light came from the end of the alleyway and was of little help to him.

He lowered one knee to the rough cobbles and turned back the clothes, knowing what he would find. He had seen many dead bodies before, here in Whitechapel, over the previous few years, but it still came as a shock to him. The victim was a young girl, probably no older than twelve years of age. There were red marks round her throat where she had been strangled. A small trickle of blood, from a wound at the back of her head caused when she had hit the ground, was already staining her clothes. He placed his hand on her face; the body was still warm. A few minutes earlier she would have been making her way along the alleyways that criss-crossed this part of London, perhaps on her way home after visiting some friends or returning from her work in one of the nearby factories. She had been someone's daughter, sister, friend, helper — and now the people that had been known her would be anxiously awaiting her arrival, wondering what was keeping her and why she had not returned.

Ravenscroft searched in the pocket of the girl's apron, placing the contents on the ground. A broken comb, two farthings and the remains of a half-eaten sweet were all that was left behind — all that was left of a life of so few years. In a few minutes he would summon his colleagues and she would be taken away; notices would be posted in the vicinity and within a day or so someone would reclaim the body — and after the inquest she would be buried in an unmarked grave, mourned for a while by those that had known her, but ignored by all those who would come after her. Life in Whitechapel would continue, as it had done before, and whoever had committed this deed would fade back into the shadows, until perhaps someone who knew him gave him away — or worse still, until he struck again.

He covered over the face of the young girl with her shawl, and as he did so, he suddenly became aware of another's presence further down the darkened alleyway. His first impulse was to cry out and request the other's assistance, but then the possibility that it might be the perpetrator of this terrible outrage who now stood silently in the shadows took root in his mind. Ravenscroft realised that he must have arrived on the scene only seconds after the girl had been killed. Her attacker, who must now face a blocked exit at the end of the walkway, had in all probability retreated into the darkness and was waiting his opportunity to make good his escape.

Slowly Ravenscroft rose to his feet and turned in the direction where he sensed the killer was waiting.

'Now then, sir. Step forward and show yourself!' He tried to make his voice confident and full of authority, but he could feel a cold sweat forming on the inside of his collar.

He waited for a few seconds, and receiving no reply took a step forwards.

'It's no good you know. My colleagues will be here in a minute. You cannot escape—' but before he could finish, he found himself thrown against the wall by a force that had emerged from the darkness. Instinctively he reached for his whistle from his coat pocket as his attacker pounded down the narrow passageway.

Ravenscroft sprang to his feet, gave a quick blast on his whistle, and set off in quick pursuit. As he reached the end of the alleyway, he could see his attacker running away from him down the street. A tall figure, his black cloak flapping behind him. Ravenscroft knew that he stood little chance of keeping up with him, even less of apprehending him, but he also knew that he would be expected to make the effort at least. There always remained the possibility that the other would fall or be caught either by one of his colleagues or a passer-by.

He blew his whistle again and shouted, 'Stop!' in a strange voice that seemed unlike his own, before resuming the chase.

The cloak turned left at the end of the thoroughfare. By the time Ravenscroft reached the corner he could feel his breath coming in wheezing gasps, and his face wet with perspiration. He blew on his whistle again, but although the street was full of men returning home from work, old ladies and small children trading their wares, and young women offering their services, no one seemed to be at all interested in either the gentleman in the black cloak or in his pursuer.

He could still see his quarry in the distance and redoubled his efforts. If only the other would turn, perhaps he would be able to catch a glimpse of his features under one of the flickering lights. There was always the chance that Ravenscroft had encountered him in the past, and that such a simple recognition would provide him with a later opportunity for apprehension, but it seemed that he was to be denied even that hope.

Ravenscroft could feel his chest tightening as his lungs began to cloud over with the old affliction. Surely one of his colleagues must have heard the blast from his whistle and come to his aid?

Turning around yet another corner, he briefly lost sight of the black cloak for a moment or so, as he pushed his way through the throng of people who seemed intent on blocking his way. As he drew his sleeve across his spectacles in a futile attempt to clear the sweat that was clouding his vision, he could feel his heart beating loudly and his head throbbing with pain.

As the ever-decreasing black figure disappeared finally from view, Ravenscroft knew that the chase was almost at its end. As he fought for every breath in his body, he felt his world becoming increasingly darker. The buildings on either side began to crowd in on him, as the voices of the street receded into the distance.

'Here look out, mate!' shouted a voice, as he stumbled into one of the passers-by.

Ravenscroft could feel his descent towards the ground and flung out one of his arms in a forlorn attempt to help steady his fall. A sharp pain vibrated through his body, as he hit the hard surface.

As he looked up at the strange faces who stared down at him, he knew that he had again failed to carry out his duty — and felt the darkness of despair closing in upon him.

Then he heard the sound of grinding glass, as someone stamped on his spectacles.

* * *

'Come!'

Ravenscroft opened the door of the office and stepped inside, coughing as he did so.

'Ah, Ravenscroft, take a seat. Be with you in a minute.'

He inched forwards into the centre of the room and seated himself on the carefully placed chair. He hated this inner sanctum of the Yard, with its dusty carpet, drab furniture and rows of ancient ledgers. The familiar smells of damp, decaying wallpaper, and yesterday's stale tobacco smoke, hung together in the air. The solitary, hissing gas lamp on the far wall barely penetrated the gloom and the fire, lit earlier in the day, gave out its last dying glow.

Ravenscroft sighed and recalled the other times when he had been summoned to this room, when the interview had always been depressing, and when the outcome had always been bad — and he knew that after the events of the previous evening he could expect little difference this time. The old clock in the corner ticked out its relentless pattern of sound, as the Commissioner continued his writing.

Ravenscroft attempted to stifle his cough, but without success.

'Won't keep you long,' said his superior, busily engaged in writing on a sheet of paper.

Ravenscroft gazed out of the tiny window, at the grey streets, and the enveloping fog beyond, and wished he was elsewhere.

'Now then, Ravenscroft, this won't do,' said the Commissioner suddenly looking up from his work. 'It will not do at all!'

'I'm sorry. I did my best. He was just too quick for me,' he offered in his own defence, but knowing that his argument would fall on unresponsive ears.

'Yes, but it's not exactly the first time, is it? Look at that fiasco last month, when you let that pickpocket walk out of the station without charging him, to say nothing of the time when that swindler walked out the back door of the bank, just as you were coming in through the front entrance.'

'I wasn't to know he was there, sir.'

'Your conviction rate is the lowest in your division,' said his superior, ignoring his last remark and studying an open file in front of him. 'No, Ravenscroft, this will just not do. It will not do at all. Look at yourself, man. When was the last time you thought of purchasing a new suit? You look absolutely terrible.'

'It's my asthma, sir. I've been plagued with it since I was a boy.'

'What's that do with it? And what has happened to your head?'

'I caught it on the pavement where I fell. The bruise should be gone in a day or so.' He coughed again and felt his chest tightening, as it always did in moments of anxiety.

'How old are you Ravenscroft? Forty-nine, is it?'

'Forty-two last month, sir.'

'Not married, are you?'

'No, sir.'

'Pity, a good wife would take you in hand.'

Ravenscroft allowed himself a brief smile.

'I'm relieving you of duty, as from now,' announced the Commissioner, closing the file shut with a finality that indicated the interview was nearly at its conclusion.

'But, sir, we have a full case load at the present. If only—' he began, though he knew already that his protest would have little success.

'Abberline will take over your cases. I'm ordering you to take two weeks' leave. I will review your future with this force upon your return.'

The Commissioner picked up his pen again and resumed his writing. Ravenscroft rose slowly to his feet. He knew that it would be futile to engage in any further debate. He made his way across towards the door.

'Malvern!' shouted the other suddenly.

'I'm sorry, sir?'

'Malvern! Go to Malvern and take the water cure. My wife went there last year and came back several pounds lighter and with a fresh glow in her cheeks. She swears by it. Yes, Malvern, that's the place. It will do you a world of good. Plenty of fresh air and exercise, that's what you need. Malvern might also help to get rid of that damn cough of yours.'

'Yes, sir,' replied Ravenscroft unenthusiastically.

He closed the door behind him and made his slow way down the old, well-worn staircase, and along the dank corridor, until he emerged once more into the fog-bound streets of London.

* * *

6

The guard had already raised his flag as Ravenscroft hurriedly made his way along platform number 7 of Paddington Station. The reception hall had been filled with crowds of people, and he had been forced to queue for his ticket and was now in grave danger of the train leaving before he could find a seat. He peered anxiously into several of the compartments but found them all fully occupied. He paused for a moment and lowered his case to the floor, as his cough threatened to erupt for the third time since his arrival at the station.

At the sound of a whistle blowing, he realised that the train was about to leave without him. Quickly he swept up his case, dashed further along the platform and flung open one of the doors just as the train began to move.

'I'm so sorry,' he apologised breathlessly to his fellow passengers, as he hastily placed his case on the rack and found himself sitting in the only available seat. He removed his handkerchief from his pocket and wiped his brow and spectacles, coughing again as he did so, before letting out a deep sigh. At least he had not been compelled to wait for the next departure.

As the train began to draw away from the station, Ravenscroft opened his newspaper and turned to one of the inside pages, where a certain story caught his attention.

YOUNG FEMALE KILLED IN
WHITECHAPEL

On Tuesday evening a young female, not above thirteen years of age, was found murdered in the Whitechapel area of London. An inquest held yesterday revealed that the girl had been strangled by a person or persons unknown in a narrow alleyway leading off Brick Lane. At present the identity of the girl is unknown, but we have learned that the police authorities have posted several bills with details of her identity in the hope that someone who knows the deceased may come forward to claim her. Several citizens of the area stated that they saw a tall figure wearing a long black cloak leaving the scene of the crime in some haste. We learn that a member of the local constabulary gave chase but that he was unsuccessful in his attempts to apprehend the felon . . .

Ravenscroft lowered his paper — 'a member of the local constabulary gave chase but was unsuccessful'. He closed his newspaper, placed his head on the back of his seat and looked out of the window. The train was beginning to pick up speed as it passed the long rows of ugly tenement buildings on either side of the track.

He turned to study his travelling companions. Ravenscroft occupied the corner seat by the window. Next to him a young couple were looking fondly at each other, while talking in hushed tones. Next to them a lady, dressed entirely in black, evidently a widow, a veil covering her face, was occupied in some fine needlepoint. In the seat opposite him, a large elderly lady sat looking out at the passing scenery, her hands neatly folded in her lap. Next to her, a young boy was reading a book, accompanied by a middle-aged woman who Ravenscroft concluded was either his nurse or his mother. In the opposite corner of the carriage, an elderly grey-haired gentleman was deeply intent on reading his newspaper, occasionally writing down items in his notebook.

Ravenscroft closed his eyes. There seemed little to engage his attention in regard to his fellow travellers. As he listened to the sound of the train running over the tracks, he found his mind returning to the events of earlier that week. If only he had been quicker, he would have caught the killer and been commended for his endeavour by his colleagues. But instead his wretched cough had slowed him down yet again, and the opportunity had been lost.

He fell into an uneasy sleep, in which the sounds of the train, the occasional whisperings of the young couple and the turning of pages seemed to mingle with the noises of running feet, laughter and his own shortness of breath.

'Oxford!'

He awoke with a start to see that the train had stopped and that several of his travelling companions — the young couple, the elderly lady, the boy and his guardian — were busying themselves with leaving the compartment. Ravenscroft assisted the lady who had sat opposite him with her case onto the platform, and then settled down once more to read the remaining pages of his newspaper.

As the train began to pull out of the station, the door of the compartment was suddenly flung open.

'Begging your pardon for the intrusion, lady and gentlemen, I thought I was going to miss the train.'

The new arrival was a young man of around twenty years of age, with a healthy, ruddy complexion and an easy-going manner.

'No intrusion, I assure you,' ventured Ravenscroft.

The young man grinned and reached into his pocket of his jacket, from where he produced a small packet covered in brown paper.

'Weather looks set fair for the next few days,' said the new arrival, untying the string on his parcel.

'I would hope so,' replied Ravenscroft, turning away and looking out of the window.

'Be bound for Malvern, I would say.'

'How on earth do you—' began Ravenscroft.

'We gets lots of visitors on this train who are going to Malvern. Water cure, that's what they go for. Think the water and all that fresh air will do them good.' The young man bit into one of the large sandwiches that he had removed from his parcel.

'And does it?' asked Ravenscroft, becoming intrigued by his new travelling companion.

'Not for me to say, sir. Not being in need of a cure, myself!'

'And you, sir, are?'

'I am a man of the soil! Born on a farm I was, and glad of it as well. Tom Crabb, at your service, sir.'

'Samuel Ravenscroft.'

The two men shook hands.

'You from London then?'

'You are correct in your assumption, sir — and yes, I am going to Malvern for the water cure.'

'I knew it! As soon as I saw you, I thought, this gent looks a bit peaky and is off to Malvern for his health,' said Crabb, leaning back in his seat and taking another mouthful of his sandwich. 'And I wish you well of it, sir.'

'I thank you, Master Crabb,' smiled Ravenscroft, resuming his reading.

The train continued on its way, the neat fields and hedgerows soon giving way to a more open, rugged countryside. The four occupants of the compartment continued with their various activities in silence.

Presently the train slowed and made its way into another station, the sign announcing that they had arrived in the town of Evesham.

The young man rose from his seat.

'Well, Mr Ravenscroft, this is where I must leave you. Perhaps I might see you in Malvern during your stay.'

'You never know, Master Crabb. We might well meet again.'

'Good day to you, sir, I wish you well of Malvern' — and with those words the young man was gone from the carriage.

'Insufferable fellow!' pronounced the elderly gentleman in the corner, speaking for the first time on their journey. Ravenscroft smiled politely and resumed his reading.

Fifteen minutes later the train drew into Worcester station. Ravenscroft took out his pocket watch and sighed.

'It can sometimes seem like a long journey,' said the elderly gentleman breaking the silence. 'I could not help hearing that you are travelling to Malvern. May I enquire where you will be staying?'

'I have made a reservation at the Tudor Hydropathic Establishment.'

'Ah, a good choice, my dear sir, if I may say so; you could not have done better. Doctor Mountcourt, the proprietor, is an acquaintance of mine. Mention my name and he will provide you with the greatest personal attention.'

'Thank you, sir. And you are?'

'Jabez Pitzer at your service, sir. A long-standing resident of Malvern Wells.'

The two men shook hands.

'Allow me to give you my card.'

'I thank you, sir.'

'I think you will like Malvern a great deal.'

'I'm sure I will.'

'Many of our visitors laud the water treatments and return time and again.'

'The cure is not that effective, then?' Ravenscroft replied light-heartedly.

Pitzer smiled. 'We have many good reports. Perhaps if you are free tomorrow evening you would care to dine with us?'

'That is most kind of you, sir.'

'Take a cab from Great Malvern. Everyone knows where we reside. My wife and I will expect you around seven thirty.'

'That is most generous of you, sir.'

The two men resumed the reading of their newspapers as the guard announced the departure of the train from Worcester station. As they travelled across the bridge which spanned the river, Ravenscroft turned to admire the view of the cathedral in the distance, and puzzled over why he had so readily accepted a dinner invitation from this man whom he scarcely knew.

A few minutes later the train stopped again.

'This is Malvern Link Station,' announced Pitzer. 'Your stop is at Great Malvern.'

The woman with the dark veil rose from her seat.

'Allow me to assist you, ma'am,' said Ravenscroft, standing and reaching out for her bag from the rack above.

'That will not be necessary, sir.'

'But I insist.'

She stepped onto the platform. Ravenscroft followed her with the bag and called out to one of the porters.

'I thank you, sir,' she said from behind the veil. He had expected a much older voice and wondered how it came that she had been widowed so young.

He climbed back into the train and watched the veiled lady and the porter make their way out of the station.

The train continued on its way, and Ravenscroft began to gain views of his approaching destination. A large hill towered upwards on his right-hand side, with a collection of fine buildings on its lower slopes. Shortly the guard announced that they had arrived at Great Malvern Station.

As he lifted his bag down from the rack, his travelling companion leaned forwards, and said, 'Until tomorrow evening, then.'

'I look forward to it, sir.'

The two men shook hands again and Ravenscroft alighted from the train.

After admiring the brightly painted wrought-iron decorations that adorned the station platform, he handed his ticket to the guard and made his way outside to where he found a number of horse-drawn cabs waiting to collect the newly arrived passengers.

'Where you going, sir?' asked one of the cabmen, reaching down for his bag.

'The Tudor Hydropathic Establishment, if you please.'

The driver nodded as Ravenscroft mounted the cab. The man cracked his whip and the vehicle set off at a brisk pace.

Ravenscroft leaned back in his seat. Their journey took them gradually upwards along a wide tree-lined avenue, with individually styled, well-built houses on either side of the road. Clearly Malvern had done well out of the water cure, thought Ravenscroft. At the end of the avenue the cab swung sharply to the right, before climbing up another steep incline. Now they passed offices and shops, and then a fine medieval church. At the top of the incline, the cab veered abruptly to the left and climbed yet again, before finally coming to a halt outside a large early Victorian building. A hanging sign indicated that they had arrived at the Tudor Hydropathic Establishment.

'Tudor, governor,' said the man, steadying the horse.

Ravenscroft paid the driver, took hold of his bag and made his way through the doors of the building. A clerk was writing at a desk in the entrance hall.

'Good afternoon, sir.'

'I believe you are expecting me. Samuel Ravenscroft.'

'Ah, yes, sir. We received your telegram this morning. It is my pleasure to welcome you to the Tudor. Stebbins, will you show this gentleman to his room.'

A youth, whom Ravenscroft judged to be no older than ten or twelve years of age, stepped forwards from out of the shadows, to claim his bag.

'Doctor Mountcourt will see you at precisely four thirty this afternoon,' announced the clerk, looking down at his ledger.

'So soon?'

The clerk looked up from his work and smiled. 'Doctor Mountcourt always likes to see his patients as soon as possible following their arrival.'

Ravenscroft followed the boy along the corridor.

'Come from London?' enquired the youth as they made their way up a flight of stairs.

'Yes.'

'Never bin there.'

'You might not like it. London is not all that it appears to be.'

'Got to be better than this place,' sniffed the youth, coming to a halt outside one of the rooms.

'After you, sir.'

Ravenscroft stepped into the bedroom.

'I'll put yer case 'ere, sir.'

He observed that the room was simply furnished — a bed, table, chair, wardrobe, washstand and basin.

Stebbins coughed and shuffled his feet.

'Oh yes, of course,' he replied, taking a coin from his pocket and giving it to the young boy.

'Thanking you most kindly, sir. I hopes you will enjoy your stay, though not many do. If there's anythin' I can do, like calling a cab, telling you where the best places are, then Stebbins is your man.'

Ravenscroft smiled. 'Thank you, Stebbins. I will try and remember.'

The boy touched his head and left the room.

Ravenscroft walked over to the window and looked out at the fine view, which stretched outwards from the lower slopes of the town and out across the ever-diminishing fields, until it reached another large hill in the far distance.

He turned as the door suddenly opened and Stebbins reappeared once more.

'Doctor Mountcourt, he ain't believin' in giving his guests much food. All part of the treatment. So if you gets hungry, at any time, you just have a quiet word with Stebbins 'ere. I'll see you right. I won't tell, if you don't.'

'Thank you, Stebbins. I will remember that.'

The boy grinned and closed the door once more.

Ravenscroft thought that life at Malvern and the Tudor might just prove interesting after all.

CHAPTER ONE

MALVERN 1887
'Cough!'

Ravenscroft obliged.

'That is not good, my dear sir.' The speaker was a middle-aged man of slender build and serious formal manner.

'I've had the complaint since I was young.'

'I can see that. Not helped by living in London. You should have come to us sooner.'

'Then am I too late?'

'It's never too late, Mr Ravenscroft, but there is a lot to do. Plenty of brisk walks, a change of diet, remedial baths should all help. You could also do with losing a few pounds in weight as well. It appears that you have been most negligent in safeguarding your health. We must act quickly to halt the decline. I'll have my assistant draw up a programme of treatment for you and have it delivered to your room this evening. We will commence the cure tomorrow.'

'Thank you,' replied Ravenscroft, feeling apprehensive.

'I must emphasise, however, that the plan must be strictly adhered to. There must be no deviation from the course on your part either during the treatment or after your return to the capital, otherwise all the good work that we do here at the Tudor will be undone. I think I make myself clear on that point?'

'Yes, of course.' Ravenscroft looked away. He felt as though he was back at school.

'Have you always had poor eyesight?'

'Since I was young.'

'I detect a slight tremor in your left hand. Does it concern you?'

'Only when I feel nervous.'

'You can get yourself dressed now. I will see you in three days' time when I will expect to observe a marked improvement in your condition.'

'Thank you,' replied Ravenscroft somewhat meekly.

'Good day to you, sir,' — and with those words, Doctor Mountcourt, chief physician and proprietor of the Tudor Hydropathic Establishment, swept quickly outwards from the room.

* * *

The following morning Ravenscroft was awakened by a loud banging on the door of his bedroom. He reached for his pocket watch that lay on the table at the side of his bed and in the gloom of the room could just make out the time to be seven o'clock.

Before he had time to consider turning over in his bed, the knocking was repeated and the door flung open.

'Good morning, Mr Ravenscroft. It is time to commence yer treatment, sir.'

'Go away, Stebbins. It's only seven in the morning.'

'We believes in an early start at the Tudor, sir.' Stebbins was already drawing back the curtains, letting in the half-light of the early morning. 'If you would care to follow me, sir, when you're ready.'

Ravenscroft, realising that it would be futile to argue, climbed out of bed, put on his slippers and his dressing gown over his night shirt, and followed the youth along the many dim corridors of the Tudor.

Three floors below they arrived at a door, which bore the words *Bath House* on its exterior. Stebbins indicated that Ravenscroft was to enter.

'A very good morning to you, sir.' The speaker was a stocky, middle-aged man of military bearing. 'Now, sir, you will oblige us by stepping into this bath.'

Ravenscroft peered down into the bath and hesitated. The water looked decidedly cold.

'You will soon get used to it, sir. No one likes it at first. Gently does it.'

Ravenscroft removed his dressing gown and nightshirt, and stepped into the icy water. He gasped at the cold.

'Now, sir, if you would care to sit in the bath.'

A shivering Ravenscroft had no desire whatsoever to comply with this request.

'Best get it over with, sir. You'll feel a lot better afterwards,' said the attendant, attempting to reassure his patient.

Ravenscroft doubted whether that would indeed be the case, but gingerly lowered his body into the tub.

'Good, sir. As I said, you'll soon get used to it. Now I'll just add a little more water,' said the attendant, pouring more of the arctic liquid from a metal jug into the bath.

'My God, man!' exclaimed Ravenscroft. 'Does it really have to be so damn cold?'

'Doctor Mountcourt's instructions, sir,' replied the man in a firm voice.

During the following ten minutes, Ravenscroft shuddered in the freezing water thinking that he had never experienced such unpleasantness in all his life and wishing that he had ignored his superior and taken in the pleasures of Brighton instead.

'Now, sir, if you could ease yourself out of the bath, we'll rub you down and take you back to your room.'

Ravenscroft, relieved to be allowed out of the bath, stood creaking with cold and reached for the outstretched towel.

Five minutes later he found himself back in his room, but the treatment had apparently not yet been completed.

'If you would care to stand by your bed, sir,' instructed the attendant.

Ravenscroft wondered what new torture was about to be inflicted upon him. Stebbins and the attendant produced a number of damp sheets which they proceeded to wind tightly round his body, before tipping him backwards onto his bed. He felt like one of the Egyptian mummies he had seen recently at the Kensington Museum.

'If you would now remain there, sir, until we return.'

What other choice did he have, he thought, wryly. His two tormentors left, leaving him with little to do but look up at the ceiling of his room.

Gradually he began to feel his body recovering its warmth and his limbs slowly stopped shaking within the tightly bound sheets. He wondered what the point of that ghastly experience had been and whether he would have to go through with it every day during his stay. He felt a desperate urge to scratch the back of his left shoulder. Letting out a deep sigh, he closed his eyes and prayed that his jailers would soon return to bring an end to his ordeal. He closed his eyes. The events of three days previous now floated before him. If only he could have stopped that man.

After what had seemed like an eternity, Stebbins and the attendant returned and unwound the sheets. He gave out a sigh of relief and suddenly realised that he had acquired quite an appetite.

'Now then, sir, once you are dressed you are to make your way up to the well house at St Ann's to partake of the waters,' said the attendant.

'I was rather hoping that I might be allowed to have my breakfast first.'

'Not until you return, sir. Doctor Mountcourt's orders.'

Ravenscroft thought he detected a slight sadistic tone in the military man's voice. The others left the room, leaving him to dress as quickly as he could. The sooner he journeyed to the well house and back, the quicker he could partake of some food.

Leaving the Tudor, he crossed over the road and walked up a flight of steps that presently bought him onto a narrow path. He turned around and as he looked down on the town, he could just make out the outline of the church through the morning mist. A sign indicated that he was to turn upwards, and he soon found that his footsteps took him to the base of another winding path, which seemed to stretch for ever upwards into the distance.

He began to make his way slowly up, the path growing ever steeper the further he ascended. Soon he felt his chest tightening and was forced to rest on one of the wooden benches at the side until he recovered his breath.

He struggled to his feet and looked upwards. Tendrils of morning mist still clung to the sides of the hills. He realised he had not encountered anyone else on his journey and wondered why. Gradually he could see the outline of what appeared to be a building of some kind ahead of him. As he drew near, he saw that it was a small octagonal structure situated in a clearing, nestling between two rising hills. A babbling spring cut through the scene and down the slopes.

A lone figure seemed to be awaiting his arrival.

'Good morning to you, sir, can I be of assistance to you?'

The speaker was an old woman, who was neatly dressed, wearing a shawl and apron.

'My name is Ravenscroft. I was told to take the waters here.'

'Ah, yes, sir. I have been expecting you. You are staying at the Tudor. Doctor Mountcourt has left instructions that you are to drink three containers of the waters.'

She dipped one of the beakers into the flowing spring and handed it to him.

The fresh, cold water was reviving, and he soon drained the glass. The old woman smiled and replenished it.

A few seats were situated to one side of the well house. He made his way across to one of them, welcoming the opportunity of being able to sit quietly.

Yet as he looked across to the other side of the clearing, he suddenly became aware of another's presence. Sitting on one of the benches was a woman dressed entirely in black. He had not seen anyone at the well house when he had first arrived. The woman must have been inside the building at the time. She seemed familiar to him. He studied the veiled lady without drawing notice to himself. Then he placed her: she was the same person who had shared his train compartment the day before. He wondered why she had visited the well house, unattended, and at such an early hour.

Not wishing to disturb her, he gazed back down the path he had just climbed. When he sneaked another glance, he discovered she had risen from her seat and was leaving the well house. He half stood in surprise, then checked himself. Chasing after her might cause alarm. Instead he lowered himself uneasily back into his seat and watched the black figure make its way slowly down the path, until she disappeared from view and was no more.

Ravenscroft reproached himself for his uncertainty. He should have addressed the widow when he had first noticed her presence at the well. He wondered whether another opportunity might present itself during his stay.

His stomach suddenly gnawed with hunger. He quickly downed his second and third beakers of spring water, gave the elderly attendant a coin and began his descent back towards the town.

* * *

The meagre breakfast at the Tudor did little to satisfy his hunger. Determined to find something more substantial to eat, Ravenscroft decided that he would take the opportunity to explore the town.

Following along the road outside his hotel, he soon found himself on a terrace that overlooked Great Malvern. After walking past a large boarding house with extensive gardens, he passed the local wine cellars, the Malvern and Worcestershire Bank, the local Oddfellows Hall, and one or two shops, until he reached a large building situated on the corner of the road. A sign stated that he had arrived at the Malvern Library and Reading Rooms. He pushed open the door and entered the building.

'Good morning to you, sir, would you like to avail yourself of our facilities?' asked a smartly attired gentleman.

Ravenscroft said that he would, and his host led him into to a large room furnished with tables, chairs and bookcases.

'Perhaps you would care to read the morning papers, sir? We also serve coffee, if you so wish?'

'I would indeed like to read the morning papers, and a cup of your coffee would be very welcome.'

The gentleman bowed, then handed Ravenscroft a newspaper. Five minutes later he returned with a cup of steaming coffee and a piping hot muffin oozing butter, on a silver tray. Ravenscroft breathed a sign of relief and reached out to take them. There was evidently more to Malvern than cold baths and arduous walks.

'You are staying at the Tudor, I believe?' asked the librarian.

'Yes — but how did you know that?'

'Malvern is a very small town, sir. I believe I might have caught sight of you leaving the building earlier this morning. I presumed you might also be hungry, sir,' he said, gesturing to the plate.

Ravenscroft took an enormous bite and nodded gratefully.

'Will that be all, sir?'

'Yes, thank you.'

The librarian gave another bow and returned to his station.

An hour later, Ravenscroft left the Reading Rooms feeling rested and refreshed. He made his way down the steep road towards the Priory Church. Here a boy in a patched jacket insisted on showing him the various medieval tiles, fine windows and interesting carvings that adorned the building.

Giving the young guide a coin for his troubles, Ravenscroft consulted his pocket watch and realised that his next treatment at the Tudor would begin within the hour. He made his way across the churchyard and up the steps that lead to the top part of the town. When he paused at the summit to regain his breath, he looked up and saw a familiar figure entering the doorway of the Malvern and Worcestershire Bank. Clearly Mr Jabez Pitzer had business to attend to there.

Back at the Tudor, Ravenscroft changed into his dressing gown and lay down on his bed. After a few minutes he felt his eyes beginning to grow heavy, as his mind played over the events of the past few days. He again saw himself running along the narrow streets of Whitechapel, the black cloak billowing in the distance. Then the garment gradually seemed to turn into the black dress of the veiled lady; and the noise of a clattering train in his mind began to mingle with the sounds of running water and shallow breathing.

* * *

A sudden loud knock on the door, made him wake with a start.

'Time for yer next treatment, Mr Ravenscroft,' called out Stebbins from the other side of the door. Ravenscroft rose from his bed. What kind of torture was he to experience now, he wondered.

He followed the cheery youth along the numerous corridors and flights of stairs of the Tudor, until they reached the Bath House.

'Good afternoon, sir, are we ready to continue our treatment?'

There was something about the attendant's brisk, military no-nonsense approach that Ravenscroft was beginning to dislike. He looked down at the bath of water. At least there was steam rising from it this time.

'Now, sir, you will oblige me by stepping into the bath.'

Ravenscroft complied with the request. 'Good God, man, it's scorching!' he exclaimed.

'You may find it a little warm at first, sir, but your body will soon adjust itself to the heat. The temperature has been laid down exactly by Doctor Mountcourt.'

He gave the attendant a black look, and then lowered himself slowly into the waters.

'There you are, sir. Not so bad, is it?'

The man was insufferable, but Ravenscroft realised he now had little choice but to clench his teeth and try to put the extreme heat out of his mind.

He laid his head back against the rim, and after a few minutes, during which the attendant busied himself in another part of the room, he could almost begin to relax in the scalding waters.

'Now, sir, we'll just add another jug of water,' said the attendant pouring the boiling contents of the vessel into the bath.

Ravenscroft cursed the man under his breath and vowed that this was positively the last time he would undergo this torture. Beneath the surface of the water, his body was turning a bright red colour. He raised his arm to wipe the beads of perspiration away from his brow.

At long last, he was instructed to step out of the bath and, after replacing his robe, was escorted back to his room, where Stebbins and the attendant again busied themselves in wrapping his body tightly with thick sheets.

As he lay on his bed feeling the sweat slick beneath the confines of the bindings, he resolved that in the morning he would announce his immediate departure from Malvern and the Tudor Hydropathic Establishment and escape towards the more soothing pleasures of Brighton — but before then, there was that matter of a dinner engagement to be fulfilled.

* * *

Later that evening, Ravenscroft took the cab that Stebbins had arranged for him and set off in the direction of Malvern Wells. The cab drove him past several fine buildings, before which a lamp lighter was busying himself with his work. The ornate iron lanterns cast pockets of light on either side of the road. Then the road opened out into open countryside. Ravenscroft could make out the contours of a large hill on his right, whereas the land on his left sloped gently away into the far distance. Small isolated gleams of light could be seen shining out from the interiors of the houses, which appeared to cling perilously to the sides of the hills.

Suddenly his driver swung the cab round to their left and they travelled up a long driveway towards a large imposing house.

'Pitzers!' announced the man, bringing the vehicle to a halt.

Ravenscroft alighted from the cab and, after giving his driver some coins, he pulled the wrought-iron bell handle at the side of the door. As the light from the cab disappeared into the gloom, he could hear the sound of the bell ringing from inside the building.

'Good evening, sir,' said a young woman, as she answered the door. 'You must be Mr Ravenscroft.'

He stepped into the hallway and handed his coat and hat to the maid. 'If you would care to follow me, sir, I will tell Mrs Pitzer that you have arrived.'

Ravenscroft admired the fine furniture and paintings, as the maid lead the way across the hall.

'Mr Ravenscroft, madam,' announced the maid, ushering Ravenscroft into the drawing room.

'Mr Ravenscroft, so good of you to come and join us.' The speaker was a tall elderly lady, elegantly attired in a blue velvet evening gown.

'It was very good of your husband to invite me, especially as I only made his acquaintance yesterday.'

His hostess smiled indulgently. 'My husband is detained at the moment on urgent business but will join us presently. May I introduce you to our two other guests? Mr Sommersby is the Assistant Master at our fine Malvern College, and the Reverend Touchmore is the vicar of our splendid Priory Church in Great Malvern.'

Ravenscroft shook hands with both men. The former was an elderly gentleman of slender build, with a pair of pince-nez perched upon his long, thin nose; the latter a well-built and bald gentleman whose red face sported an expansive set of side whiskers.

'So, Mr Ravenscroft, how do you find our town?' asked Touchmore, resuming his seat.

'I find it well, sir, what little I have seen of it.'

'You must visit our Priory Church.'

'I did so today, sir. One of your guides was kind enough to show me around the interior. I found it a most interesting building.'

'You are here to undertake the water cure, I believe? May I ask where you are residing?' asked the cleric brushing an imaginary hair from one of his trouser legs.

'I am staying at the Tudor.'

'An admirable choice, if I may say so. Doctor Mountcourt has only been at the Tudor for three years but has already built up a significant reputation. I am sure you will be most comfortable there. We accommodate many esteemed visitors who come to Malvern to take the waters.'

'You live in London, sir?' interjected Sommersby, leaning forwards in his seat, and peering over his pince-nez at Ravenscroft. 'And what line of work are you engaged in?'

'I am engaged in work in the City,' replied Ravenscroft carefully, beginning to think that perhaps he had been unwise to have accepted the dinner invitation. He had no wish to reveal he was an inspector.

'The City! I have had the misfortune of finding myself in the metropolis on a number of occasions and have always been glad of my safe return to Malvern,' said his questioner in a dry tone.

Ravenscroft moved uneasily in his seat, sensing that the two men had decided that their new arrival was of little interest.

'We must consider at our next meeting how we are to raise the requisite funds for the improvements to the church roof,' said Sommersby, turning towards the clergyman and Mrs Pitzer.

'I must confess that the problem has caused me a number of unsettled nights,' replied Touchmore. Mrs Pitzer nodded sympathetically.

Ravenscroft took the opportunity of being ignored to sit back in his chair and study the room. An upright piano was to be found in one corner of the room, the top of which was adorned with framed photographs of his host and hostess. There were paintings of rural rustic scenes on the walls and a large quantity of leather-bound volumes in the tall, wooden bookcases. It all suggested that Jabez Pitzer was a man of conservative and refined taste.

'We hope that Mr Pitzer will be able to present the prizes for us at the college at the end of term.' Sommersby was speaking to his hostess.

'I am sure that my husband will be delighted.'

'He must be a busy man these days, my dear lady. We all expect him to be elected mayor quite soon,' said Touchmore.

Their conversation was interrupted by the opening of the door.

'Please, ma'am. Cook says dinner will be served in five minutes,' announced the maid, standing in the doorway.

'Thank you, Susan. Would you be so good as to inform the master? He should still be in the study.'

'Very well, ma'am.'

The maid closed the door behind her.

'That must be for the council to decide,' said Mrs Pitzer addressing the cleric.

'I'm sure you will have no problems on that account. Mr Pitzer has done most valuable service to the town and its inhabitants over the past twenty or thirty years, and it is only his just reward that he should be recommended by the members of our council for the highest position in Malvern. And I might add, my dear lady, that you will make an admirable mayoress.'

Ravenscroft was beginning to find his mind wandering on to other matters when suddenly the door was thrown open.

'Ma'am, something terrible has happened! It's the master!' cried the maid, in some distress.

'Calm yourself, Susan. Whatever is the matter?'

'The master — I think, I think — he's dead!'

Sommersby was already on his feet and rushed from the room, quickly joined by Touchmore. Ravenscroft and Mrs Pitzer followed them across the hallway and into the study.

'Touchmore, see to Mrs Pitzer,' instructed Sommersby as he leaned over the desk. Ravenscroft saw their host slumped in his chair, his head and outstretched hand lying across the desk in front of him. 'It looks as though poor Pitzer has had a stroke or a seizure of some kind.'

'Is he—' began Touchmore.

'I'm afraid he's dead,' announced Sommersby, shaking his head, after taking Pitzer's hand and feeling his pulse.

Mrs Pitzer let out a sob.

'Susan, take your mistress quickly into the drawing room. Touchmore, go and fetch Gladwyn,' instructed Sommersby.

'Come now, ma'am,' said the maid, as she and her mistress left the room.

'Should we not call for the local constabulary?' broached Ravenscroft, casting a glance around the study.

'Whatever for, man? Poor Pitzer has clearly had a seizure. Anyone can see that. There is little the police can do,' said Sommersby, clearly becoming annoyed that anyone should question his authority.

'Nevertheless, I do think—' began Ravenscroft, but he was cut short by Touchmore.

'I think our guest is correct. There is a correct procedure to be followed, Sommersby.'

The schoolmaster glared at the clergyman. 'Oh, very well then, have it your own way, Touchmore. You go and inform the constabulary, and I will go and fetch Doctor Gladwyn. Perhaps our guest would attend to Mrs Pitzer?'

'Of course,' replied Ravenscroft.

The three men walked out of the room, Sommersby closing the door behind them. As the other two men left the house, Ravenscroft made his way into the drawing room where he found a distressed Mrs Pitzer being comforted by her maid.

'I am so sorry that this has happened during your visit to our household, Mr Ravenscroft,' said his hostess, looking up.

'My dear lady, do not worry on my account. I am only sorry your husband has been taken from us. Mrs Pitzer, I'm afraid I must enquire: did he receive any visitors in his study this evening?'

'No. No. But why do you ask?'

'It is no matter. Might I suggest that your maid escort you to your room? I will await the return of the others and can inform you of anything of importance.'

'Thank you, Mr Ravenscroft. You are most kind.'

Mrs Pitzer and her maid left the room. Ravenscroft waited for a few moments, before making his way back to the study. Walking over to the desk, he knelt by the side of the dead man and examined the contents of his pockets but found little of interest. He glanced at the top of the desk, which was empty except for the usual writing materials and an open diary. Ravenscroft looked down at the day's entry, which read, *Seven thirty. Touchmore, Sommersby and Ravenscroft for dinner.*

Looking up, he observed that the window was slightly ajar. He stepped out into the garden and crouched down to examine the ground.

At the sound of people returning to the house he stepped back quickly into the study.

'Ah, there you are, Ravenscroft,' said Sommersby, entering the room. 'May I introduce you to Doctor Gladwyn.'

Ravenscroft shook hands with the new arrival.

'Well, this is a sad state of affairs. Poor Pitzer, I had warned him that he must take greater care of his health,' said Gladwyn, in a pronounced Welsh accent.

'It must have happened quite suddenly. We were in the main room at the time,' said Sommersby, as the doctor began to examine the deceased.

'Yes, I am inclined to agree with you, Sommersby. It does appear that Pitzer died of a seizure of some kind.'

'You are sure of that diagnosis?' asked Ravenscroft, examining the contents of a small silver tray on one of the side tables.

The two men, surprised by his comments, looked sternly in his direction.

'My dear sir, I am a qualified medical practitioner,' said Gladwyn drawing up to his full height.

'Doctor Gladwyn has been practising medicine in this town for over forty years, my dear sir. You of course are a doctor yourself?' snapped Sommersby.

'No, I was merely—'

They were interrupted by the sound of the outside door opening once more. Clearly Touchmore had returned with an officer of the local constabulary.

'If you would care to follow me into the study, Constable,' said Touchmore entering the room. He was followed by a uniformed officer.

'You say, sir, that Mr Pitzer died earlier this evening? Why bless my soul, if it isn't Mr Ravenscroft!' said the constable.

'Mr Crabb, we meet again. I was under the impression that you were a member of the farming fraternity. I was not aware that you were also a member of the local constabulary.'

'Indeed so, sir. It is my mother who runs the family farm near Evesham. I serve with the Malvern Constabulary and live here in the Wells,' replied Crabb, shaking Ravenscroft's hand.

'You two know each other?' asked Touchmore, a puzzled expression on his face.

'Mr Ravenscroft and I had the good fortune to meet one another on the Malvern train yesterday,' answered Crabb.

'Constable, can we now proceed?' said Sommersby in an irritated voice.

'By all means, sir. You say that Mr Pitzer died earlier this evening?' asked Crabb, taking out his notebook from the inside top pocket of his tunic.

'Constable, if I may,' said Gladwyn. 'Poor Mr Pitzer appears to have died as the result of a seizure.'

'Had he been ill, sir?' asked Crabb beginning to write in his pocketbook.

'He did consult with me two or three weeks ago, and I found him a little tired and recommended that perhaps he and his wife would benefit from a holiday.'

'I see, sir. It would appear that the gentleman did not take your advice. Well, I will have to inform the coroner of course. It's just a formality,' said Crabb closing his pocketbook once more.

'Constable Crabb, I wonder if I might have a private word with you, before you leave?' asked Ravenscroft. The two men looked at one another.

'Of course, sir. I wonder if I could ask you other gentlemen to go into the drawing room, while I have a word with Mr Ravenscroft.'

'Really, Crabb, this is most irregular,' protested Sommersby.

'I'm sure we won't detain you long, sir,' said Crabb.

'Oh, come along, Sommersby. Let's do as he says,' said Gladwyn.

Sommersby gave Ravenscroft a stare as he left the room, followed by Touchmore and Gladwyn.

'Now, sir, I guess that you know something about this affair that does not seem at first evident?' said Crabb closing the door behind the departed trio.

'I do indeed, but before that, I should inform you that I hold the rank of Inspector in the Whitechapel Division of the Metropolitan Police.'

'I knew I was right! When I saw you yesterday, I said to myself, ten to a penny that gent is a policeman — and look here we are again,' smiled the young constable.

'The other gentlemen here tonight would have it that Pitzer died of a seizure of some kind.'

'But you know differently, sir, I'll be bound.'

'I do indeed, Constable Crabb. You see, I think that Pitzer did not die of a seizure or as the result of any other natural causes or ailments. I have every reason to believe that Pitzer was murdered in this room earlier this evening!'

CHAPTER TWO

'Well, sir, that seems rather a bold statement to make, if you don't mind my saying so. What evidence do you have to suggest such a possibility?' asked Crabb.

'When I arrived at the house earlier this evening, Mrs Pitzer informed me that her husband was detained, in this study, on urgent business. I believe that he was expecting a visitor, and it was that person who entered this room and killed him.'

'But surely the maid would have seen such a person when she showed the visitor into the study?'

'I believe that the visitor did not wish to announce his, or her, presence to the rest of the house, and that the person entered through that window.'

'How do you know that, sir?'

'When I entered the study tonight, I observed that the window over there was slightly ajar. It leads directly onto the garden. Whoever was in this room with Pitzer tonight must have entered and left by that same entrance. That the window is not closed properly suggests he left in a hurry.'

'You think the killer was afraid of being interrupted?' enquired Crabb.

'I am sure of it. Furthermore, outside the window I found marks caused by a shoe or boot on the earth directly below it. A path from the house then leads across the garden to a gate. It would have been easy for our visitor to have slipped out of the grounds without being seen by anyone, and once outside he could have made his way anywhere.'

'He could even have returned to the house later,' suggested Crabb.

'Indeed. If Pitzer was killed at approximately half past six, let us say, there would have been ample time for either Mr Sommersby or the reverend to have returned to the house to keep their dinner appointment.'

'You suspect either of these two gentlemen, sir?'

'We must keep an open mind to all possibilities, Constable Crabb. Certainly, Sommersby was quick to assume that Pitzer had died of natural causes and Doctor Gladwyn seemed only too obliging to agree with him.'

'Begging your pardon, sir, but you keep saying that Mr Pitzer was killed?'

'There are two glasses on this tray by the decanter. Both appeared to have been used recently, but one of them has the remains of what looks like a powdery substance at the bottom,' said Ravenscroft, holding the suspect glass up to the light.

'Then you think, sir, that Mr Pitzer was poisoned?'

'It would appear so. There is a slight bitter smell. Clearly our murderer did not have time to swill out the remaining contents of the glass before he left, but then again he probably assumed that everyone would accept that Pitzer had died of natural causes and would have no need to make an examination of the room.'

'So our visitor pours out two glasses of sherry and slips some poison into one of the glasses. Very neat, I would say.'

'Poor Pitzer then drinks the lethal concoction, and slumps forward over the desk, and if I am not mistaken, he may well have dropped the glass from his hand onto the floor. You will oblige me by studying the carpet Crabb.'

The constable crouched on the floor and ran his fingers along the carpet.

'You are correct, sir, there is indeed quite a wet patch here.'

'Pitzer dropped the glass, and our murderer, disturbed by some noise outside in the hall, picked it up quickly and replaced it on the tray before leaving in a hurry, in case he was discovered.'

'I am quite impressed by your observations, sir, but who could have done such a deed — and why?'

'That is what we have to discover — or rather what you have to discover. I have no jurisdiction here in Malvern. It must be a matter for the local constabulary to investigate.'

'I think we will be a bit out of our depth with this one, sir. We don't tend to have any murders here in Malvern. I'll have a word with my sergeant. I'm sure he would be most obliged if you were to take over the case, sir.'

'I do not think I am able to comply with your request, Constable. I am supposed to be here for the water cure, and I had planned to leave tomorrow for Brighton.'

Crabb looked crestfallen. 'I see, sir. Well then, that's a great shame. It looks as though our murderer may escape the gallows. Perhaps you could just stay for a day or so until the investigation is under way and we have apprehended the felon?'

'I'm not so sure, Constable,' protested Ravenscroft.

'We would be grateful for your expertise, sir,' pleaded the constable.

Ravenscroft thought deeply for a moment.

'As you wish, Constable Crabb — but just for a day or so.'

'That is excellent news, sir. You will of course take over the investigation?' asked Crabb enthusiastically.

'If your sergeant agrees, Constable,' sighed Ravenscroft. 'Then let us make a start. If you would have a word with our three guests, inform them as to my true role, but on no account mention that we suspect that Pitzer was murdered. Just say we have to make further enquiries.'

'I understand, sir.'

'Tell them to go home but make appointments for us to see each one of them individually tomorrow. Then I suggest you return to your station and inform both your sergeant and the coroner. Then meet me tomorrow morning outside the Tudor at ten o' clock.'

'And you, sir?'

'I will have words with the maid, Susan, before returning to the Tudor.'

* * *

'Sit down here, Susan,' said Ravenscroft, indicating a seat on the sofa. 'I believe that Constable Crabb may have told you that we are making enquiries into the death of your master.'

'Yes, sir,' replied the maid, dabbing the corner of her eye with a handkerchief.

'I realise that you have suffered an unpleasant shock, but I would like to ask you a few questions, if you feel you can manage that?' asked Ravenscroft, trying to sound as sympathetic as he could as he sat down beside her.

'Yes, sir. I will do my best.'

'I'm sure you will. How long have you been working for Mr and Mrs Pitzer?'

'For about ten years, sir. I came first as a scullery maid. After a few months Mrs Pitzer asked me to be her personal maid.'

'Did Mr and Mrs Pitzer ever argue or quarrel?'

'Oh, no, sir, they were very much devoted to one another. There was never anything like that.'

'Would you say that your master was the kind of man to have any enemies?'

'Enemies, sir? Why bless me, sir, everyone seemed to like Mr Pitzer. I never heard anyone have a bad thing to say against him.'

'Did Mr and Mrs Pitzer have any family? I see no evidence in any of the photographs on display.'

'No, sir. There was never any talk of a family or such like.'

Ravenscroft paused as the maid dabbed her tearful eyes with her handkerchief.

'I want to turn to the events of earlier this evening. Did anyone, other than the dinner guests, visit the house either late this afternoon, or earlier this evening?'

'No, sir. No one called.'

'Are you sure?' asked Ravenscroft moving closer to the maid.

'Quite sure, sir. Mr Pitzer received no one. There was only the boy with the letter.'

'The boy with the letter?'

'Yes, sir. A boy came with a letter for Mr Pitzer.'

'What time was this?'

'About half past four, sir. I told the boy to wait while I took the letter into Mr Pitzer.'

'What happened next? What did your master do with the letter?' asked Ravenscroft anxious to learn more.

'He read the letter and gave me a sixpence to give to the boy to send him away.'

'Had you ever seen the boy before?'

'No, sir. He must have been someone from the town.'

'Tell me, Susan, how did Mr Pitzer seem when he read the letter?'

'I don't understand, sir.'

'Did he seem angry or displeased?'

'No, sir. He just read the letter and placed it on his desk. He did say that on no account was he to be disturbed until dinner time.'

'I see,' said Ravenscroft standing up. 'You have been most helpful, Susan.'

'Can I go now, sir?'

'One more question. You say that no one else came to the house after the boy left?'

'That's correct, sir.'

'During the evening you would have had cause to pass by the study many times. Did you, at any time, hear voices coming from inside? Think carefully.'

'No, sir, I heard no voices.'

'Did you hear any other noises from inside the room?'

'No, sir. There was only the sound of something falling as I passed the door.'

'Falling?'

'Yes, it sounded as though Mr Pitzer had dropped something on the floor.'

'Excellent, Susan, you are doing very well. Tell me at about what time you heard this noise?'

'At six thirty, sir,' replied the maid, a puzzled expression on her face.

'How can you be sure as to the exact time?'

'Why, by the clock in the hallway, sir. I remember it chiming the half hour, just after I heard the noise.'

'And you did not go into the study to investigate what had caused the noise?'

'No, sir. I did tap on the door, but Mr Pitzer had left strict instructions that he was not to be disturbed, on any account, and there was no response.'

'Thank you, Susan. I am obliged to you for all your assistance. I think it would be well if you returned to your mistress. She will have need of you tonight. I will let myself out.'

The maid left the room. Ravenscroft stared into dying flames of the fire for some minutes, deep in thought. It had only been yesterday that he had spoken with Pitzer on the train, now here he was in the poor man's house enquiring into the nature of his demise. It was ironic that his holiday now looked more likely to take second place to his investigations. Quite why he had allowed himself to be persuaded to take on the task of solving the crime by the youthful enthusiastic constable, he was at a loss to comprehend. Then he returned once more to the study where he made a search through the drawers of the desk, before casting a final look round the room.

A few minutes later he began to make his way back along the dimly lit road in the direction of Great Malvern. The gas lamps threw pools of light onto the path before him, each one guiding him onwards towards the next, like islands in a sea of darkness. He drew the collar of his coat tighter round his neck and pulled down his hat to protect him from the wind that blew off the common. Eventually the lights of the town came into view.

He now knew that Pitzer had been poisoned at six thirty that evening, and that whoever had written the letter arranging the meeting had not only sworn Pitzer to secrecy, but had also been careful to remove the same letter before he had hurriedly left the scene of the crime.

It looked to Ravenscroft that he would be staying in Malvern for a while longer. The case looked a challenging one, and he was now resolved to solve it. The pleasures of Brighton would have to wait for a while longer.

As he approached the Tudor, he suddenly became aware of his own hunger and realised that he had not eaten since lunchtime. Perhaps if he was fortunate, Stebbins would still be up at such an hour and be able to procure him a dish or two from the kitchens, before he retired for the evening.

CHAPTER THREE

A loud banging on his bedroom door woke Ravenscroft from the deep sleep he had finally fallen into.

'Go away, Stebbins! Leave me alone!' He turned over on his side and buried his face in the pillow.

'Can't do that, sir. Orders is orders. Doctor says you must have your bath, and the bath you shall have,' said the youth, entering the room, throwing open the curtains and reaching for Ravenscroft's robe.

'Why are you always so damn cheerful, Stebbins?'

'No time to be miserable, sir.'

'And where were you last night when I got back to the Tudor? I hadn't eaten all evening and could have done with a morsel or two before retiring,' grumbled Ravenscroft rising from his bed.

'Say no more, sir. Stebbins is yer man. After yer bath, sir, how about I arrange for a nice juicy slice of lamb and a lump of cheese to be brought to yer room?'

'Stebbins, I see that we might be friends yet. Here is a shilling.'

'Thank you, sir,' said the smiling youth, biting on the silver coin with his crooked teeth.

The prospect of finally satisfying his deepening hunger encouraged Ravenscroft to make his way to the bath house where he forced himself to give even the attendant a brief smile. Returning to his room, after his treatment, he found the food and a jug of ale waiting for him on the table at the side of his bed.

After consuming the contents of his unexpected breakfast, he dressed quickly and began to make his way slowly up the hills towards St Ann's well house. Pausing halfway up the winding path, he wiped his brow and stood admiring the view below him. Duty required him to present himself for his three containers of spring water when he arrived at the well house, but he also hoped that he might find his mysterious travelling companion again. In this he was disappointed. There was no sign of the black-veiled woman. His curiosity on that score would have to wait for another day. There were only three persons present — the attendant, a young boy playing with his hoop, and his nurse.

Ravenscroft raised his hat to the nurse, smiled at the child, and then went over to the old woman who poured him a container of water.

'Perhaps you might care to read the local paper, sir?'

'Thank you. That would be most kind.'

Ravenscroft accepted the newspaper from the old woman and made his way across to one of the seats.

The *Malvern News* contained little to interest him — reports of Temperance Meetings, lists of important people visiting the town, the previous week's Council meetings, advertisements for patent medicines and wine cellars — until a certain article caught his attention—

THE SHADOW OF THE RAGGEDSTONE
ANCIENT MALVERN CURSE

Our readers will be interested to know that the ancient legend of the curse of Raggedstone Hill has been revived in a new novel written by Doctor Charles Grindrod. The Shadow of the Raggedstone *is based on the old monkish legend and the curse upon its shadow. Many of our older readers may recall the legend of the dying monk who had been turned out of his dwelling by the local people and who before dying on the slopes of the Raggedstone Hill cursed all that would for ever fall beneath its shadow. While we can inform our readers that there is little evidence to support the truth of the legend, we know of several of our more elderly readers who swear that they would never go anywhere near the hill. This reporter however can reassure his readers that he has walked both on the hill, and beneath its shadow, on a number of occasions, and that to date he has never met with any misfortune—*

'Good morning to you, sir.'

Ravenscroft looked up from his reading, to see the figure of Doctor Mountcourt standing before him.

'I see you are studying our local paper.'

'I was just reading about the curse of the Raggedstone Hill.'

'Stuff and nonsense, sir! A mere folk tale written to scare the feeble minded away from the hills. Good to see you taking the waters before breakfast, Ravenscroft. Keep up the good work.'

Before Ravenscroft could reply, Mountcourt had resumed his walk, striding along the path, his cane tapping the ground at his side as he did so.

The doctor slowly disappeared from view. Ravenscroft continued reading the *Malvern News* before handing the paper back to the attendant.

'Thank you for the newspaper. I have just been reading about Raggedstone Hill and the old curse. Where is the Raggedstone?' he asked drinking his second beaker of water.

'Over there,' replied the old woman jerking her thumb in the air.

'Do you believe in such things?'

The woman said nothing, instead turning quickly away and making her way back inside the building.

Ravenscroft downed his beaker of water before retracing his steps back towards the town.

* * *

Later that morning he met Crabb outside the Tudor.

'Good morning to you, Mr Ravenscroft,' said the constable in a cheerful manner.

'And to you, Master Crabb. Where are we going first?'

'I thought you might want to speak first with Mr Sommersby at Malvern College. If you would care to follow me, sir, you will find it to be about ten minutes on foot. That's the trouble with Malvern — all hills. Easy enough going downhill; not so easy coming up.'

'So I have observed.'

'I have had a word with my superiors, Mr Ravenscroft, and they are more than pleased that you have taken an interest in this case. We are quite a small station here in Malvern and welcome any help we can receive.'

'I am glad to be of assistance,' said Ravenscroft warmly. He briefly wondered if he should inform the Commissioner of his secondment, but was soon distracted by matters at hand.

As the two men walked, Ravenscroft recounted his meeting with Susan the maid from the night before. Presently they approached an austere building, which bore the name 'Malvern College'. Crabb rang the bell and the door was opened by a uniformed servant.

'Good day, my man. We are here to see Mr Sommersby, if you please,' said Crabb, stepping into the hall.

'Please follow me, gentlemen.'

The two policemen followed the servant across the wide hallway, and along a cloister like corridor, until they reached a large oak door.

'If you would care to wait here, I will see that Mr Sommersby is informed of your arrival.'

Ravenscroft and Crabb found themselves in a large library. Books adorned not only the shelves that ran around the walls of the room, but also occupied a number of tall bookcases in its centre.

'Lordy me! They certainly likes their books here! Don't think I have ever seen so many books before. Wonder they have time to read them all,' said Crabb walking around the room. Ravenscroft looked through the leaded windows out towards the quadrangle and wished he had been sent to such a school as this in his youth.

The door opened and Sommersby strode into the room.

'Mr Ravenscroft and Constable Crabb, I am sorry to have kept you waiting. Please sit down. We are very busy with examinations at the present time. I warn you that I can only give you a few minutes of my time.'

Ravenscroft was reminded of the academic's dry, off-hand manner of the night before.

'Thank you, sir. As you are probably aware, both Constable Crabb and I are investigating the death of Mr Pitzer,' began Ravenscroft.

'I would have thought there was little to ask about. Pitzer died of a seizure I believe,' replied the schoolmaster, in a dismissive tone.

'How long have you known Mr and Mrs Pitzer?' asked Ravenscroft, ignoring Sommersby's last remark.

'I have known them for about thirty years or more. I am a native of Malvern, and when Mr Pitzer arrived here, he and his wife were most generous towards me.'

'In what way, sir?'

'The life of a schoolmaster can sometimes be a lonely one, Inspector, and Mr Pitzer and his wife invited me into their home and accorded me their kindness and hospitality,' replied Sommersby, staring at Ravenscroft through the lenses of his pince-nez.

'I believe that Mr Pitzer was a busy man and that he took a prominent interest in the affairs of the town?'

'That is indeed so. He was a member of the town council, a prominent member in church circles, the local bank, temperance hall, Old Lechmere's Almshouses, to name but a few. But really, I don't see the relevance of all this. Poor Pitzer is dead and nothing will bring him back. Now if you will excuse me, I have a Latin examination class which I must invigilate,' said Sommersby, rising from his chair.

'We are here, Mr Sommersby, because we have strong grounds to believe that Mr Pitzer was poisoned last night,' said Ravenscroft in a matter-of-fact voice.

'Poisoned! That is quite ridiculous. Both Doctor Gladwyn and I are of the same mind that Pitzer—'

'We found poison in a glass that Pitzer had been using,' interjected Ravenscroft, leaning forwards in his chair.

'This is quite terrible. Why would Pitzer take poison?'

'He did not take the poison. He was given it. Someone killed him.'

'But . . . I don't . . . Pitzer never had an enemy in the world,' stuttered Sommersby.

'He certainly had one, sir,' ventured Crabb, replacing one of the books on the shelves.

'What time did you arrive at Pitzer's last night?' asked Ravenscroft.

'I arrived at a quarter past seven, a few minutes before your own arrival.'

'And the Reverend Touchmore?'

'He was there already.'

'How did you travel to the house?'

'I walked. Yes, I walked. It is not far from here. I left here just before seven, and walked through the wood, and across the common until I reached the house.'

'Even although it was getting dark, sir?' asked Crabb.

'I know the path well. I have been that way many times, Constable. Now if you will excuse me,' said Sommersby, recovering his composure. 'I really do have to go.' He walked over to the door.

'One more question, Mr Sommersby. Did you see anyone either leaving the house when you arrived, or even anyone loitering in the near vicinity of the building?'

'No.'

'You are sure on that point?'

'Of course, I am not in the habit of telling untruths, Inspector. Now I wish you good day. I am sure you can make your own way out.'

'We may need to see you again,' called out Ravenscroft — but the schoolmaster had already left the room.

'Well, he's a fine fellow and no mistake,' said Crabb, as the two men made their way back along the corridor.

'I think our fine Mr Sommersby could tell us a lot more, Crabb. He was more than anxious last night to see that everyone should have assumed that Pitzer had died of natural causes.'

'I think you rattled him, sir, with your questioning, if you don't mind my saying so, sir.'

'Well, we will certainly need to return to question him further. Where next, Crabb?'

'I thought you might want to see the Reverend Touchmore at the Priory Church, sir.'

'Then lead on. Upwards this time, I believe.'

'Afraid so, sir,' said Crabb, ruefully.

* * *

The church clock of the Priory church sounded out the hour of eleven, as the two policemen made their way through the churchyard towards an old building situated at the entrance to the site.

'The reverend gentleman has his office up these stairs, sir,' said Crabb, pushing open the heavy door. They made their way up the winding staircase until they reached a landing, where they found a doorway facing them.

Crabb banged his fist on the door.

'Ah, Inspector Ravenscroft, the constable said that you would want to speak with me. Do please come in,' said Touchmore ushering the two men inside. 'I'm afraid you will have to take me as you find me. Paperwork, you know. Never-ending paperwork!'

The clergyman picked up a stack of old papers that had been placed on one of the chairs and threw them into a corner of the floor. Ravenscroft observed that Touchmore's desk was littered with piles of books and ledgers; while other old papers, charts and artefacts seemed to be gathering dust in every inch of the room.

'Do take a seat, Inspector,' said the cleric, indicating the empty chair with one hand, while using the other to mop his sweating brow with a large red spotted handkerchief. 'Dear me, there never seems enough hours in the day to fulfil all the tasks one has set oneself. Oh, my cane. I've been looking for that all morning. So that's where it was all the time, on the chair under all those papers.'

Ravenscroft passed over the silver-handled cane to its owner and sat down.

'I'll stand, thank you, sir,' said Crabb, closing the door to the room.

'This is a very sad business. Poor old Jabez. He will be a sad loss to us all, a very sad loss,' said Touchmore, sitting down behind his desk.

'You had known Pitzer long?' asked Ravenscroft.

'For nearly thirty years or more,' sighed Touchmore, wiping the top of his bald head with the handkerchief.

'Would you say that Mr Pitzer had made many enemies during that time?'

'Good lord, no,' replied Touchmore laughing. 'Jabez had not an enemy in the world. Everyone liked him. Had he lived he would almost certainly have become mayor of the town in a few months' time. No, in all my years I have never heard anyone say a cross word about him.'

'He was very active in a number of spheres, I understand?'

'Why yes. He had been a member of the town council for fifteen years or more. He was also one of our church wardens and was a prominent member of the vestry.'

'Did Mr Pitzer have any other interests?'

'Well, there was the Temperance League, the bank — and Mrs Pitzer, she also served on a number of local committees directed towards the welfare of our less fortunate citizens,' replied the cleric, returning the handkerchief to his coat pocket.

'But Mr Pitzer left all that side of things to his wife?' asked Ravenscroft.

'Well, er, yes, I suppose so.'

'Mr Pitzer himself was not involved in any kind of charity work then?'

'No, I suppose not, — although he was a trustee, like myself, of Old Lechmere's Almshouses.'

'Old Lechmere's Almshouses?'

'Yes, they can be found at the nearby village of Colwall. One of the Lechmere's, a local family, left a sizeable sum of money in the sixteenth century for the foundation and building of a group of almshouses for the aged and infirm of the village. There are a group of trustees appointed from amongst prominent persons in the area, whose duty it is to see that the almshouses are administered correctly.'

'How long had Mr Pitzer been a trustee?' asked Ravenscroft.

'For about fifteen years, like myself. Yes, I remember, we were both appointed at the same time. But can I ask, Inspector, as to the reasoning behind all these questions? They won't bring back poor old Pitzer you know. It is my understanding that the poor man died from a seizure of some kind.'

'We have reasons to believe, sir, that Mr Pitzer was poisoned,' said Crabb.

'Poisoned! Surely there must be some mistake? Both Gladwyn and Sommersby stated that in their opinion Pitzer had died as the result of a seizure,' said Touchmore, retrieving his handkerchief from his coat pocket and dabbing it onto his reddened, perspiring face.

'Both gentlemen were incorrect in their assumption. We believe that Pitzer was poisoned at around six thirty in the evening. At what time did you arrive at the house?' enquired Ravenscroft rising and walking over to the window.

'I, er —well — are you sure Pitzer was poisoned? Dear me, this is terrible. Who can have done such a terrible thing? The man had not a single enemy in the whole wide world,' Touchmore repeated. 'A terrible, unforgivable thing! But to answer your question, Inspector, I arrived at the house just after seven.'

'Did you see any person leaving the building, or anyone lingering about in the neighbourhood?'

'No. I don't think so. I remember leaving the vicarage at around ten minutes to seven. The cab dropped me off at the end of the drive, as I said, just after seven. Really, Inspector, I cannot accept this at all. I can think of no reasons as to why anyone would want to kill Pitzer. I'm sure you must be mistaken. For all these years . . .'

As Ravenscroft looked out of the window, he suddenly noticed a familiar, black-attired figure walking up the path that threaded its way between the gravestones in the churchyard. The veiled lady of the train and the well house had reappeared yet again to distract his thoughts and to arouse his curiosity. He watched her for some moments, until she sat on one of the benches near the flight of steps leading up from the churchyard onto the upper terrace of the town.

'Jabez and I had spent many a pleasant evening together.' Touchmore was still recalling the past. 'I can't imagine how poor Mrs Pitzer must be feeling. She must be distraught, the poor lady. She will find his passing such a sad loss.'

'I understand that the couple do not have any immediate family?' said Ravenscroft, turning away from the window. 'There were no children?'

'Alas, no, it was a great sadness in their lives that they were not granted God's gift. Mrs Touchmore and I had one child, a boy, but he died of the fever when he was quite young, many years ago of course.'

'I'm sorry for your loss.'

'Thank you, Inspector. Is there anything else I can help you gentlemen with?'

'Not at the present, Reverend, although we may need to ask you some more questions at a future time. Meanwhile, if you can remember seeing anyone near the house when you arrived last night or if you can think of anyone at all who might have had a grudge against Pitzer, or with whom he might have had a recent falling out, I would be obliged if you would let me know. I can be contacted at the Tudor or you can leave a message for Constable Crabb at the police station. I wish you good day, sir.'

Ravenscroft and Crabb turned to leave the room.

'Well, I suppose there could — but no, that is foolish thoughts. Good day to you, gentlemen.'

'There was something?' enquired Ravenscroft, returning to the desk.

'No. It is nothing.'

'It may have some relevance, sir.'

'Well, there has been a recent disagreement over the almshouses.'

'Go on, sir,' urged Crabb.

'Recently the trustees and the warden of the almshouses have had — well, shall we say, a slight falling out or difference of opinion, over certain matters.'

'A difference of opinion?' asked Ravenscroft, sensing that Touchmore was clearly feeling ill at ease.

'The warden, a young impulsive fellow by the name of Armitage, was appointed to the position at the almshouses about three years ago. If we had known at the time that he is of a radical, dissenting disposition, I'm sure we would never have appointed him, but then sometimes one is led astray in these matters. I know that Mr Pitzer in particular had taken a dislike to the fellow and that the two of them had disagreed over certain matters in regard to the financial affairs of the almshouses. Dear me, I have perhaps said rather too much. Ignore what I have said. I'm sure that Armitage was not the sort of fellow to kill Pitzer over such a trifling matter. Now if you will excuse me, I have to prepare for a service in the priory.'

'Of course, Reverend, you have been most helpful.'

Ravenscroft and Crabb made their way down the stairs.

'Quickly, Crabb, there is someone in the churchyard I caught sight of.'

The two men walked swiftly out of the building, and Ravenscroft led the way across the churchyard.

'She was sitting on this bench, not five minutes ago.'

'Whoever it was, sir, has flown the nest, as they say.'

'Yes indeed.'

'Who did you see, sir?' asked Crabb, puzzled.

'It is of no matter. Tell me, what did you make of our reverend gentleman?'

'Well, sir, he seemed quite surprised when we told him that Pitzer had been poisoned.'

'Yes, I think the two men were friends.'

'The reverend is quite liked in the town, I believe. Been here almost as long as the church, I should think.'

'Strange how he remembered about the disagreements at the almshouses just as we were leaving, and yet he was quite adamant when we arrived that Pitzer had not an enemy in the world.'

'Just slipped his mind, I suppose.'

'Then at the end of our visit, he thought that he had said too much. Anyway, I think you and I should make a visit to these almshouses and have a few words with this Armitage fellow. Where are they again?'

'At Colwall, sir, that's about four miles away, over the other side of the hills.'

'Good. Unfortunately, I have to return to the Tudor for my next treatment now so meet me there at three this afternoon. I'll have someone arrange a cab for us to travel over to Colwall. Until then, Crabb, I wish you adieu.'

'And you, sir. I hope you enjoy your bath,' shouted Crabb, as he walked away down the road.

* * *

After suffering the rigours of yet another warm bath and being bound tightly like an Egyptian mummy for what had appeared to be an eternity, Ravenscroft was pleased to be closing the door of the Tudor behind him, and to be climbing into the cab that was to take Crabb and himself to the nearby village of Colwall.

'And how goes the water treatment with you this afternoon, sir?' asked Crabb, in a jovial tone.

'Exceedingly badly, thank you, Crabb. I cannot understand what on earth possessed me to make the decision to subject myself to such strange tortures,' replied Ravenscroft.

'I'm sure it must be doing you a power of good, sir. You will no doubt feel the benefits when you return to London.'

'I should doubt that very much. But enough of the water cure and the Tudor. It is a fine afternoon, and I am looking forward to our excursion to Colwall. Drive on!'

Ravenscroft sat back in the cab and prepared to enjoy the scenery. During the next twenty minutes or so, their journey took them first towards the direction of Pitzer's house, before a sharp turn to their right took them up a long steep road almost to the top of the hill, enabling the two men to enjoy the wide, ranging views over the Worcestershire countryside. Reaching the summit, the cab navigated carefully over the narrow road before pausing for a moment or so, enabling Ravenscroft and his companion to marvel at the rugged landscape that opened up before them.

'This is known as the Wyche, sir, so called after the old salt route that ran over the hills between the counties of Worcester and Hereford. Colwall is just down there,' informed Crabb, pointing to the winding route that lay before them.

'I see now why this area attracts so many visitors.' replied Ravenscroft, his face turned towards the welcoming rays of the afternoon sun.

The cab man flicked his whip and the cab continued its journey, turning first left, then right, then left again, and so on, down the steep meandering road, until the way ahead finally became straight and stretching into the distance. As they entered the village of Colwall they passed between two rows of cottages, each with their own neat little gardens, until the cab halted on the edge of what Ravenscroft supposed to be the village green.

The two men alighted from the cab, and Crabb gave instructions to the driver that he was to wait for their return. There in front of them lay a line of black and white thatched cottages.

'These are Old Lechmere's Almshouses,' said Crabb, nodding at the buildings.

Outside the nearest cottage, two old men sat talking together and smoking long clay pipes.

'Good day, my man,' said Crabb, addressing the first man. 'We have come to speak with Mr Armitage. Do you know where he is?'

'No good asking him. He can't speak. Lost his tongue in an argument with his wife,' said the second man indicating his companion.

'Can you tell me where Mr Armitage is, then?' asked Crabb.

'No good asking me. I can't 'ear yer. Lost me 'earing on account of my wife shouting so much!' answered the first old man, laughing.

'Come on Crabb, we will perhaps do better looking for him ourselves,' interjected Ravenscroft, realising that any further attempts of conversation would be futile.

'I think you're right, sir. Thank you, gentlemen,' said Crabb.

The two policemen moved on.

'What did they want then?' asked a voice behind them.

'Wanted to know where young Armitage was,' replied the second old man. 'Told him we can't help him on account of our wives.'

The two men chuckled.

'Take no notice of them, sir. Their brains are addled,' said Crabb, shaking his head.

They continued walking past more cottages until they reached a slightly larger building, which was separated from the rest of the row.

'I fancy this might be where the warden lives,' suggested Crabb, walking up a path that ran between rows of red and white rose bushes, towards the front door. Before they could raise the knocker however, they were interrupted by a voice coming from the corner of the garden.

'May I be of assistance to you two gentlemen?'

The speaker was a tall, thin gentleman, dressed in country attire and a garden apron, and sporting a fine long, red, flowing beard. Ravenscroft guessed his age to be around thirty years or so.

'Do we have the pleasure of addressing Mr Armitage?' enquired Ravenscroft.

'You do,' replied the other.

'My name is Inspector Ravenscroft. This is Constable Crabb. We are investigating the death of Mr Jabez Pitzer of Malvern Wells.'

'Pitzer dead, you say? I was not aware that he had died,' replied Armitage, placing his gardening bucket on the ground before him, before wiping his dirty hands on his apron.

'He died yesterday evening, sir,' said Crabb, taking out his pocketbook from his tunic.

'What terrible news. How did he die?'

'We have reason to believe that he was poisoned,' said Ravenscroft.

Armitage turned away. 'I don't see what this has to do with me.'

'We are trying to build up a picture of Mr Pitzer's business concerns, and we think you could be of assistance. I understand that he was one of the trustees of the almshouses?'

'As indeed were a number of other gentlemen. The trust deed states that there shall always be ten trustees of the almshouse. They were founded in the sixteenth century, by a local benefactor, Sir Nicholas Lechmere.'

'How long have you been warden here?'

'Three years.'

'We understand that you and Mr Pitzer had a falling out over a few matters concerning the running of the alms-houses,' said Ravenscroft, closely observing the young man's expression.

'Ah, I see you think I killed Pitzer because we had a "falling out", as you so eloquently put it, Sergeant,' laughed Armitage, picking up his bucket and moving off towards his doorway.

'Inspector,' corrected Ravenscroft.

'Inspector? Well, then, this must indeed be a serious matter, if the Malvern Constabulary has secured the services of an inspector to investigate Pitzer's death.'

'This is not a matter to be taken lightly, sir,' said Crabb.

'I am sure not. There was no offence intended.'

'And none taken, Mr Armitage,' said Ravenscroft. 'You would oblige us, though, by informing us as to the nature of these differences of opinion, if you would be so kind.'

'Oh dear, Inspector, I'm sure that if I told you all about our little matters of difference of opinion, I would be in danger of detaining you here until the sun sets over that field.'

'We have plenty of time at our disposal.' Ravenscroft was becoming irritated by the warden's casual manner.

'Well, I'm afraid I haven't. Good day to you two gentlemen.'

Armitage went to enter his cottage but Crabb smartly moved to one side of the path, blocking his way.

'Mr Armitage, you will oblige us, sir, by answering our questions,' said Ravenscroft, using his best voice of authority. Armitage gave him an unwelcome stare, and sighed.

'When I came here three years ago, I could see that the almshouses were in a poor state of disrepair. The buildings had been sadly neglected for many years and the previous incumbent had spent the majority of his time in Tewkesbury, instead of supervising the health and education of the old people. I merely suggested, upon a number of occasions, that the trustees spend more of the money that has been invested from old Lechmere's bequest, on the improvement of the houses for the benefit of the residents.'

'And the trustees refused?' suggested Crabb, looking up from his notebook.

'Let us say that they were not forthcoming. I know that some of them regard my ideas as being somewhat too liberal. Malvern is a very conservative town. It does not welcome change, Inspector.'

'What radical ideas were those, Mr Armitage?' asked Ravenscroft, anxious to know more of the rift between Armitage and his employers.

'I felt that we should be adopting a more outgoing approach; that we should extend our mission, for want of a better word, out towards the less fortunate members of the village. I wanted to start classes for not only the residents but also any of the poorer villagers who would benefit from them. I am a great believer in education for the working classes, Inspector.'

'It all sounds a noble idea to me, Mr Armitage. I cannot see why the trustees would object.'

'Ah well, Inspector that is where you are wrong. Pitzer and several of the trustees thought that my ideas would prove too radical for the people of Colwall, who might be tempted to stray from the straight and narrow. In other words, I was regarded as a corrupting influence. Some of the trustees tried to remove me and replace me with another, one who would be more in tune with their conservative thinking.'

There was no doubting the bitterness of tone in Armitage's voice.

'The Reverend Touchmore spoke of financial irregularities in the running of the almshouses,' said Ravenscroft.

'Touchmore is a silly old man who ought to keep his idle thoughts to himself.'

'You have charge of the finances of the almshouses?'

'I have access to some finance. As the warden, I am expected to attend to bills that may arise from time to time, from the food, clothing and daily expenditure of the inmates.'

'For which you keep accounts, sir?' asked Crabb.

'For which I keep detailed accounts. Look, I really don't see the relevance of all this,' replied Armitage, throwing up his arms in the air.

'It is for us to decide what is relevant, Mr Armitage, and what is not. So, Mr Pitzer and the reverend Touchmore and some of the other trustees thought that the accounts were not in order?'

'I have said, Inspector, that some of the trustees wanted to remove me because of my reforming views. If they could have found some financial irregularities in the accounts, well, that would have provided them with the excuse they were looking for to dismiss me.'

'And did they find any such irregularities?'

'Certainly not!'

'Then you would not object if we studied the accounts?'

There was silence for a moment or so, before Armitage spoke. 'I do not have the accounts here.'

'Where are they then, sir?' asked Crabb.

'The accounts are at my sister's house. She resides in Ledbury.'

'That is a rather strange state of affairs. Surely it would be more convenient to keep the account books here at the almshouses?' asked Ravenscroft

'I visit my sister usually once a week and it is an easy matter for me to bring the books up to date. I do not like leaving the account books here.'

'And why is that, sir?'

'There have been one or two burglaries recently at the almshouses. I removed the books and one or two more valuable items to my sister's house, where I considered they would be safer.'

'You did not report these burglaries to the police station at Malvern, sir,' ventured Crabb, writing down something in his notebook.

'No, I did not consider they were important, although I may have mentioned it to the constable on duty at the Ledbury station. Look, I really must go now.'

'Very well, Mr Armitage. That will be all for now. I should warn you, though, that we may need to talk with you again, and that we might require access to the accounts of the almshouses.'

'Of course,' nodded Armitage, turning away.

'Good day to you, sir.'

Crabb and Ravenscroft made their way up the garden path, as Armitage opened the door of his cottage and went inside.

'Good day to you, gentlemen,' said Crabb, as they passed by the two old men.

'What's he say?' asked one of the other.

'Says he has to go home, lest his wife tell him off!'

The two men laughed.

'Well, that Armitage is a tight fellow and no mistake,' said Crabb, as they made their way back to their waiting cab. 'All that nonsense he gave us about the almshouses being burgled.'

'He was certainly reluctant to let us view the accounts. I find it very difficult to accept that the books are lodged with his sister in Ledbury,' said Ravenscroft, climbing back into the cab. 'We will certainly need to speak with him again. Our Mr Armitage is holding something back, I'm sure.'

'Perhaps Pitzer found that Armitage had been cheating the almshouses of money and called him to account, and rather than be discovered Armitage decided to kill Pitzer so that it would all be kept secret?'

'That is a strong possibility, but your argument has only one flaw. If we accept what Touchmore told us, namely that the other trustees knew or suspected that Armitage had been appropriating some of the funds for himself, then Armitage would have to kill the other trustees as well to safeguard his secret. To remove all the trustees would cause a great deal of suspicion, I think you would agree.'

'Pitzer might have discovered something that the other trustees did not know about and decided to keep it secret.'

'True. We must consider all possibilities. Where do you suggest we go next, Constable Crabb?'

'I thought we should call on Doctor Gladwyn, sir.'

'Then Doctor Gladwyn it is.'

* * *

Twenty minutes later the men found their cab had returned them to the town of Great Malvern.

'Gladwyn lives just below Link Top,' said Crabb, as the cab sped past the Tudor, along Belle Vue Terrace and out of the town. After passing a church on their left and the beginnings of a large expansive common stretching away on their right, their journey took them past a number of attractively designed villas, until eventually lower down the road, their driver swung the cab through a gateway that led up to an house built in the recent Gothic style.

'This is where the good doctor resides,' said Crabb stepping down from the cab and instructing their driver to await their return.

Ravenscroft walked up to the front door and pulled the bell under a brass plaque bearing the words: *Septimus Gladwyn. Physician.*

The door was opened by a maid.

'Inspector Ravenscroft and Constable Crabb, called to see Doctor Gladwyn, if you please,' said Crabb.

The girl gave him a disapproving stare, then said, 'Wait here' — and disappeared inside the building.

The two men stepped inside and found themselves in a drab, dark hallway. Ravenscroft looked at the faded photographs on the walls and across towards the cluttered hallstand, full of battered hats and ancient walking sticks. A plant, which had clearly seen better days, spread out from a large cracked pot in the corner.

'Whatever is that smell, sir?' whispered Crabb

'I think the maid has been somewhat overzealous in her cleaning of this floor,' replied Ravenscroft.

'Smells more like the leftover cabbage from yesterday's dinner,' sniffed Crabb.

'Gentlemen, do come this way,' said Gladwyn, suddenly in the hallway. 'I think I can spare you a few minutes, before I commence my rounds.'

The two detectives followed the physician into what Ravenscroft supposed to be Gladwyn's consulting rooms.

'Do sit down.' Gladwyn indicated two chairs situated in front of his desk. 'How may I help you?'

'We are investigating the death of Mr Pitzer, Doctor Gladwyn,' began Ravenscroft, accepting the seat.

'There is nothing to investigate, Inspector. Pitzer died from natural causes. I am sure the coroner's inquest will agree with my diagnosis,' interjected Gladwyn, taking his seat behind the desk.

'Would it come as a surprise to you, Doctor, if I told you that Mr Pitzer was poisoned?'

'I would say that suggestion was somewhat fanciful. I examined Pitzer myself.' Gladwyn removed his spectacles and polished the lens on a large white handkerchief.

'Nevertheless, we did find traces of poison in the glass from which Mr Pitzer had been drinking.'

'I see,' said the doctor, looking down at his desk. 'This changes everything. We will have to see what the inquest reveals.'

'May I ask how long you had been Mr Pitzer's physician?' asked Ravenscroft.

'For over thirty years. He engaged me when he and his wife first moved to Malvern.'

'And how was his health during these years?'

'Really, Inspector, such things are confidential between doctor and patient,' protested Gladwyn, replacing his spectacles.

'Surely that no longer applies now that your patient is deceased. This is a murder inquiry, Doctor Gladwyn, and we would appreciate it if you could answer all our questions,' said Ravenscroft firmly.

The two men stared at one another, before Gladwyn broke the silence.

'Mr Pitzer had generally enjoyed the best of health over the years. However, he had been working quite hard recently. I thought he could do with a complete rest for a week or two. Unfortunately, he did not take my advice.'

'I am right in assuming that Mr and Mrs Pitzer had no children?' asked Ravenscroft, anxious to continue with his questioning now that the doctor was now more forthcoming.

'That is correct. They were not fortunate in that direction.'

'Mr Pitzer never had cause to confide with you relating to any matters of a sexual nature?'

'I find that question rather offensive, Inspector. Mr Pitzer was not the kind of man to engage in extramarital affairs. He was utterly devoted to his wife,' replied Gladwyn, annoyed.

'Can I turn to other matters now? We have heard that Mr Pitzer played a prominent role in the affairs of the town.'

'That is so. We served together on a number of committees which benefited the local community.'

'Was the trusteeship of Old Lechmere's Almshouses one of them?'

'Yes, both Mr Pitzer and I were trustees, but I don't see the relevance of all this,' replied Gladwyn, a puzzled expression on his face.

'I believe that Mr Pitzer and Mr Armitage did not agree on a number of matters regarding the almshouses?' suggested Ravenscroft.

'I don't think they particularly liked one another.'

'The Reverend Touchmore says there were certain financial irregularities concerning the finances of the almshouses.'

'I was not aware that was the case.'

'You cannot recall any disagreement, concerning the accounts, between the trustees and Mr Armitage?'

'None that I recall. Look, Inspector, I have been quite patient with your questioning, but I'm afraid I must insist that we now conclude this discussion. I do have patients that require my most urgent attention.'

'Thank you, Doctor Gladwyn. We won't take up any more of your busy time,' said Ravenscroft, rising from his seat.

'I'll get my maid to see you out,' said Gladwyn, ringing a bell on his desk.

'One final question, Doctor Gladwyn — yesterday evening, did you have cause to visit Mr Pitzer, before Mr Sommersby summoned you to the house?' asked Ravenscroft.

'No. I have not visited Pitzer's house for several weeks now. Show these gentlemen out,' said Gladwyn, addressing the maid.

'Where were you between six and seven yesterday evening, sir?'

'I was here, with my wife.'

'Thank you, sir, we wish you good day.'

Ravenscroft and Crabb made their way out of the house and climbed back into their cab.

'Good to be out in the fresh air again, sir,' said Crabb, taking a deep breath.

'Doctors' waiting rooms are often like that,' replied Ravenscroft mounting the cab.

'Doctor Gladwyn was not particularly forthcoming.'

'On the contrary, whereas the Reverend Touchmore speaks of irregularities in the accounts of the almshouses, it appears that Doctor Gladwyn was not aware that there were any. One of the two men is lying, unless of course one of them has a short memory. Either way, it would appear more and more likely that those almshouses might well have played an important role in Pitzer's death.'

'You think we should return there tomorrow?'

'Perhaps.'

The cab made its way back along the drive, but as the vehicle turned into the roadway, the driver suddenly pulled up the horse, throwing the policemen back into their seats.

'There, boy! Steady! Easy does it. Look out, you fool!' shouted their driver.

The cause of the horse's fright was a tall, bearded, elderly figure who had been walking straight in front of its path.

'I think the poor man is blind!' cried out Ravenscroft.

The man in question was simply dressed, wearing a pair of old trousers, and a shirt and waistcoat under a torn, open overcoat. He was staring out vacantly ahead of him and mumbling something under his breath.

'Out of the way there!' shouted the driver.

The man swore something under his breath, before moving quickly away down the road.

'Poor fellow,' remarked Crabb, as the cab resumed its journey.

'Strange, but I seemed to think I caught sight of the same man loitering on the other side of the road, just when we arrived at Gladwyn's house,' said Ravenscroft.

'Shall I go after him, sir?'

'No. He was in all probability some vagrant on the look-out for his next meal.'

'I'll ask the station to keep a look out for him. Those types can often be up to no good. Where would you like to go next, sir?'

'I think it is time we ate. I don't know about you, Constable, but I have an increasing hunger, and have not had a decent meal since I arrived in this town. Perhaps you could recommend somewhere, Crabb, where we might procure a chop or two. The fare at the Tudor is meagre and uneatable, the surroundings dull, and the company almost non-existent.'

'I think I can suggest somewhere which I hope will be to your liking, sir. Cabbie, take us to Westminster Road, if you will.'

* * *

Ten minutes later Ravenscroft found himself alighting from the cab outside a small white cottage, situated along a narrow road, which looked down onto the main road to the Wells.

'You certainly have a magnificent view from up here,' he said, looking across the open countryside.

Crabb paid their driver and the cab trotted off. 'If you would care to follow me, sir, I'm sure my Jennie will be pleased to meet you,' he said opening the gate.

'You're a dark fellow, Crabb. I was not aware that you were married.'

Crabb smiled, opened the front door of the cottage and indicated that Ravenscroft should step inside.

'Ah, there you are, Jennie my dear. This is Mr Ravenscroft.'

'Mr Ravenscroft. My Tom has told me all about you. It is a pleasure to meet you, sir.' The speaker was a thin, rosy-cheeked woman, of homely appearance, who curtsied as they entered the tiny room. Ravenscroft estimated her to be around twenty years of age and knew straight away that he would like her.

'I said that Mr Ravenscroft would be welcome to share our meal with us, especially as I know that you always cook more than enough, my dear.'

'My dear Mrs Crabb, this is frightfully unjust of your husband to suddenly impose me upon you,' said Ravenscroft, shaking her hand.

'We would be delighted of your company, sir. Tom is quite correct when he says I always cook too much. He often chides me, saying that he will be twice the size he is now by the time he is thirty, if I carries on the same way,' she laughed. 'You are more than welcome, sir.'

'That is most kind of you,' replied Ravenscroft.

'Well, sir. If you would like to give me your coat, and then sit at the table, I'll get us a drink,' said Crabb.

Ravenscroft looked around the welcoming room, with its neat, tidy furnishings and the warm fire that glowed in the hearth. Jennie disappeared into the kitchen, as Crabb poured out two mugs of ale from an earthenware pitcher. 'There you are, sir. Taste that and tell me what you think.'

'Uncommonly good and certainly welcome after all our travels today. Have you been married long?'

'Just six months, sir.'

'And how did you come to be here at Malvern? I thought you were bought up on a farm near Evesham?' asked Ravenscroft, sitting back in his chair.

'Indeed I was, sir. But our farm did not provide enough work for the two of us, so my elder brother took over the farm when my father died three years ago and he now runs it with my mother. I saw a job going with the Evesham constabulary and applied and worked there for a while. Then I married my Jennie, and they said there was this police cottage here at Malvern Wells, so we moved here just four months ago.'

'Malvern seems a strange place, full of doctors and water cure patients,' said Ravenscroft, taking another mouthful of his ale.

'Very stuck in its ways, sir, is Malvern. Very conservative it is in all respects, and the same group of people — Pitzer, Touchmore, Sommersby, Gladwyn and their friends — seem to run everything. Nothing much seems to happen here, until now of course with this murder. I am only thankful that you were on that train, sir, as I don't think I could have conducted a murder inquiry on my own.'

'I'm sure you would have managed.'

''Tis certainly a strange affair, no mistaking it, sir. Everyone says that Pitzer didn't have any enemies, yet our reverend gentleman says that Pitzer had had a disagreement with this Armitage fellow over the accounts.'

'Now, Tom, put your police talk on one side, while we have our meal,' said Jennie, returning from the kitchen, carrying a large steaming saucepan, which she set down upon the table.

'You are quite right, Mrs Crabb, we policemen have a habit of taking our cases home with us. My, that smells incredibly good,' said Ravenscroft, leaning forwards.

'My Jennie makes the best mutton stew in the whole of Malvern,' said Crabb, hastily tucking a napkin under his necktie.

'Only Malvern! Why, Tom Crabb, you said Worcestershire last week,' laughed Jennie, ladling out the food into their bowls.

'Nay, why stop at Worcestershire, when there is the whole of the county to be fed! Let Mr Ravenscroft be the judge of your fine dish.'

Ravenscroft took a forkful. 'I swear,' he declared, 'this is the best thing I have eaten since I have been here in Malvern.'

Crabb gave his wife a wink.

'Mr Ravenscroft is staying at the Tudor, my dear.'

'Oh, you poor man, you must be quite starved!'

'Doctor Mountcourt does not believe in providing generous helpings of food for his guests — he declares the frugal fare to be part of the treatment. What few patients there are, do not seem to be enjoying the experience. The place is quite miserable. But enough of the Tudor. This really is quite excellent, Mrs Crabb.'

'Then you shall have some more, sir,' said Jennie, ladling more of the mixture into Ravenscroft's bowl.

'I will certainly not refuse. Tell me, if I am not being impolite, how did you two meet?' asked Ravenscroft, taking another mouthful of the warming food.

'Jennie and I lived in the same village,' said Crabb. 'We went to the same school together. I always knew that she was the girl for me, although it took me a while to persuade her to marry me. But I tells you, Mr Ravenscroft, I have never regretted it. Not one day have I ever woken up and regretted my choice. She is the finest, most handsome, noblest woman for miles around—'

'Stop! Tom, your embarrassing me,' interrupted Jennie, looking down at her bowl and turning a bright red.

'I admire your certainty and commitment,' replied Ravenscroft.

'And are you married, sir?' asked Jennie.

'Jennie my love, we should not ask our guests such questions,' said Tom, reprimanding his wife.

'I'm so sorry, sir, my inquisitive nature sometimes gets the better of me,' said Jennie, looking crestfallen.

'I do not mind answering. No. There is no Mrs Ravenscroft. There was someone some years ago with whom I formed a close attachment, but she went away before I could decide that I cared for her.'

'That is very sad,' said Jennie, looking across into Ravenscroft's eyes.

'Sometimes we realise that we have failed to make the best of the opportunities that are offered to us and it is only later — often much later — that we regret our lack of resolve.'

'And what happened to her? If I may be so bold as to ask you, sir,' enquired Jennie.

'She went to Australia, and I never saw her again,' replied Ravenscroft, turning away.

'Perhaps she will come back one day?' suggested Jennie.

'I would doubt it. She is probably married by now and the mother of ten lively children. You should have children, Crabb. Malvern and its hills would be a fine place to bring up a family.'

'Strange you should say that, sir—' began Crabb, but his wife interrupted him.

'Tom, please!'

'I don't care if I tells the whole world! My dearest Jennie is expecting our first child in six months' time,' said Crabb proudly.

'That is splendid news. I do congratulate you both. I'm sure you will make admirable parents,' said Ravenscroft, leaning across the table and shaking the hands of his host and hostess.

'Thank you, sir,' replied Jennie, going a deeper shade of red.

'Your children will certainly be well fed! This is the best thing that has happened to me in this town since I arrived here. I have never tasted food as good as this, even in London,' said Ravenscroft, emptying his bowl.

'Stop, sir, you're embarrassing me again,' laughed Jennie.

They were suddenly interrupted by a banging on the front door.

'If you will excuse me, sir, I'll just go and see who that is,' said Crabb, rising from the table.

'Your husband enjoys his work?' asked Ravenscroft. He could hear Crabb, talking to someone at the front door.

'Tom enjoys being out and about,' replied Jennie. 'And yes, he likes his work, sir.'

Crabb returned to the room, studying a piece of paper, and looking very solemn.

'Trouble, Crabb?' enquired Ravenscroft, sensing that something was wrong.

'A note, sir, delivered from Malvern College. It says we are to come straight away. It seems that Mr Sommersby has met with a fatal accident!'

CHAPTER FOUR

As Ravenscroft and Crabb made their way down the winding path that lead to Malvern College, they were overtaken by a trap that drew up sharply at the front entrance of the building.

'It seems as though our Doctor Gladwyn has been sent for as well,' said Crabb.

'News travels fast,' remarked Ravenscroft.

'Good evening to you again, gentlemen,' said Gladwyn, alighting from his trap. 'Have you heard the news about Sommersby?'

The door was opened by the porter, who was clearly in an agitated state. 'Thank goodness you gentlemen have come. Mr Sommersby seems to have met with a terrible accident. If you would all come this way.'

The porter led the way across the hall and down the cloister like corridor, until they reached the library. 'I think perhaps you should enter first, gentlemen.'

'Good heavens!' exclaimed Gladwyn.

The floor was littered with books and Ravenscroft noticed that one of the large bookcases had been pulled to the side of the room.

'Mr Sommersby must have been working in the library when one of the bookcases fell on top of him. We lifted the bookcase from off him, and placed it over there,' said the porter.

Sommersby lay on his back, surrounded by the fallen books.

Gladwyn knelt to examine the body.

'Have you moved the body at all?' asked Ravenscroft.

'No. We naturally moved some of the books that were on top of him, to see if we could render him any assistance, but all to no avail.'

'He must have been killed instantly by the force of the bookcase and the falling books,' said Gladwyn.

'The bookcase cannot have been very secure. He must have been reaching up for one of the books, when the bookcase toppled over,' suggested Crabb.

'The other bookcase, which is also in the centre of the room, looks pretty secure,' said Ravenscroft, placing his hand on one of the shelves. 'It would require quite a lot of force for the case to come down on one. On the other hand, if someone gave it a hard thrust from the other side, I have no doubt it would come down easily enough.'

'Poor man, what a terrible accident to have happened. First Pitzer and now Sommersby.' Gladwyn got to his feet and shook his head.

'I don't think it was an accident,' said Ravenscroft, kneeling by the side of the deceased. 'Look how the body is situated, on his back with his two arms at either side. It is almost as though the body had been arranged in this position before the bookcase was pushed over on top of him. If he had been placing a book on the shelf, and the case had begun to move suddenly, I believe Sommersby's instant reaction would be either to move back quickly, or at least attempt to cover his head with his hands, or even turn away. I can see a line on the floor where the edge of the bookcase stood. Sommersby is far too close to the line. Whoever killed him tried to make it look like an accident.'

'Good heavens!' exclaimed Gladwyn.

'Look for his pince-nez, Crabb. They are not on his face. Again, if the bookcase fell on top of him, they would have broken the glasses and yet I cannot see them anywhere,' said Ravenscroft. Crabb began to look around the room, searching through the piles of books on the floor as he did so.

'Doctor Gladwyn, can we turn Sommersby over?' asked Ravenscroft.

The two men moved Sommersby over so that his face lay to the floor.

'Ah, it is just as I suspected. See at the back of his head. He had been hit by a hard instrument of some kind. That is what killed him.'

'It could have been one of the books that hit him?' suggested Gladwyn.

'But the body was positioned on its back when we entered the room. It seems unlikely that after a falling book hit him on the head Sommersby would have turned around to face the rest of the falling books. If the first book hit him on the back of the head, he would have fallen in a different position.'

'I suppose you could be correct, Inspector,' replied Gladwyn somewhat grudgingly.

'Ah, here we are, sir. I've found them on the floor over here,' announced Crabb, holding up the glasses.

'I think you would agree, Doctor Gladwyn, that the position of the glasses in the room is too far away from the body,' said Ravenscroft.

'Sommersby could have taken them off, before he moved over to the bookcase,' suggested Gladwyn.

'And left them on the floor? I don't think so.' Ravenscroft knelt down on the floor and pushed the books to one side.

'What are you looking for, sir?' asked Crabb.

'I'm examining the carpet to see — ah, here we are. Do you see, Crabb? Look at this patch of blood on the carpet. This was where Sommersby was killed. He was struck on the back of his head by a sharp instrument of some kind, fell to the floor where some of the blood from the wound stained the carpet. He was then dragged across the floor to the base of the bookcases, which were then toppled over on top of him to make it look like an accident.'

'My word, sir!' exclaimed Crabb. 'Then it now seems that we now have two murders on our hands.'

'It would appear so. Did you see Mr Sommersby enter the library?' Ravenscroft addressed the porter.

'He came in here about an hour ago, sir.'

'Did you see anyone else enter or leave the library after Mr Sommersby?'

'No, sir. But my station is in the entrance hall, and I do not have a view of the library from where I am situated,' replied the porter.

'So it would have been comparatively simple for someone to enter the library from either the other end of the corridor or through one of these windows, and you would not have seen them?' asked Ravenscroft.

'That is correct, sir.'

'Did you hear the sound of the bookcase fall?'

'Yes, sir. There was an almighty crash.'

'And what did you do?'

'I ran into the library. I saw what had happened and ran off to the kitchens to summon help, so we could lift the bookcase off Mr Sommersby.'

'You saw no one in the library or running away?' asked Crabb.

'No.'

'How long were you away from the library fetching help?'

'About a minute or so, sir. We came back as quickly as we could.'

'It would have been easy for the murderer to have hidden himself in another part of the library when you entered the room, and for him to slip away unnoticed while you were away,' said Ravenscroft, staring out of the window. 'Tell me, was Mr Sommersby a single man?'

'He was as far as I know, sir.'

'Did he have rooms in college?'

'Yes, sir. As the assistant master he was entitled to reside in the college. His rooms are upstairs,' replied the porter.

'Then perhaps you would be kind enough to allow my colleague and myself to view them,' asked Ravenscroft.

'Do you want me any further, Ravenscroft?' asked Gladwyn.

'No, thank you, Doctor. You have been most helpful.'

'I'll arrange for the collection of the body and inform the coroner.'

'Thank you, Doctor Gladwyn.'

Ravenscroft and Crabb followed the porter up two flights of stairs and down a long corridor until they reached a door at the end of the passageway.

'These are Mr Sommersby's quarters,' said the porter, unlocking the door.

'Thank you. We will look round on our own, and let you know when we have finished,' said Ravenscroft, entering the rooms as the porter made his way back along the corridor.

The two policemen found themselves standing inside a comfortably furnished living room. A table was situated in the centre of the room, which also contained a desk and an armchair. The walls were lined with rows of books.

'Right, that must be the bedroom over there. I'll take this room, you look in there,' instructed Ravenscroft.

'What are we looking for, sir?' asked Crabb.

'I don't really know, Crabb, until I find it. Papers, documents, anything I suppose that might tell us more about Mr Sommersby and answer the question as to why he was murdered.'

Crabb disappeared into the bedroom as Ravenscroft looked at the many books that lined the dead man's bookcases. He then crossed over to the table and examined the papers lying there. Sommersby had evidently been making notes for an impending Latin lesson. On top of the desk was a pile of unmarked exercise books. Ravenscroft sat down on the chair behind the desk and went through the drawers, taking out the papers and examining them one by one. As he reached the bottom drawer on the left-hand side of the desk he found it locked. Taking out his pocket-knife, he slipped the blade between the wood and the lock until he was able to open the drawer fully. Inside he found yet more papers, which he placed on the desk and began to go through.

'Nothing in the bedroom, sir,' said Crabb, returning to the room. 'Have you found anything of interest there?'

'This document would appear to be a copy of Sommersby's last will and testament, made five years ago. Nothing particularly startling though. He leaves everything to Malvern College, although there does not appear to be much to leave — a hundred pounds, his watch, some pictures, and the books.'

'Not much to show for a life of school mastering,' said Crabb.

'In my experience, Crabb, schoolmasters are not particularly well paid, just as policemen are not, and he does not seem to have come into any legacies. It does not look as though he was killed for his money then. There was no inheritance to pass on. Ah, this looks interesting. Something to do with Old Lechmere's Almshouses in Colwall,' said Ravenscroft opening out the document. 'It names Sommersby as one of the trustees, and was drawn up about twenty years ago, by the look of it, when Sommersby was appointed. It names the other trustees. There is Pitzer and Touchmore, and Gladwyn as well. I don't know the others. Make a note of their names, Crabb. So Sommersby was also a trustee of the almshouses. Something he and Pitzer had in common. It is interesting how those old almshouses keep arising in our investigations,' said Ravenscroft, replacing the papers in the bottom drawer.

'I knew that Armitage fellow was hiding something. I didn't like the look of him at all,' replied Crabb, shaking his head.

'I certainly think the warden was not exactly forthcoming when we questioned him. I think you and I need to have more words with Mr Armitage. It is too late this evening but in the morning, another outing to Colwall is called for,' said Ravenscroft, closing the drawers of the desk. 'Before we leave, let us look around the rest of this room, Crabb. Is there anything you think we have missed? What does this room tell us about its occupant?' he said, rising from his seat.

'I can't see anything of note.'

'Our Mr Sommersby seems to have lived a frugal kind of existence. There is nothing here to suggest a vast expenditure. The contents of this room indicate a comfortable but not an overly indulgent life. Our good doctor was not a man to go about wasting his money. What's this?' said Ravenscroft. He lifted up the cane from a stand that lay near the doorway.

'It looks a fine cane to me. Silver handle, I'll be bound,' said Crabb.

'You are right, Crabb. The handle is well worn, indicating that it was purchased many years ago. What is interesting though, is the monogram. Looks like a large B interlocked with an M and a W.'

'May have been the initials of someone in his family?'

'There is no S for Sommersby, though. Nor an L, which might have stood for Lechmere's almshouses. M, B and W. No doubt the letters held some significance for Sommersby to have gone to the trouble of having them engraved on the handle of the walking stick.'

'Perhaps it was given to him by a grateful parent.'

'You could well be right, Crabb,' said Ravenscroft, returning the stick to its stand. 'Well, I think there is nothing else here that can shed any light on why our good doctor was murdered. I don't think we can do anything more here tonight. We will see what the morrow may bring.'

* * *

Ravenscroft woke with a start. He reached out for his pocket watch and spectacles and in the cold darkness of his room made out the hour to be not yet four.

The church clock had struck the hour of twelve when he had returned to the Tudor some hours earlier, but he had been unable to sleep for some time, his mind being occupied by the events of the previous two days. Why had Pitzer and

Sommersby been killed? Who had killed the two men? What possible reason could there be for anyone to have acted in such a way? The more he considered the matter, the more the same questions kept repeating themselves. Perhaps the answer lay in both men having been trustees of the Colwall Almshouses. He had certainly not thought that Armitage had been exactly forthcoming with his answers and had taken a dislike to the man. Pitzer and Armitage had not worked well together. What had been Armitage's relationship with Sommersby? Had they also had a falling out? Then there was Gladwyn and Touchmore, two more of the trustees. Did they know more than they were telling him?

Finally, he had drifted off into a half-sleep, during which he had seen again the old buildings in Colwall and then the gothic exterior of Malvern College. He saw himself making his way up the windy path to well house, where the dark familiar figure of the veiled lady had appeared to be awaiting his arrival. He had called out to her as he had drawn near, but as he looked upwards, the falling bookcases of the college library tumbled rapidly down towards him. Now he had awoken to find his face covered in moisture and his throat parched.

Reaching for the tumbler at the side of his bed, he poured some of the water into the glass and wiped his brow on his sleeve. After swallowing the liquid, he lay back on his pillow and stared out into the darkness of the room. What on earth had possessed him to come to such a place? Why had he so readily agreed to take on the task of solving one murder, only to be faced now with trying to solve two? How had his holiday turned into this thankless task? Ravenscroft let out a deep sigh, turned over and buried his face in the pillow.

* * *

'Good morning, Mr Ravenscroft; it's time for yer treatment, sir.'

Ravenscroft emerged from beneath the bed spread and gave Stebbins a bleary stare.

'Late night was it, sir?'

'Mind your own business, Stebbins.'

'There is a nice leg of chicken in the pantry, sir, I could get it for you.'

'That won't be necessary at the moment, but I might consider it for later,' said Ravenscroft, reaching for his dressing gown.

'Been dining out, have we?' asked Stebbins grinning. 'Doctor Mountcourt says he'll see you at ten this morning.'

Ravenscroft made the well-worn journey to the bath house.

'Good morning to you, Mr Ravenscroft. Time for your new treatment today,' said the attendant, a note of new optimism creeping into his voice. Ravenscroft's heart sank. What new torture were they about to inflict on him now, he wondered. But then he considered that nothing could possibly be worse than that which he had suffered already.

'If you would care to stand under this pipe, sir,' said the attendant indicating a cubicle situated in the corner of the room. Ravenscroft feared the worst as he began to remove his sleeping attire.

'Just stand there, sir. Be over before you can say Queen Victoria.'

Ravenscroft wondered what her majesty had to do with the situation. Nervously he stood under the pipe and looked upwards. Suddenly he felt the full force of a waterfall of freezing cold water cascading over his body. He let out a cry that was part pain and part anger.

'There you are, sir! You'll soon feel the benefit of that!' said the attendant, handing him a towel.

Ravenscroft muttered under his breath, and cursed the man, as he reached for the cloth. Now he knew what drowned rats felt like and resolved that this would positively be the last time he was going to be humiliated in this way.

After dressing he made his way up to St Ann's well. He had no desire to undertake the arduous journey yet again up the steep winding path, but he had little else to do before breakfast and thought that the exercise might at least bring some warmth back into his still-shaking limbs. There was also the prospect that he might again meet his veiled lady and learn more of her circumstances.

He found instead only the old woman and a young courting couple at the well. Sitting on the seat, outside the well house, drinking his beaker of refreshing spring water, the events of the previous evening began tumbling back into his mind. Why had two prominent members of Malvern society been killed in two days? Who would have wanted to have killed them — and for what purpose? Then he recalled that he had asked himself the same questions before he had fallen asleep. He resolved to put such thoughts away from his mind and enjoy the spring morning sunshine instead.

The young courting couple, becoming aware of his presence, moved away from the building and began to make their way upwards towards the higher reaches of the hills. Ravenscroft promised himself that once the case had been solved, and before he left the town, he might also venture forth to complete the journey towards the Beacon. Closing his eyes and letting the warm sunshine fall upon his face, his thoughts turned again to the veiled lady. She clearly had nothing to do with the deaths of the two men, and yet the mysterious woman intrigued him the more he thought about her. He half expected to see her sitting on one of the seats when he opened his eyes but knew that he would be disappointed. If only he had engaged her in conversation when the opportunity had availed itself, then his curiosity might have been satisfied. Now, he told himself, she had probably left the area and he was unlikely to see her again.

He rose from his seat, dropped a coin into the beaker for the well woman and, deep in thought, began to make his way back down the zigzagging pathway towards the town. As he reached the bottom of the path, he looked up to see a tall shambling figure coming towards him. He recognized him as the same man he had seen the previous day loitering outside Gladwyn's house. Although blind, the man seemed to be aware of the nature of the path beneath his feet. Ravenscroft uttered a few words of greeting; the other merely grunted as they passed by each other.

Upon reaching the town, instead of returning to the Tudor for breakfast, Ravenscroft decided to make his way to the Reading Rooms.

'Good to see you again, sir. The London papers have just arrived. May I serve you with coffee?' asked the attendant as he entered.

'You certainly may. Do you have any information about the ancient curse of Raggedstone Hill?' asked Ravenscroft.

'I think we might be able to accommodate you, sir. Please take a seat, and I will see what I can find for you.'

Ravenscroft made his way into the reading room and was rewarded within a few minutes by the attendant returning, carrying his coffee and holding an old, leather-bound book.

'I think you might find a summary in there,' said the attendant, handing him the volume.

The book was entitled *Old Myths and Legends of Worcestershire*.

'I think you will find what you are looking for on page thirty-five, sir,' said the librarian.

'Thank you,' replied Ravenscroft, opening the volume.

'Will that be all, sir?'

'Yes, thank you.'

Ravenscroft began to read, as the librarian gave a neat bow and left the room.

THE ANCIENT CURSE OF RAGGEDSTONE HILL

There is an ancient legend concerning a monk from Little Malvern Priory, who, contrary to his religious vows of chastity, fell in love with one of the local girls. The Prior, learning of his disgrace, ordered the monk to crawl on his hands and knees to the top of the Raggedstone Hill every day. Finally, one day, instead of offering up his usual prayers when he reached the summit, the monk cursed the hill and anyone on whom the shadow of the hill should fall. Shortly afterwards the monk died, worn out by his fatigues and harsh treatment — but the curse he had made lived on. There are numerous stories concerning people on whom the shadow fell and who subsequently suffered disasters. These include Cardinal Wolsey, the chief minister of Henry VIII who fell out with his master; and William Huskisson the famous member of parliament who fell under the wheels of George Stephenson's Rocket at the opening of the Liverpool to Manchester Railway. One wonders whether anyone else will succumb to the ancient curse?

Ravenscroft closed the book and smiled.

As he left the Reading Rooms, he enquired of the attendant as to the location of the Raggedstone Hill.

'Over here, sir,' said his informant, pointing to a map on one of the walls.

'Raggedstone is the last hill but one at the end of the range. It is just off the road that goes from Ledbury, through Eastnor, and on towards Tewkesbury,' said the attendant. 'It is quite wild and remote out there. I believe there is only a cottage or two in the area.'

Ravenscroft was relieved that the shadow from the hill did not appear to stretch anywhere near where either Pitzer or Sommersby lived.

'It is only an old legend, sir. Nothing to worry about,' said the attendant reassuringly, as Ravenscroft left the Reading Rooms.

Ravenscroft studied his pocket watch and realised that he would be late for his appointment with the formidable Doctor Mountcourt.

* * *

'I see some signs of improvement.'

The tone and manner were as brisk and efficient as before.

'I don't feel any,' said Ravenscroft, pulling his shirt back over his head.

'It is early days yet, Mr Ravenscroft. I see a slight improvement in your breathing. The water treatment and those walks over the hills must be doing you some good,' said Doctor Mountcourt. 'Although I believe you dined out last night?'

'I was fortunate to receive an invitation.'

'We would prefer it if you ate here at the Tudor, at all times, where we can see that your diet is properly regulated. I also see that you missed one of your treatments yesterday afternoon,' said Mountcourt, looking down at his notebook, a note of disapproval creeping into his voice.

'Yes, I was investigating the murder of Mr Pitzer,' replied Ravenscroft, doing up the remaining buttons on his shirt.

'I thought Mr Pitzer died from a seizure of some kind,' said Mountcourt, writing on Ravenscroft's medical card at his desk.

'He was poisoned.'

'And you would know, Mr Ravenscroft?' said Mountcourt, looking up from his writing and giving Ravenscroft a hard stare.

'It is my business to know about these things. I am an inspector with the Whitechapel Division in London,' replied Ravenscroft, trying to sound as confident as he could.

'Ah, I see that would explain your condition, but not your involvement.' Mountcourt resumed his writing. 'Malvern is clearly out of your jurisdiction.'

'I have been invited by the local constabulary to make enquiries regarding the death of Mr Pitzer, and now Mr Sommersby as well.'

'Yes, I heard about that. Poor fellow! Bookcase fell on top of him, I believe?'

'Did you know either of the two gentlemen concerned?'

'I have met them on several occasions. I have been here at the Tudor for only three years. Neither of them, of course, was my patient. I restrict my professional activities to my clientele here at the Tudor. That is more than enough to occupy my time. I expect Gladwyn was their doctor. You should speak with him.'

'I already have.'

'Good. I'm sure he has proved most helpful. Now if you will excuse me, I have another patient to see. Please continue with the treatment and walks. I'll see you again in another three days.'

* * *

The two policemen climbed into the waiting cab outside the Tudor.

'Where to, sir?' enquired Crabb.

'Back to the almshouses; I think it is about time that Mr Armitage showed us those account books,' replied Ravenscroft.

Several minutes later they found themselves outside the row of old buildings. The two men walked up the path of Armitage's cottage and knocked on the door.

'No good you knockin'. He ain't there.'

The speaker was one of the old men with whom they had spoken with the day before.

'Do you know when he will be back, my good fellow?' asked Crabb.

'Don't know. How should I know? He left last night. Just after you skedaddled,' said the old man. 'Ain't seen him since.'

'I believe he sometimes goes to see his sister in Ledbury?' suggested Ravenscroft.

'Does he now?'

'You don't happen to know whereabouts in the town that she resides?'

'Ain't been to Ledders since me wife left us.'

'Thank you. If Mr Armitage returns, will you tell him that Inspector Ravenscroft wants to speak with him urgently, and that I can be contacted at the Tudor in Malvern.'

'Ain't been to Malvern neither, since I left 'er,' replied the old man, wiping his nose on his sleeve.

'Nevertheless, I would be obliged,' said Ravenscroft firmly.

'Sees what I can do.'

'Good day to you, my man.'

'If we call in at the station in Ledbury, they will know where she lives,' suggested Crabb, as they made their way back to the cab.

'Good thinking, Crabb, then let us do that.'

Their journey continued along winding country lanes until they entered the market town of Ledbury. The cab pulled up outside the police station and Crabb went inside to consult with his colleagues, returning a few minutes later.

'It seems that there is a Miss Armitage who resides in Church Lane.'

Their driver took them on to the Market Place.

Ravenscroft and Crabb climbed down from the cab and looked around at the street full of half-timbered buildings and fine Georgian frontages.

'Can't go no further, it's up there,' said the cabman, pointing in the direction of a narrow lane in front of them.

'Will you wait for us here then, my good man?' said Crabb, patting the horse.

'I will. Old Patch could do with rest.'

The two men made their way up the narrow, cobbled street, where the old timbered buildings faced one another on either side, until they reached a black and white cottage, with neat hanging baskets of flowers outside.

'I think this is the place,' said Crabb. He reached out for the bell pull.

The door was opened by the maid.

'We understand that Miss Armitage lives here?' enquired Ravenscroft. 'Perhaps you would be good enough to say that Inspector Ravenscroft and Constable Crabb from the local Malvern Constabulary would like a word with her.'

The maid curtsied, pulled the door ajar and disappeared from view, leaving the two officers standing on the doorstep.

'The town seems a pleasant enough place,' said Ravenscroft, as they waited.

''Tis the first time I have been up this lane,' replied Crabb.

'Mistress says, would you like to enter this way, sir,' said the maid, returning.

Ravenscroft and Crabb followed the servant through a brightly lit hall and into a small drawing room.

'Mr Ravenscroft.' The speaker was a young lady of striking appearance and auburn hair, who Ravenscroft judged to be of around twenty-five years of age.

'I presume I have the honour of addressing Miss Armitage?' said Ravenscroft.

'You do, sir. How may I help you?'

'Your brother, is I believe, the warden of the almshouses at Colwall?'

'Yes. Has something happened to James?' she asked, suddenly alarmed. 'Has he met with an accident of some kind?'

'No. Your brother has not met with an accident. He is well, as far as we know.'

'That is a relief. Please do sit down, gentlemen.'

Ravenscroft accepted a seat by the table and looked around him. The room was light and airy, being comfortably but simply furnished. A small piano stood in one corner, upon which stood two vases of flowers and a framed photograph of a group of people. A round table and chairs were situated in the centre of the room, and a small but welcoming fire on one of the walls gave out a bright glow. Ravenscroft felt that its occupier had given the arrangement of the room a great deal of thought, and the more he gazed around him the more it seemed to him to be a place full of peace and calm, free from the cares of the outside world — almost a sanctuary.

'I should perhaps explain, Miss Armitage, why we have called upon you. Your brother is not here I suppose?'

'I have not seen my brother since last week,' said the lady of the house, resuming her seat.

'Constable Crabb and I are investigating the deaths of two prominent members of Malvern society. One of them was Mr Jabez Pitzer, who lived at Malvern Wells; the other a Mr Sommersby, the assistant master at Malvern College. Were you acquainted with either of these two gentlemen, Miss Armitage?' asked Ravenscroft.

'No, the gentlemen are unfamiliar to me, Inspector.'

'Did your brother ever mention their names?'

'I don't believe so,' she answered, looking puzzled by his questions.

'They were both trustees of the almshouses, Miss Armitage.'

'Ah, I see. I suppose my brother may then have mentioned them in passing. He often talks about the almshouses, but I am afraid I have no recollection of the names. I am sorry.'

'How often does your brother come to visit you?' asked Ravenscroft, trying not to be too forthright in his questioning.

'He usually calls upon me on a Saturday morning. He stays for a few hours. We go out into the town, have lunch here, talk together, and sometimes if it as a fine day we will go onto the hills.'

'Forgive the intrusion, Miss Armitage, but I could not help noticing the photograph. The people — they are other members of your family?'

'It was taken a few years ago, before my parents unfortunately died,' she replied, walking over to the piano and bringing the photograph over so that Ravenscroft might see it. 'That is my father, and there is my mother,' she said, pointing to the figures in the picture. 'We lived in Gloucestershire, near Fairford. After my parents died, James was fortunate enough to secure the position of warden at the almshouses. Naturally I could not share his abode there, so I came here to Ledbury and rented this cottage.' Ravenscroft thought he could discern a note of sadness in her voice.

'You have private means to support yourself? Forgive the question,' said Ravenscroft, beginning to feel uncomfortable with his intrusive questioning.

'I have a number of pupils who call upon me during the week. I give lessons in piano and some writing. My brother also assists me from time to time, but his income from the almshouses is fairly limited.'

'You like Ledbury, miss?' enquired Crabb.

'Yes. It is a very fine town. I have made many friends here,' she replied, smiling.

'I am glad of it, Miss Armitage. We spoke with your brother yesterday at the almshouses, but when we returned this morning we found that he had not been seen there since yesterday evening. If he is not here, can you think of anywhere else where he might be, anywhere at all?' asked Ravenscroft.

'No. I know James likes walking on the hills. We sometimes take a cab together up to the British Camp and walk down to Eastnor through the park. Is my brother in any kind of trouble?'

'No, not at all, my dear lady,' replied Ravenscroft, seeking to relieve her anxiety. 'We merely need to ask him some more questions concerning the affairs of the almshouses. Your brother mentioned that the accounts of the almshouses are kept here?'

'Yes.'

'Why is that so?'

'James, my brother, said there had been a burglary at the almshouses recently, and that the books would perhaps be safer if they were kept here. He was anxious that they would not fall into the wrong hands, and worried that he would be in trouble with the trustees if they were lost.'

'I wonder whether it would be possible if Constable Crabb and I looked at the books, if you have no objection, Miss Armitage?'

'Yes, of course. They are over here, in the bureau.'

Ravenscroft watched as their hostess walked over to the piece of furniture, opened the lid and took out a large ledger, which she placed on the table.

'Perhaps you would like some tea?'

'That would be most welcome,' replied Ravenscroft.

'I will leave you two gentlemen to your business, while I go and see to the tea.'

Ravenscroft rose from his seat as Miss Armitage left the room.

'A very pleasant young lady,' whispered Crabb.

His superior shrugged his shoulders, smiled briefly and opened the ledger.

'Now what have we here,' he said, looking at the first page. '1850. That's too early. Let us try further on.' He turned over a few more pages. '1872. Further on. Armitage came three years ago. Yes here we are. 1884. See how the handwriting changes. This must be where the old warden died, or left, and Armitage took over, Crabb. Now let us see. On this side of the page we have the income, which appears to be in the form of regular sums, probably issued every three months or so, by the trustees I would suspect. On this side we have the expenditure. Let's see what kind of money is going out. Various items on food, bills paid to local traders, then personal items — new bonnet for Martha Turner, new pair of shoes to Thomas Mason, and so on.'

'Nothing particularly startling there, sir — and both sides of the books seem to balance,' said Crabb, leaning over Ravenscroft's shoulder.

'It would appear that way, and yet there must be something. Let's proceed on over the months.' Ravenscroft turned the pages and ran his finger down the column of figures. 'This is unusual. See here, Crabb. 1885. February. Troutbridge £1 10s. — and again for March, Troutbridge £1 10s. See, it is the same again for the next month, and the next.' He turned over yet more pages. 'Yes, here we are again. Every month, the same sum, paid out on the seventh of the month to this Troutbridge. Ah, here we have an initial D. — D. Troutbridge. I wonder who this D. Troutbridge can possibly be? Paid as regular as clockwork, but not once does it say what the payment is for.'

'Looks as though we may have uncovered something here, sir,' said Crabb.

'It requires further investigation, certainly. There may be a perfect logical explanation for the payments.'

'Or our Mr Armitage has been paying himself out of the money?'

'Shush, Crabb, I think Miss Armitage is returning.'

The door opened and the lady in question entered, followed by her maid carrying a tray.

'Did you find what you were looking for, gentlemen?'

'Yes, thank you, Miss Armitage,' replied Ravenscroft, closing the ledger and walking over to the table.

'Good. Do sit down, gentlemen. That will be all, Sally. I'll serve the tea. How do you like your tea, Mr Ravenscroft?'

'Lemon and a little sugar, thank you, miss,' replied Ravenscroft.

'And you, Constable?'

'Oh, I'll have the same, thank you, miss,' said Crabb, pulling his collar in an uncomfortable manner.

'You do not sound as though you are a native of this area, Mr Ravenscroft,' she said, pouring out the tea and handing the cup to him.

'No. I live and work in London, in the Whitechapel area.'

'So what brings you to Malvern then, Inspector?' his hostess asked, smiling as she did so.

'I came to Malvern to take the water cure.'

'Ah, the famous water cure! And how have you found the water cure, Mr Ravenscroft? To your benefit I trust? Here is your tea, Constable.'

'Thank you, miss,' said Crabb, accepting the cup.

'I doubt that very much, Miss Armitage, although I am informed by the physician that I can expect an improvement any day now.'

'I think you are a born sceptic, Inspector,' she laughed.

'Perhaps you may be correct,' replied Ravenscroft, drinking his tea. 'Can I ask you if the name D. Troutbridge means anything to you?'

'No,' she replied, turning away suddenly.

'Your brother never mentioned anyone of that name to you?'

'No. There was a village, close to where we used to live, called Troutbridge. That is all the name means to me.'

'Thank you, Miss Armitage. You have been most helpful to us. If your brother should return here within the next day or so, I would be obliged if you would ask him to contact me at the Tudor in Malvern,' said Ravenscroft, standing up.

'Of course, Inspector, although I sense that my brother is in some kind of trouble,' said their hostess, rising and looking away sadly.

'My dear Miss Armitage, I am sure you have nothing to worry yourself about,' replied Ravenscroft, feeling compelled to lay a comforting hand on her arm. 'We merely need to meet with your brother again and ask him a few more questions. I am confident he will be able to answer all to our satisfaction.'

'I know my brother. He is a good man. He would not be involved in these murders you speak of,' she said suddenly, looking deep into Ravenscroft's eyes.

'I am sure not, Miss Armitage.'

'Lucy.'

'Lucy,' repeated Ravenscroft slowly, removing his hand. 'Be assured we will keep you informed of any developments. I will let you know when we have made contact with your brother.'

'Thank you, Mr Ravenscroft, I would appreciate that.'

'Now, Miss Armitage, Lucy, I'm afraid we must continue with our investigation. I thank you for your hospitality, and for the tea.'

'I will see you both out,' she said, smiling.

Crabb hastily drank down the contents of his cup, placed it upon the table and followed his superior out of the room.

* * *

Ravenscroft and Crabb made their way down Church Lane, towards their cab, which was waiting for them in the marketplace.

'Do you think she was telling us the truth about her brother, sir?' asked Crabb.

'I have no cause to doubt her.'

'She could be hiding him, somewhere in the house.'

'I doubt it.'

'Then it seems, sir, as though our Mr Armitage has gone to ground.'

'It would appear so. Did you notice how she blushed and turned away when I mentioned the name Troutbridge? Crabb, I think it would be useful if we could make enquiries regarding this D. Troutbridge. Perhaps you would be good enough to ask questions at the Ledbury station to see if they are familiar with the name. While you are doing that, I'll take a brief walk around the town and see you back here in, say, fifteen minutes.'

'Very well, sir.'

Crabb set off to the station, after exchanging a few words with the cab driver. Ravenscroft stood back and admired the features of the fine marketplace, then retraced his steps up Church Lane. He paused outside Lucy Armitage's cottage for a moment or so, looking up at the windows, half expecting to see the young lady gazing down upon him, and then continued upwards until he reached the church yard. Opening the door of the church he went inside the building. A figure was standing by the altar and called out to him. 'Welcome to our church, sir.'

'Thank you. You are the incumbent here?'

'I am indeed. How can I help you?' asked the clergyman, peering through his round spectacles.

'You have been here a long time, vicar?'

'More years than I sometimes care to remember,' laughed the other.

'So, I would be correct in assuming that you know everyone in these parts?'

'Well, nearly everyone, but may I be so bold, sir, as to enquire the nature of your questions?'

'I am a police inspector. What can you tell me about Miss Armitage?'

'A charming lady, she lives just down the lane. She arrived about three years ago, if I recall. One of my daughters goes to her house once a week for piano instruction. Surely the good lady is not in any trouble?' asked the vicar anxiously.

'Do not alarm yourself my good, sir. I am sure the lady is of an impeccable character. I understand she has a brother?'

'Yes, I think he is the warden of some almshouses, over at Colwall, I think.'

'What can you tell me about him?'

'Very little I'm afraid. I think he came to church once with his sister. He seemed an agreeable fellow, but really I don't recall much about him.'

'And does the name Troutbridge mean anything to you? D. Troutbridge, to be precise?'

'Troutbridge, Troutbridge? Yes, I have heard of the name, but I must confess I cannot put a face to it.'

'But the name is familiar to you? I believe it is a local name. The family may reside in the vicinity. If you could try and recall the name, I would be most grateful,' urged Ravenscroft.

'Well — but — ah, yes, I have it. I believe there is a family called Troutbridge out near Mathon. Yes, Troutbridge, that is the name. They live on a farm, if I recall correctly. Yes, that's it,' replied the vicar scratching his head.

'Thank you. Mathon, you say? You have been most helpful,' said Ravenscroft turning away.

'Glad to have been of service. Come to one of our services if you have the time officer.'

'I'll bear it in mind,' said Ravenscroft, as he closed the door behind him on the way out.

He found Crabb waiting for him back at the market place.

'I have it, sir. Troutbridge—' began Crabb.

'—has a farm in Mathon,' interrupted Ravenscroft.

'How did you know that, sir?'

'Divine inspiration, Crabb! Divine inspiration! Cabbie, take us to Mathon if you please.'

* * *

Their journey now took them along country lanes, lined with overhanging trees, and bordered with wild flowers and long grass. Thirty minutes after they had left Ledbury, they arrived at the small village of Mathon. As the cab drew up outside the village inn, Ravenscroft looked around at the church and the untidy cottages.

'Here, my man,' shouted Crabb to a figure who was sitting on a bench outside the inn drinking ale. 'We are looking for Troutbridge's farm.'

The man wandered over and gave them a vacant stare.

'Troutbridge's Farm,' repeated Crabb, in a louder voice.

'Oh, that will be Denis Troutbridge you want. Go up this road, turn up lane on right, and follow track that goes off to right. Mind, you'll not be welcome, like,' answered the man, beginning to walk away.

'Why not?' enquired Ravenscroft.

'Denis, he don't take too kindly to strangers. I'd have a care if I were ye,' laughed the man, as he made his way back inside the inn.

They resumed their journey, and soon found themselves making their way up an old rutted track, which eventually ended in a yard full of a collection of dilapidated farm buildings. The two men alighted from the cab.

'Where first, sir?' enquired Crabb, looking around him at the half-ruined buildings.

'Let's try in that one,' suggested Ravenscroft, indicating a large barn which lay in the centre of the complex.

Making their way across the muddy farmyard, the two men entered the building, which turned out to be a milking shed.

'Mr Troutbridge?' called out Crabb.

'Who wants him?' said a gruff voice from somewhere inside the barn.

'Police. Malvern Police. Can you spare us a minute or two of your time, Mr Troutbridge,' shouted Crabb.

'Don't have much time,' said the voice emerging from behind one of the cows.

'I believe you are Mr Denis Troutbridge? My colleague and I are making enquiries regarding the murders of Jabez Pitzer and Mr Sommersby in Malvern, and believe you may be able to assist us with our enquiries,' said Ravenscroft.

'Never heard of them, don't mean nothing to me it don't. I never goes into Malvern,' said Troutbridge, stepping forwards. Ravenscroft looked at the tall and well-built late middle-aged man. A large scar scuttled into an untidy beard on one side of his face. The farmer banged his pail of milk on the floor, slopping some of its contents over the side and onto Ravenscroft's boots

'You know Old Lechmere's Almshouses at Colwall?' continued Ravenscroft not put off by the white liquid dribbling over his walking apparel.

'I might,' replied the farmer grudgingly.

'Do you know the warden there, a Mr Armitage, Mr James Armitage?'

'Never heard of him, don't know anyone called Armitage.'

'He appears to know you. He pays you one pound and ten pence every month.'

'I should be so lucky,' laughed the farmer picking up his bucket and moving on to milk the next cow.

'You don't know Mr Armitage then?'

'That's what I said.'

'You don't have any dealings with the almshouses, then?' continued Ravenscroft, determined to persist with his questions.

'No.'

'Do you supply the almshouses with food or any other type of goods, for which you receive payment?'

'No.'

'You never have cause to go to the almshouses?'

'No.'

'And you don't receive money from Mr Armitage?'

'No.'

'What would you say if I told you that someone saw you there last week, talking with Mr Armitage?' said a frustrated Ravenscroft, deciding to try another line of questioning.

'I'd say he were a damned liar! I'm getting tired of all these damnable questions. Who did you say you were?' replied the farmer becoming increasingly surly in his manner.

'We are both from the Malvern Constabulary. I am Inspector Ravenscroft and my associate here is Constable Crabb.'

'That's as may be. I've told you I don't know anything about any almshouses. Now let me get on with my milking.'

'You have never met with a Mr Pitzer?'

'No.'

'What about Mr Sommersby from Malvern College?'

'No. I've just about had enough of these stupid questions,' said Troutbridge laying down his bucket, walking over to Ravenscroft and thrusting his features close up before his face. 'If you don't get off my farm within the next minute, I'll set the dogs loose on you!'

'Now then, my fellow, have a care. This is the law you're talking to,' interjected Crabb, drawing himself up to his full height.

'I don't care a damn whose law it is. If you ain't off my farm in next minute I won't be responsible for who gets hurt!' snapped the farmer, glaring at the constable.

'If you set your dogs on us, you'll find yourself up before the bench tomorrow morning and no mistake,' said Ravenscroft firmly.

'Maybe you won't live to tell the tale, if the dogs have you first!' growled Troutbridge.

'Don't you threaten us, my man!' continued Ravenscroft.

Troutbridge and Ravenscroft stared at one another, each determined to hold their ground and to test the mettle of the other. Finally, Ravenscroft turned away. 'Come, Crabb. We have done all we can do for now. Mr Troutbridge, you should be warned that we will return, next time with constabulary assistance, and that you may be taken into custody.'

'On what charge?' snarled the farmer.

'Threatening behaviour, wasting police time, keeping savage animals on the premises — that will do for a start,' said Ravenscroft walking away.

'If you come back again, I'll have the dogs ready. I warn you!' threatened Troutbridge as the two policemen left the barn.

'What an unpleasant fellow,' remarked Crabb as they mounted their cab.

'I quite agree with you, but I have seen his type, many times before and in my experience, they are all bravado and bluster and soon break down when you take them into custody. Our Mr Troutbridge certainly has a great deal to hide. I noticed the way he looked when I mentioned Armitage's name. He certainly knew him all right. It would seem that our decision to visit here was the right one, but there is little we can do on our own. I am not inclined to have a piece of my leg being removed for some animal's supper.'

'We can come back tomorrow, sir, with more of my colleagues if you so wish. A few days in the cells should cool his temper.'

Their driver turned the cab round and they started to drive away from the farm buildings. Suddenly Ravenscroft gripped Crabb's arm. 'Don't look over there at the house!' he instructed, aware that Troutbridge was standing outside the milking shed, observing their departure.

The cab sped out of the yard and down the trackway.

'What was all that about, sir?' asked a bewildered Crabb.

'If I was not very much mistaken, I would say that someone was watching us from one of the upstairs windows of the house, as we drove away!'

* * *

After stopping for refreshment at one of the inns situated on the western slopes of the hills, the two men returned to Great Malvern and made their way to the recently opened Assembly Rooms where the coroner's inquest was to be held into the death of Jabez Pitzer.

'Make a note, Crabb, of all the people who are present at the inquest,' said Ravenscroft as they entered the building. 'It will be interesting to see who attends.'

'I can see Mrs Pitzer with her maid sitting near the front, sir, and Doctor Gladwyn and the Reverend Touchmore. Who the other people are, I don't know, sir.'

'It would be useful at the end of the proceedings if you stopped them all on their way out, take their names and addresses and ask for their interest in this affair.'

'That may prove difficult, sir. Mr Pitzer was well known in the town and a great many people seem to be arriving to attend the inquest,' said Crabb as the two men took their seats.

The coroner entered and took his place at the large desk, which had been placed at the front of the assembly.

'We are here today to hold an inquest into the death of Mr Jabez Pitzer of Malvern Wells,' began the coroner in a formal, dry tone. 'However, before we begin, I'm sure you would all join me in extending our condolences to his widow, Mrs Pitzer, who is with us today. Madam, we all sympathise with your great loss' — sounds of affirmation rang from across the room — 'Mr Pitzer was a highly respected figure, and will be a sorely missed in the community here in Malvern' — hear, hears from various sections of the room — 'We will begin today by calling Doctor Gladwyn to the stand, as I understand he was the first to examine the deceased.'

Gladwyn took his place and began to answer the coroner's questions. Ravenscroft looked around him. The room was certainly full. He estimated an audience approaching a hundred, and wondered why so many people had taken the trouble to attend the inquest — out of respect for the dead man, or was it just a simple curiosity to learn more about the events of the night in question and an opportunity to confirm or deny the many rumours concerning Pitzer's death that must have been circulating around the town. Many of those attending wore black, no doubt out of respect for the deceased. Some would undoubtedly have been his business associates, his fellow councillors, his friends and neighbours; others would merely have known about the man and would have wanted to learn more about his demise. As Ravenscroft examined the rows of seated figures he looked in vain for Armitage or the veiled lady and wondered whether one of these highly respectable citizens present was in fact the murderer of Jabez Pitzer.

'Thank you, Doctor Gladwyn. I would now like to hear from Inspector Ravenscourt.'

Ravenscroft made his way over to the witness stand and took the oath.

'Now, Inspector Ravenscourt—'

'Ravenscroft, your honour.'

'Ah, Ravenscroft, yes of course, would you care to give your evidence, sir?'

Ravenscroft coughed and cleared his throat. 'My name is Samuel Ravenscroft. I hold the rank of police Inspector in the Whitechapel Division of the London Constabulary.'

'Forgive me,' interrupted the coroner leaning forwards. 'If you are an inspector with the, er—'

'Whitechapel Division,' helped Ravenscroft.

'Quite. If you are an inspector with the Whitechapel Division, perhaps you would care to explain why you are investigating this case? I would have thought that London was too far removed from Malvern to warrant such interest, or perhaps Mr Pitzer had business interests in Whitechapel?'

'I believe not, sir. I met Mr Pitzer a few days ago on the London train. We conversed together, the result of which he kindly invited me to dine with him on the night in question. That was how I came to be present at the murder scene. Since then I have been engaged by the local Malvern constabulary to carry out further investigations into Mr Pitzer's death.'

'Very well — I understand. Please proceed with your evidence, if you will,' said the coroner, leaning back in his chair and looking over his spectacles at Ravenscroft.

'I arrived at the deceased's house at seven thirty and was shown into the drawing room where I met Mrs Pitzer, the Reverend Touchmore and Mr Sommersby. We conversed for a few minutes, and then Mrs Pitzer instructed the maid to call for her husband, who was in the study at this time. When the maid returned, she informed us that Mr Pitzer was in fact dead. We all then entered the study. Mr Sommersby was the first to examine the deceased and declared that in his opinion, the deceased had died from natural causes, such as a seizure, or heart failure. When Doctor Gladwyn arrived he also gave cause of death due to a seizure. I had cause to think otherwise, sir.' Exclamations of surprise came from various sections of the room.

'Quiet from those attending this inquest!' interrupted the coroner. 'Please continue with your evidence, Inspector.'

'Thank you, your honour. The deceased had been drinking from a glass that had been replaced on the decanter tray. When I examined this glass, I found a residue of a powdery substance which was later confirmed as being poison.' This prompted more exclamations from the room.

'Quiet! Quiet!' said the coroner, banging the table with a small wooden hammer. 'I will not hesitate to clear this courtroom if we have any more interruptions. Please continue.'

'I also noticed that the window to the study was open, and when I stepped into the garden, I discovered evidence of a recent footprint on the ground beneath the window. When I later questioned the maid, she stated that she had heard the sound of something like a glass falling onto the floor at around six thirty in the evening. When I examined the carpet, I found that part of it was damp where the glass had fallen. I also discovered that Mr Pitzer had received a letter that afternoon, which had necessitated his being closeted in his study. It is my contention that someone entered the study at six thirty that evening and administered poison to Mr Pitzer's glass.'

'Can you tell me, Inspector, whether you have recovered this letter, the one that you have just mentioned?'

'No, sir. I believe the murderer took the letter away with him.'

'I see. That is most unfortunate. I understand there have been some developments in this case, since then, Inspector.'

'Yes, sir. Mr Sommersby of Malvern College has also been killed.'

'The court has been led to believe that Mr Sommersby met his death from a fallen bookcase?' asked the coroner, staring at Ravenscroft.

'We believe that Mr Sommersby was killed before the bookcase fell on him.' Further gasps echoed from the audience.

'Quiet! I see, Inspector. Are we to assume therefore that investigations concerning the deaths of these two men are still continuing?'

'Your assumption is correct, sir.'

'And can we expect a swift conclusion to these investigations?'

'We are endeavouring to do all that we can to expedite matters your honour, and are hopeful of an arrest,' replied Ravenscroft, trying to sound as convincing as possible.

'The court thanks you for your evidence, Inspector. You may step down. I would now like to call upon the Reverend Touchmore to give evidence.'

Ravenscroft let out a sigh of relief as he resumed his seat. Although he had given evidence many times before in numerous courts of justice during his career, he had never particularly enjoyed the experience, always fearing that he would fall foul to some over-zealous barrister, or be reprimanded for his lack of enterprise by some supercilious judge, and be made to look a laughing stock by the many people who were hanging on his every word.

He looked out of the window of the Assembly Rooms at the trees and flower beds that had been recently planted in the grounds, and his mind began to dwell on the events of the previous three days. He had little realised when he had arrived in Malvern that he would have been called upon to solve not one, but two murders, of its prominent citizens. The more and more he thought about this, the more and more he found himself returning yet again to the old almshouses. Was it Armitage who had killed the two men because they had uncovered his payments to Troutbridge from the accounts? Why was Armitage paying Troutbridge every month, — and where was Armitage now? Was Troutbridge sheltering Armitage? Had the face at the window of Troutbridge's farm been that of Armitage — or had it been someone else? Perhaps Troutbridge was perfectly innocent and Armitage had merely inserted his name in the accounts while pocketing the money for his own use? The possibilities seemed endless; one question led on to another and the more he thought about it, so the maze seemed to deepen. Then there was the cottage in Ledbury with its occupier, Lucy Armitage, appearing to know nothing of either her brother's involvement with Troutbridge or his whereabouts. He had not wished to consider anything against the lady but felt forced to concede that she had not exactly been forthcoming with her answers.

'Ladies and gentlemen, the court has heard evidence from a number of witnesses concerning the demise of Mr Jabez Pitzer,' said the coroner announcing his summing up. 'It is our opinion that Mr Pitzer was murdered by a person or persons unknown, and accordingly we enter such a verdict. The court stands adjourned until the police have completed their enquiries.'

The coroner banged his hammer down sharply on the table before him, gathered his papers together, stood up, and left the room, leaving an excited and animated gathering behind him busily discussing the events of the afternoon.

'I'll go by the door and get as many names as I can, sir,' said Crabb rising from his seat quickly. Ravenscroft remained seated, studying the various groups of people as they began to leave.

'Mr Ravenscroft. I thank you for all your efforts in this case,' said Mrs Pitzer addressing him as she attempted to make her way out of the room.

'Rest assured, ma'am, that Constable Crabb and I are quite determined to bring to justice whoever perpetrated this deed, and that we will not rest until we have done so,' said Ravenscroft, rising from his seat.

'I thank you for your encouraging words, Inspector. And now poor Mr Sommersby has been killed as well,' she said, tears beginning to form in her eyes.

'It is indeed so. I am sure that whoever killed your husband also killed Mr Sommersby.'

Susan began to lead her mistress away.

'Good day to you, Mrs Pitzer,' said Ravenscroft. He began to make his own way out of the hall. He pushed his way through the throng, avoiding the stares of some of their number, seeking only one more person before he should leave.

'Ah, Reverend, I wonder if I might have a word with you,' he said catching hold of Touchmore's arm, once they were out of the Assembly Rooms.

'Why yes, of course, Inspector.' The clergyman seemed surprised to be singled out by the policeman.

'Perhaps we could talk outside, away from these people?' suggested Ravenscroft.

The two men moved away from the hall and walked out across the lawn.

'When I came to see you in your office the other day, Reverend, I happened to look out of the window, and I saw a widow dressed in black walking across the churchyard. I wondered whether you would be able to assist me in discovering the identity of such a lady,' began Ravenscroft.

'We have a number of ladies who visit the churchyard from time to time. They are often in mourning. It is usually the men who die before their wives.'

'I understand that. This lady would perhaps be aged around forty or so, although I must admit that I have never seen her face. She must be quite active, as I have seen her walking on the hills near St Ann's. I would suppose that her husband had been taken from her within the last year or so, for her to be still in mourning. She may well have been visiting one of the graves in the churchyard when I saw her.' Ravenscroft realised that his line of encouraging questioning with the clergyman might yet bear fruit.

'I see,' replied Touchmore, deep in thought. 'Within the last year or so, I can think of perhaps five or six occasions when we have buried a husband, and the wife has been left to grieve. I would have to consult my records of course, to provide you with their names. Although most widows might tend to wear their widow's weeds for a few months or so, it is not uncommon for them to remain in black for a number of years.'

'And that would make our search even more difficult,' sighed Ravenscroft.

'Have you also considered the possibility, Inspector, that such a lady might be grieving for the loss of a child, rather than for a husband, or indeed for both of them? Unfortunately, quite a number of our children still die as the result of a fever.'

'You have not been aware of one particular person who has visited the graveyard a number of times in recent weeks?'

'No, I must say that I have not been aware of such an instance. As I say, I will consult with my records and let you know of any particular instances that might be of help.'

'Thank you, Reverend, I would appreciate that.'

'This lady to whom you refer, has she anything to do with Pitzer's murder?'

'I think not.'

'Then may I ask, Inspector — why are you so interested in her?'

'Let us say, that it is a policeman's curiosity. Thank you Reverend, you have been most helpful.'

Ravenscroft began to walk away, but then turned around once more.

'Oh, Reverend — one more question. Were Mr Sommersby and Mr Pitzer involved in any other activities together, other than the fact that they, like you, were trustees of the almshouses in Colwall?'

'They were both members of the town council. That is all, I believe.'

'Thank you again for your assistance. I would be obliged if you could contact me, if you recall any further information.'

'Of course, Inspector. I wish you a good day.'

Ravenscroft walked back to the entrance to the Assembly Rooms where he found Crabb studying his pocketbook.

'Ah, there you are, sir. I think I have most of the names down. Most people were forthcoming; one or two were more reserved. There were certainly a lot of them. I should think that nearly the whole town must have turned out today.'

'There is nothing like the prospect of an inquest that suggests murder to bring out the crowds, Crabb. Keep all your names. We may have need of them later.'

'Do you think our murderer may have been amongst them?'

'That is a distinct possibility. Murderers often have a great curiosity to revisit the scenes of their crimes. On the other hand, the killer may well have wanted to keep well away from the inquest, for fear of giving himself away in some incriminating way.'

'Like Armitage, sir.'

'Like Armitage. Talking of Armitage, it might be to our advantage to return to the almshouses and make a close search of his cottage. We might just find something there that links him to the killings. Let's see if we can acquire a cab to take us there.'

'Can I make a suggestion, sir? If we walk through the gardens here and walk out through the other side, a ten-minute stroll will take us to Great Malvern Station. We could then take the train to Colwall. The almshouses are quite near the station at the other end. There may be a train due soon, sir, in which case our journey may prove of a quicker duration.'

'That seems a good idea to me Crabb. After sitting in that stuffy court room for the last hour or so, and listening to all that evidence, I could do with stretching my legs and clearing my mind. A walk would be most acceptable.'

Ten minutes later found the two men standing on the platform of Great Malvern station. They did not have long to wait for the next train, which took them onwards, past the common at Malvern Wells, before plunging into darkness as it entered the tunnel that ran beneath the hill.

'It must have been quite a feat of engineering to have tunnelled through all this rock,' remarked Ravenscroft.

'Only done about thirty years ago, sir, I believe,' informed Crabb.

'Rather them than me.'

'After Colwall, sir, the train goes on to Ledbury and then to Hereford.'

The train exited the tunnel and began to slow down as it approached the small country station of Colwall. Crabb and Ravenscroft alighted from the train and made their way out through the gate and along the path until they reached the almshouses. Here they found the two old men still sitting in the same place, and smoking the same pipes, as they had done when the two detectives had seen them on their first visit.

'Good day to you gentlemen again,' said Crabb.

'What's that he says?' asked the one of his companion.

'Says weather don't look too good.'

'Oh, that's alright then. As long as he don't be lookin' for makin' gammets of us.'

'Has Mr Armitage returned?' asked Ravenscroft.

'Nowt seen Armitage,' replied the elder of the two.

'We'll just have a look in his cottage,' shouted Crabb.

''Tis no need to shout,' sniffed the old man, shrugging his shoulders and resuming his smoke.

Ravenscroft made his way down the path towards Armitage's cottage. 'The door appears to be unlocked,' he remarked entering the tiny building. 'Just two rooms, by the look of it, simply furnished. You take the bedroom Crabb, while I have a look through these papers on the table.'

The two men set to their work.

'Only old letters, one or two bills, some notes he has been making from this book of philosophical thoughts, nothing incriminating here,' said Ravenscroft.

'There's nothing in the bedroom, sir, just a bed and a few old clothes. It's all a bit spartan if you ask me. There's still bread and cheese on the side here, as though he intended coming back, sir.'

'What's this old photograph on the wall? Very similar to the one we saw at Miss Armitage's in Ledbury, almost the same family group I would say, probably the father, mother, and the two children. It was obviously taken some years ago, in better times. Well, Crabb, I can't see anything here that might suggest that young Armitage killed either Pitzer or Sommersby. We will just have to ask the men to keep a look out for him. We best make our way back to Malvern. What's this on the chair?'

'Looks like a pile of old newspapers, sir,' suggested Crabb.

'They appear to be back copies of the *Malvern News*. You take that half, Crabb, and I'll take these.'

'What am I looking for, sir?'

'Look at each page and see if Armitage has marked any articles, adverts, anything in fact,' said Ravenscroft placing the newspapers on the table.

Crabb looked puzzled but complied with Ravenscroft's request.

The two men worked in silence, turning the browning sheets of the old newspapers one at a time, running their fingers down the columns of newsprint, examining the advertisements, until suddenly Ravenscroft let out a cry, 'See here, Crabb! Armitage has drawn a line all the way round this article!'

'What does it say, sir?'

'"A new company has been formed to raise issue of shares for the construction of the proposed Tewkesbury to

Leominster Railway,"' said Ravenscroft, beginning to read the sheet.

'What was there to interest Armitage in a new railway company?' asked Crabb. 'He surely is not wealthy enough to afford the purchase of any shares.'

'This is most interesting, Crabb. It says here that the proposed line will commence at Tewksbury, run through Upton, then through Colwall and on through various villages until it arrives at Leominster. Ah, here we have it — "the building of the line will necessitate the removal of several buildings which may lie in its intended route, particularly at Colwall where the proposed line would cross the existing Malvern to Hereford line." Are you thinking what I'm thinking, Crabb?'

'If the line was built, the almshouses might well have to be demolished to make way for it.'

'Exactly, Crabb, this is why Armitage has marked this article. As the warden of the almshouses he had a decided interest in opposing such a scheme. If the almshouses were knocked down, the old people would be turned out and he would in all probability lose his position as warden. We need to find out more about this new railway company. I wonder if we can discover who is the agent for the new company? Ah — here we are — "should any members of the public be interested in purchasing shares in the new Tewkesbury to Leominster Railway, they can view the prospectus at the Malvern Library and Reading Rooms. The issue will continue until either all the shares of the new company are fully subscribed or by the twenty-third of April, 1887."'

'That must be in about a fortnight, sir,' said Crabb. 'What is the date of the paper?'

'Published about five weeks ago,' replied Ravenscroft.

'Perhaps Armitage knew who the proposed shareholders were?'

'Let us return to Malvern and see what else we can discover about the company and its shareholders,' said Ravenscroft. 'Somehow, Armitage took an interest in this newspaper item.'

The two men closed the cottage door behind them and walked towards the two old men. Ravenscroft reached into his pocket and took out a silver coin, which he placed on the old wooden table in front of them. 'Should Mr Armitage return, send urgent word to Malvern Police Station,' he said.

One of the old men picked up the coin and tested it with his teeth. 'A nimble ninepence is better than a sleepy shillin', sir,' said his companion with a broad grin.

'I can hear a train approaching, sir. If we are quick enough, we can catch it back to Malvern,' said Crabb.

'Lead on Crabb, and I will follow.'

* * *

Upon their return to Great Malvern station, Ravenscroft and Crabb hired a cab from outside the building, which took them upwards, back towards the town. Alighting at the top of Church Street they walked across to the Library and Reading Rooms, only to find the doors locked.

'Looks as though we are too late, sir? Closed up for the day,' said Crabb.

'I suppose it is rather late,' said Ravenscroft consulting his pocket watch. 'I think that is all we can do for today. Go home, Crabb; your lovely wife will be pleased to see you, no doubt. I must return to the Tudor and make my excuses for not undertaking my treatment this afternoon. Meet me outside the Reading Rooms tomorrow morning at nine, and we will see what we can discover.'

The two men parted company and Ravenscroft made his way back to the Tudor, where he was confronted by an anxious Stebbins.

'There you are, sir. I've been lookin' all over for you, on account of yer treatment, sir.'

'Detained on important police business, Stebbins,' said Ravenscroft sweeping past the youth and seeking the sanctuary of his room. Here, he lay on the bed going over the events of the day in his mind.

After a few minutes he walked over to the window and gazed out at the view that had now become familiar to him. If only he could solve this case, he could make some excuse to terminate his treatment at the Tudor and leave the town. There would still be a possible second week of his leave to take in the pleasures of Brighton. His eyes wandered over to his left where he could see a part of the churchyard. The light was beginning to fade, but there was no mistaking the lone figure kneeling by one of the graves. Quickly gathering up his coat, he closed his bedroom door behind him and set off at a brisk pace. If luck was with him, this time, he might surely be able to confront the mysterious woman who had so occupied his thoughts.

Exiting the Tudor, he made his way down the steep road, and then down the steps that led into the church-yard — only to find it empty. He looked around frantically. Where had the woman in black gone to? He had not passed her on his progress into the grounds, so she could not have left the churchyard that way. He ran down the path leading out of the grounds into the main street of the town and peered anxiously down the road, but in vain. He ran back to the church and made his way into the building to see if she had entered it to worship, but although he searched every-where, he found no one.

Wearily he made his way back outside. Yet again his quarry had eluded him. It seemed that destiny would always prevent him from meeting the veiled lady. He turned to make his way back to the Tudor, but then remembered that he had seen the figure kneeling by one of the graves. If only he could recall which one? There were so many stones, a number of which were quite recent. It would be like looking for a needle in a haystack. But then he remembered. The figure had been kneeling by a grave and had appeared to have placed a basket of some kind on the seat situated near the wall. Of course, she had been placing flowers on one of the graves!

He walked up the path towards the bench and stopped at one of the stones. This must have been the grave, he told himself, for there were some fresh flowers placed before the headstone. Ravenscroft moved the vase of flowers to one side and began to read the inscription on the stone:

Sacred to the memory of
Anthony Stewart Kelly (1840-1886)
and
Mark Richard Kelly (1885-1887)
Always Remembered.

Ravenscroft had found the husband and child of the veiled woman in black!

CHAPTER FIVE

'Good morning, gentlemen. It is a pleasure to see you again.'

It was the following morning and Crabb and Ravenscroft had entered the Malvern Library and Reading Rooms, in their quest to discover more about the railway company and its shareholders.

'Your usual coffee and papers, sir, or is there something more pressing that I can help you with, Inspector?' asked the attendant.

'How did you know that I was a police inspector?' asked Ravenscroft.

'I attended the inquest yesterday.'

'And you, sir, are?' asked Crabb

'Ronald Clifford, manager and owner of the Malvern Library and Reading Rooms,' smiled the attendant.

'Mr Clifford, we have come to make enquiries of you regarding the proposed Tewkesbury to Leominster Railway. I understand you are the local agent for the company?' asked Ravenscroft.

'That is so.'

'You appear to be a man of many parts.'

'One has to diversify in such a small town as this, Inspector.'

'Quite. What information do you have, regarding the railway company?'

'If you would care to follow me this way, sir,' said Clifford leading the way into a back room, which appeared to serve as his office. He walked over to a large cabinet and opening the top drawer removed a map which he unfolded on the table.

'This chart, gentlemen, shows the proposed route of the railway. As you can see the line begins here at Tewkesbury, cuts across here to Upton, then on to Colwall before travelling on to Leominster,' said Clifford tracing the route with one of his fingers.

'Are there not plenty of railway routes already in this area?' interjected Ravenscroft.

'Indeed so, but if one wants to travel from Malvern to Leominster at present, one is either faced by a long journey overland through Bromyard or be compelled to travel down to Hereford, where one has to change trains in order to reach one's destination. Once this line has been constructed, the traveller would be able to travel from Malvern to Colwall and on to Leominster in a single journey. Travellers from the east would likewise find it much easier to travel from Tewkesbury straight through to Leominster. Upon arrival at that town passengers would either be able to connect with the main line to Shrewsbury and the north or travel down to south Wales. Either way, the proposed line will save the traveller a great deal in time and expense.'

'You are a good salesman, Mr Clifford.'

Clifford smiled. 'I sense however, Inspector, that you are not interested in purchasing shares?'

'I could not afford them, sir. A policeman's salary is not a great one. Do you have a more detailed plan showing how the route will affect the village of Colwall?' asked Ravenscroft.

Clifford crossed over to the cabinet, looked through his collection of maps until he eventually found the one for which he was looking.

'Here we are, gentlemen. This shows the alterations that will have to be made to Colwall station so that it can accommodate the new line. As you can see, several of the existing buildings in the village will have to be removed.'

'Including Old Lechmere's Almshouses?' enquired Ravenscroft.

'Yes, I'm afraid so. There are always some casualties if progress is to be maintained.'

'I doubt that the inmates would see it that way,' said Crabb.

'What would happen to the old people?' asked Ravenscroft.

'That would be a matter for the trustees of the alms-houses and the directors of the new company to decide,' said Clifford.

'The original charter setting up the establishment of the almshouses might prevent such a demolition,' suggested Ravenscroft.

'I would think not.'

'Might we see who the directors of the new company are — and could you also provide us with a list of subscribers?' asked Ravenscroft.

'Of course, if you will just bear with me, Inspector,' replied Clifford, crossing over to a bookcase and removing one of the ledgers.

'Here we are, gentlemen. I will have to ask you to look through this on your own, as I have just heard the bell ring and must attend to my customers.'

As Clifford left the room, Ravenscroft turned over the pages of the ledger.

'Now let us see. The Leominster and Tewkesbury Railway Company, apparently formed in July of last year. Here is the List of Directors. Good heavens, Crabb, see who is listed as one of the directors!' exclaimed Ravenscroft.

'Jabez Pitzer!' said Crabb.

'So our Mr Pitzer was a director of the company, as well as being a trustee of the almshouses. That would explain why Armitage and Pitzer fell out. Armitage must have found out about Pitzer being a director. There would certainly be a conflict of interest there, and I have no doubt that once the line had been built our Mr Pitzer would have received a good return on his investment, at the expense of the inmates of the almshouses. Let's look down the rest of the list of directors. No, I don't see either Touchmore, Sommersby or Gladwyn listed. The other names appear to be outsiders, possibly directors of other railway companies. Ah, here is a list of subscribers. There is Pitzer's name again. He appears to have taken up quite a few of the shares. Besides being a director, he was also one of the major shareholders. Our Mr Pitzer was certainly well committed to the project. I can't see any other names I recognise in this list of subscribers.'

'It seems to me, sir, that Mr Pitzer was using his influence to have the almshouses demolished, so the new line could go through,' commented Crabb.

The two men had not noticed that Clifford had returned silently to the room.

'I trust you found what you were looking for, gentlemen?'

'Yes indeed, Mr Clifford. Can I enquire as to whether the shares are fully subscribed?' asked Ravenscroft, looking up from the ledger.

'Not at present, Inspector.'

'What percentage has been subscribed?'

'I would say about sixty per cent.'

'That would still leave nearly half the issue under-subscribed,' said Ravenscroft.

'It would appear so, Inspector, but I must say there have been a great number of enquiries from both town and country gentlemen.'

'Tell me, Mr Clifford. If the issue is not fully subscribed by the closing date of the twenty-third, am I right in assuming that the proposed development will not go ahead?'

'That is correct, sir.'

'And the shareholders would lose all their money?' asked Crabb.

'No, Constable. If the line does not go ahead, then the proposed shareholders are released from their pledges,' replied Clifford.

'But the directors—' began Ravenscroft.

'They would lose any initial capital investment they made in establishing the company. Can I help you further with your enquiries, Inspector?'

'No thank you, Mr Clifford. You have been most helpful,' replied Ravenscroft.

'I am glad that I have been of some assistance,' smiled Clifford, giving a little bow.

Ravenscroft and Crabb made their way out of the Reading Rooms, to find that the skies had clouded over and that rain was beginning to fall.

'Well, it seems as though our Mr Armitage had good cause to want Mr Pitzer dead, what with him being the director and main shareholder of the railway company,' said Crabb.

'That does not mean to say that he murdered him. You also forget that Sommersby was neither a director nor a shareholder in the company, and if our killer is Armitage there would have been little point in killing him as well. No, although we may be getting nearer the truth, Crabb, we seem as far away as ever from finding out who killed the two men — and why,' replied Ravenscroft.

'Can't say I cared for your Mr Clifford.'

'Why ever not, Crabb? I found him most helpful.'

'Bit too silky for me.'

Ravenscroft smiled. 'I think I see Stebbins running in our direction, and trying to attract our attention?'

'Mr Ravenscroft, sir, I thought I might find you 'ere. This letter was delivered to the Tudor about thirty minutes ago, sir,' said the youth, handing over the rain-spattered envelope.

'Thank you, Stebbins,' said Ravenscroft, giving the messenger a coin from his pocket.

Stebbins ran off, as Ravenscroft opened the letter. 'It's from Doctor Gladwyn. "Dear Inspector Ravenscroft. Can you come and see me as soon as possible. I think I may have some important information regarding the deaths of Pitzer and Sommersby, which may be of value to you." It's signed: Septimus Gladwyn.'

'That's a turn up for the books,' said Crabb.

'Let's see if we can secure a cab,' said Ravenscroft, turning up the collar of his coat.

'I don't fancy walking down to the Link in this weather. The heavens look as though they are about to open up on us.'

The two policemen walked up onto the Terrace where they hailed a cab and set off for Gladwyn's house. The rain began to fall more heavily.

A few minutes later, they arrived at the doctor's residence.

After climbing down from the cab, Crabb instructed the driver to wait, and rang the doorbell.

'Yes, sir. Can I help you, sir?' said the maid opening the door.

'Inspector Ravenscroft and Constable Crabb, to see Doctor Gladwyn, if you please,' said Ravenscroft attempting to shelter under the entrance porch. 'We are expected.'

'Sorry, sir. Doctor Gladwyn has been called away on urgent business, to attend to a sick patient I believe,' replied the maid.

'That's alright, my girl, we'll wait inside. I'm sure your master won't be long,' said Crabb.

'I believe he has gone to Hollybush, sir. He may be some time.'

'At what time was he called out?' enquired Ravenscroft.

'It was about thirty minutes ago, sir.'

'Must have been after he had sent the letter to us,' said Ravenscroft. 'Can you tell me who it was who called at the house?'

'Yes, sir. He was a strange-looking gent. Quite tall he was, dressed in a ragged overcoat — and yes, sir, he was blind as well.'

'Must have been the same fellow who we saw hanging about outside here the other day, Crabb. What happened when this man called? Do you remember? I am a police officer and it is important that we speak with your master as soon as possible,' said Ravenscroft quickly.

'Well, sir. I remember the gentleman was quite agitated. He kept saying his wife was dying and could the doctor come urgently and try and save her. Doctor Gladwyn said he had to see someone else first, but the man was quite insistent that Doctor Gladwyn come immediately. He kept repeating that his wife would surely die if the doctor delayed. Finally the doctor got out the horse and trap, and the two of them left together.'

'Thank you. You have been most helpful. You say they set off for Hollybush?'

'Yes, sir,' replied the maid, looking concerned.

'Where is this Hollybush, Crabb?'

'It's a good few miles away from here — on the other side of the hills, sir. Just off the Ledbury to Tewkesbury Road — past the village of Eastnor. It's near the Golden Valley, close to Raggedstone Hill. Should take us about thirty or forty minutes to get there, sir,' began Crabb

'What was that you said?' asked Ravenscroft.

'I said it's on the Ledbury to—'

'No, what did you say after that?'

'I said it's near the Golden Valley, close to Raggedstone Hill.'

'Raggedstone Hill,' repeated Ravenscroft, deep in thought.

'Yes, sir,' replied Crabb, looking puzzled.

Ravenscroft thanked the maid, and the two men climbed back into the cab and gave instructions that the driver was to proceed with all haste in the direction of Hollybush.

'Rather a coincidence that just after Gladwyn had sent us a letter, he should be called out to attend to a patient,' said Crabb.

'I find it more than a coincidence, Crabb. I don't like the sound of this blind fellow, who was hanging about the house the other day. I fear that Doctor Gladwyn's life may be in danger. I'll instruct the cab driver to go quicker. We are on urgent police business my man. Drive as quickly as you can!'

'Old Patch will do his best, sir. Weather is breaking up badly though. Are you sure you wants to go to Hollybush?' enquired the driver.

'We do indeed. A man's life may be in danger.'

The cab sped on at a fast pace, travelling through the Terrace at Malvern, on past the Tudor, the Wyche Common, and Pitzer's house, and out towards the Wells, spraying water onto the sides of the roads as it did so. The skies had now become black, and to Ravenscroft looking through the falling rain, the hills seemed to be taking on a more overpowering and sinister appearance.

They passed a collection of elegant buildings before the cab made its way up a winding road, until they reached the top of the hill. Ravenscroft could just make out the outline of a large inn on their right-hand side, and Crabb informed him that they had arrived at the British Camp.

'This road will take us down towards Ledbury, sir,' said Crabb.

After a few more turns the cab hurried quickly down the road that lead away from the hills. Ravenscroft could now barely see the sides of the road through the driving rain.

'Not the best of days to be going out to Hollybush,' shouted Crabb.

'I thought the sun always shone on Malvern,' said Ravenscroft.

The cab made a sharp turn to the left and they found themselves leaving the main road and heading out in an easterly direction along a country lane. After going through a small village and past a large house which was hidden from the road by a long tall wall, they found themselves climbing upwards again.

Suddenly their driver pulled up the cab. 'Hollybush, sir,' he called through the noise of the falling rain.

Ravenscroft and Crabb alighted from the cab and looked around. They appeared to be at a crossroads. To the left and right of them were large hills towering up into the mist and rain. Ahead of them the road seemed to drop sharply away from the range.

'That's Hollybush Hill over on our left, sir, and I believe the other hill on our right is the Raggedstone,' said Crabb, closely clutching the top of his tunic around his wet neck.

Ravenscroft stared up at the forbidding hill on his right and felt a cold shudder travel down the spine of his back.

'Are there any cottages around here that you know of my man?' asked Crabb.

'There's one or two further on past church at Hollybush, and one down track there,' replied their driver pointing in the direction of the Raggedstone.

'Let's try that one first' replied Ravenscroft, climbing back into the cab.

'Right you are, sir. Up there, Patch!'

The cab turned off the road and made its way along the bumpy track, the two men straining to see if they could see any other signs of life at the base of the hill.

Suddenly Ravenscroft cried out, 'Over there. I can see a building of some kind — and yes, there is a horse and trap in front of it!'

'Could be Gladwyn's, sir,' said Crabb anxiously.

As their cab came to a sudden halt and the two police-men jumped down and ran over to the empty trap.

'This looks like a medical bag of some kind,' said Ravenscroft, holding up the article in question from the seat of the trap. 'Now where is Gladwyn?'

'Over here, sir!' called out Crabb, running towards the old stone cottage.

'God, we are too late!' exclaimed Ravenscroft.

Lying on the ground, face down, was the body of a man.

Ravenscroft quickly turned him over. 'It's Gladwyn — and look here, there is blood on the side of his head where he has been hit by a weapon of some kind.'

'This is it, sir,' said Crabb picking up the item from the ground. 'There's still blood on it. Whoever killed him used this stone, and then threw it to one side.'

'The cottage, Crabb! Our murderer may still be inside. Draw your truncheon and follow me,' said Ravenscroft, racing up the path. Upon reaching the door of the cottage he lashed out with his leg and kicked it open.

The two men rushed inside. Ravenscroft looked frantically around the empty room.

'Looks as though he's got away, sir,' said Crabb.

'Quickly! Outside!' instructed Ravenscroft, turning on his heel.

The two men ran up the path towards the trap.

'Look around you, Crabb. Whoever killed Gladwyn must have left only minutes ago,' said Ravenscroft, looking around frantically in all directions. 'We obviously passed no one on either the road, or the path coming here. Therefore our killer has either made his escape by going further down this track, or by climbing upwards to the top of the hill.'

'There is no sign of any other vehicle having been here recently, other than Gladwyn's trap and our own cab,' said Crabb.

'My God, Crabb! Look up there on top of the hill, just where the sun is breaking through all that cloud. There's someone up there looking down on us! Can you make out who it is?'

'All I can see is a tall figure wearing some kind of long coat,' said Crabb.

'Precisely! Our friend is the blind man, who called on Gladwyn and lured him out here to his death.'

'I'll get up there after him,' shouted Crabb.

'Wait. He's heading back over the hill towards the road. If you take the path up to the hill, I'll head back to the road in the cab, and see if I can cut him off. At least this damned rain is easing.'

Crabb set off up the path. The figure on top of the hill had now completely disappeared.

'Quickly back towards the road,' instructed Ravenscroft to the cab man.

The driver turned the cab slowly, and with care, in the confined space, Ravenscroft irritably stamping his feet on the ground as he did so. The manoeuvre completed, Ravenscroft jumped in, and they set off at a brisk pace. After what seemed an endless eternity to Ravenscroft, they gained the main road and turned to their left before the cab came to a halt in the space between the Raggedstone and Hollybush hills.

Ravenscroft jumped down from the cab and looked anxiously all around. A path on his left appeared to go up onto the Raggedstone. If the blind man was still on the hill, he must surely come this way, thought Ravenscroft. On the other hand, if he had arrived too late the fellow could have crossed the road by now and have headed on over the Hollybush hill. Who would come down the path first — Crabb, or the mysterious blind man? If it turned out to be the latter, he would be ready for him; he was determined that this was one quarry that he would not let escape.

Suddenly Crabb came crashing down the path.

'Damn it. He's gone from us!' exclaimed Ravenscroft.

'I ran all the way, sir,' panted Crabb.

'Did you see the fellow at all?'

'No, sir, but he must have come this way. There is only this one path that leads down from Raggedstone.'

'Then he was too quick for us! Damn the man. For someone who is supposed to be blind, he seems to know these hills remarkably well,' muttered Ravenscroft.

'He moves at the speed of lightening, I know that,' complained Crabb breathlessly.

'You did your best, Crabb. He had a good start on us. He must have run down here, shortly before I arrived, and made his escape up there over the Hollybush hill. See here,' said Ravenscroft examining the ground. 'If I'm not mistaken these are boot marks going in that direction.'

'We may still be able to catch him, sir. If he carries on over the hills, he will eventually reach the British Camp. If we return to Malvern, I could have some men searching the hills from there.'

'That seems a good idea, Crabb. At least the sun is starting to come out at last. The rain has cleared up and we have several hours of daylight left to catch the villain. You take the cab back to Malvern and get your men out on the hills. I'll go back to the cottage, make a search there, and put poor Gladwyn's body in the trap, then join you all at the British Camp,' said Ravenscroft, sneezing. 'Go quickly, Crabb.'

Ravenscroft watched as the cab drove off down the road and into the distance, then made his way back down the track towards the cottage. It was obvious that the blind man had lured Gladwyn out to Raggesdstone on the pretext that his wife was seriously ill, and that once there, he had killed the doctor. But why had the blind man committed such an atrocity? Then he remembered the note that Gladwyn had sent, and wondered what had been the urgent news that Gladwyn had been so anxious to tell him. Gladwyn had said that he had some important information regarding the deaths of Pitzer and Sommersby. Could it have been that Gladwyn had discovered who had murdered the two men, and that knowledge had now cost him his own life? If only he and Crabb had arrived a few minutes earlier, they might have been able to have saved the doctor's life. But they had not and now he had three bodies on his hands; three crimes to solve. Worse than all that — he had let the killer slip through his hands yet again!

Dejectedly, Ravenscroft walked into the cottage and looked around at its meagre contents — a broken chair and a pile of old rotten rags in one corner of the room — there was certainly no evidence that a sick woman could have been dying there.

He made his way out into the overgrown, abandoned garden, gazing down at the ground, looking for anything that might yield a clue as to who the perpetrator of the crime might be, even though aware that his search would probably prove futile. There was poor Gladwyn still lying in a pool of blood on the ground. Ravenscroft made a search of his pockets but could find nothing that might have identified the killer of the three men.

Slowly, he edged the body upwards and dragged it over towards the trap. With all his strength he managed to lift it into the vehicle. Then, finding a blanket, which the late doctor had evidently used to wrap round his feet and legs on his journeys, Ravenscroft draped it over the dead body. He returned to the garden, recovered the blood-stained rock and placed it by the side of the deceased man.

Pausing to regain his breath, he looked up towards the summit of the Raggedstone Hill, where the blind man had stood but a few minutes previous, and the longer he stared at the hill top the more it seemed to Ravenscroft that he was imagining the man still standing there, pointing down at him — and almost mocking his failure.

And then he suddenly realised, that although the rain had cleared and the sun was shining brightly, the shadow of the Raggedstone had fallen not only upon the old deserted cottage — but upon himself as well!

CHAPTER SIX

Ravenscroft drove quickly away from the cottage, anxious to escape from the shadow of the hill, seeking the sun so that his wet clothes might dry and so that some warmth might return to his aching body.

As he entered the grounds of the inn, at the clearing below the British Camp, he found that Crabb had preceded him.

'There you are, sir. I've sent three men up onto the hills. If he comes this way, we will surely have him.'

'Then let us go and join them,' said Ravenscroft, tying the reins of the trap to a post. 'I best go into the inn first and explain our presence here. Poor Gladwyn is there in the back of the trap.'

'I've done that already, sir. They have also sent three of their hands from the inn onto the hills to assist us in our search.'

'Good thinking, Crabb,' replied Ravenscroft, sneezing and blowing his nose.

'You could do with getting in the dry, sir,' suggested Crabb.

'It is of no concern, Crabb. The sun and the breeze will soon help to dry me out.'

The two men began to make their way up the slopes of the hill and after a steady climb found themselves on the summit. From here, they looked out onto the many fields of the three counties, which spread out before them like a patchwork quilt. Ravenscroft was glad that they had reached the end of their climb and could feel his heart pounding, and his breathing coming in short gasps.

'He could be coming this way, sir,' said Crabb. He gestured to the range of hills that stretched into the distance. 'Our men and the servants from the inn are making their way along the top of the hills as well as searching the lower slopes. I've also sent word to Ledbury and asked them to send some men to make their way up from the Eastnor side, in case he decides to go that way. It's only a matter of time before we have him, sir.'

'I sincerely hope so,' gasped Ravenscroft. He wiped his wet face and spectacles with his handkerchief.

'My word you look bad, if you don't mind my saying so, sir.'

'It's just the wet and the climb, Crabb,' replied Ravenscroft coughing. 'We'll just rest here for a time, before we go on. I'll be alright in a little while. It certainly is a grand view.'

'Over there is Malvern with Worcester beyond,' said Crabb pointing. 'And there is the River Severn in the distance. Behind us is Ledbury and they do say you can see Hereford on a fine day, and half of Wales as well, if your luck holds.'

'Let's go on, Crabb. The sooner we catch this fellow the better it will be for all of us.'

They began to make their way gradually along one of the ridges that ran alongside the top of the hill. Despite the temporary shelter from the wind, Ravenscroft began to find that his whole body was beginning to shake from the cold and wet. 'Damn it, Crabb. I don't feel that I can go on for much longer,' he said sneezing again.

'You look decidedly ill, sir. Perhaps you are going down with a chill? May I suggest that you go back to the inn and wait there? I'll inform you if there are any developments,' suggested Crabb.

'I think I will take your advice. If I hear nothing from you, I'll come and re-join you later,' replied Ravenscroft.

Clutching the collar of his wet coat with one of his hands, he made his way back down the slippery slope, until he eventually found himself in the clearing once more. He paused at the entrance to the inn, coughing to clear his lungs from the congestion that threatened to engulf him.

'My word, sir, you look as though you could do with a drink. Sit yourself down there, sir, in front of the fire, and I'll bring you some of our finest ale,' said the landlord as he entered the bar.

Ravenscroft thanked the man, walked over to the log fire, removed his wet overcoat, cleaned his spectacles and warmed his hands near the welcoming flames.

'There you are, sir. I could bring you some bread and cheese, and a slice of meat pie if you would like, sir.'

'That is an offer I cannot refuse,' replied Ravenscroft, coughing and then blowing his nose. He took a welcome swig of the ale, and stood before the fire attempting to dry out his wet clothes but although he could feel the heat from the flames on his hands, he found that his body was still shaking with the coldness that had seemed to enter his very bones.

The landlord returned presently bearing a plate of food which he placed on the table near to Ravenscroft. 'No luck catching that ruffian yet then?' he asked.

'Crabb and the men are searching the hills,' replied Ravenscroft, slicing a piece of cheese. 'I hope we may be able to apprehend the fellow before dark. You may know the man. Tall, blind, wears a long, ragged overcoat. Perhaps he has been in here?'

'I knows the man you mean, and no mistake. He ain't been in here, but I have seen him a few times on the hills. Locals call him Old Penny.'

'Old Penny?' enquired Ravenscroft, eating a piece of bread.

'Folks call him that, on account of him not havin' two pennies to rub together like. They says he lives wild on the hills, although some folk says he lives in some old cottage out near Hollybush, while others swear they have seen him living in some old cave or other. Always seemed harmless enough, but now he's gone and killed our Doctor Gladwyn, so your constable says.'

'It would seem highly likely. He was certainly seen in the vicinity of the crime. We will know more when we catch him. My word this cheese is good,' said Ravenscroft.

'If you thinks that's good, sir, wait until you has tried the meat pie,' said the landlord, cheerfully leaving the room. 'I'll bring you a slice of wife's apple pie as well, in a few minutes.'

Ravenscroft settled down to enjoy his lunch and gradually began to feel his strength returning. After consuming the meat pie and then the apple pie, and downing another tankard of ale, Ravenscroft stood in front of the fire and felt the steam rising from his damp clothes. He took out his pocket watch. One thirty. They would have another four or five hours of daylight left; long enough, he considered, to make their arrest. After all, the man was blind and could not have gone far. Soon he would need to make his way back up the hill and join in the search, but first he would spend a few more minutes warming his aching limbs before the flames. He drew up the chair in front of the crackling log, and gazed into the flickering flames, thinking he saw the features of the blind man in the red glow there. He let a loud yawn, stretched out his legs, and gradually felt his eyelids growing heavy as his head fell on his chest.

He awoke suddenly with a start. He must have fallen asleep. The fire had burnt down to its embers and the new log which had recently been placed there was gently hissing. He reached for his pocket watch and found he had been asleep for three hours. Cursing his own negligence, he looked out of the window. The sun had disappeared, and the skies looked grey and threatening.

Ravenscroft rose from his seat and stretched his aching limbs. His forehead felt wet and clammy to the touch, his cough as persistent as it had been previously. Crabb and the men would be wondering where he had got to. He must re-join them as soon as possible. He reached for his coat, left some money on the counter for his host, and made his way out of the inn.

Slowly he made his way up the same path he had climbed that morning, pausing every so often to ease his congested lungs, and wipe the sweat away from his brow. He had been instructed by his superior to take a holiday, a rest cure, and now here he was struggling up a lonely hill, on the edge of civilization, feeling as though he was but an inch away from dying of a fever brought on by the morning's awful weather, and wishing that he could be somewhere warm and comfortable where he would not have to worry about catching criminals ever again.

After what seemed like an eternity, he reached the summit of the hill and as he looked up at the sky, he fought to clear his head from the dizziness that he felt would overwhelm him. Feeling alone and dejected on the top of the great hill, he peered into the distance and was relieved when he thought he detected a group of figures standing on the next hill in the range. He started to walk towards the group and as he drew nearer, he saw Crabb raising his hands in the air and frantically beckoning him to join them. He increased his pace. Perhaps they had been successful in tracking down their quarry? As he clambered down the slope of the hill, towards the lower hill, Crabb came forwards to meet him.

'We've got him, sir.'

'Well done, Crabb.'

'It's not all good news though. Follow me, sir.'

Ravenscroft followed his constable along the path that ran along a kind of plateau high up between the two hills.

'One of the men found him down there,' said Crabb, pointing below them, towards a clump of trees.

The two men scrambled down the side of the hill. There, lying on the ground, was the body of the blind man.

'He must have lost his footing on the path above and rolled all the way down here, hitting his head on the rocks as he fell, until this clump of trees halted his fall,' said Crabb.

The other policemen and searchers began to gather around, as Ravenscroft knelt by the side of the body. 'He doesn't seem to have any possessions on him,' he said, after examining the man's pockets.

'There appears to be a kind of cave up there, sir, where he may have lived. He must have been making his way back there, when he fell.'

Ravenscroft made his way back up the slope and followed Crabb into a small cave that had been made on the side of the hill.

'It's a bit smelly and wet, sir. I don't think I would like to live here,' said Crabb.

'Me neither, Crabb,' replied Ravenscroft, searching through a pile of old rags that lay on some straw bedding in one corner of the cave. 'Looks as though this is the remains of his breakfast,' he said, turning over some crusts of bread and a half-eaten apple with his foot, and sneezing violently as he did so.

'Poor chap,' muttered Crabb.

'A pity we didn't have chance to speak with him before he died. Well, this looks like all we can do here. It will be dark soon, and in another half hour we will have difficulty making our way down off these hills. Get the men to pick up the body and we will all make our way back to the inn,' instructed Ravenscroft, attempting to stifle his cough with his hand.

The policemen recovered the body of the blind man, and the silent group began to make its way slowly down the sides of the hill, Ravenscroft leading the way and Crabb bringing up the rear.

Upon their return to the inn, Crabb instructed the men to place the body of the dead man into the rear of the police cart, then transferred Gladwyn's body to the same vehicle before telling them to set off for Malvern and the mortuary with their load. Ravenscroft thanked the landlord for the loan of his men, before he and Crabb climbed into Gladwyn's trap.

'I think that is all we can do today, Crabb. It will be dark before we get back to Malvern. If you could drop me off at the Tudor on the way, I would be obliged to you,' said Ravenscroft.

'If you don't mind my saying so, you look quite terrible. I should see Doctor Mountcourt when you get in,' said Crabb, looking at his superior with a degree of concern.

'I'll be alright, once I've got out of these wet clothes and had a good night's rest. I'll see you at nine tomorrow. It's been a long day, Crabb, a very long day.'

* * *

Upon returning to the Tudor, Ravenscroft instructed Stebbins that on no account was he to be disturbed until the morning. He removed his damp clothes, put on his night attire and was relieved to find his aching body sinking into the comfort of a warm, dry bed. Within a few minutes he began to feel himself drifting off into a deep sleep.

He slept badly. At first he thought he saw again the figure of the blind man mocking him from the summit of the Raggedstone, then the hill seemed to fall in on him, and he felt himself suffocating in the damp cold earth as it engulfed him. A range of faces now thrust themselves before him — the bearded features of Armitage, laughing at him for his failure to catch him; then the crooked smile, snarling leer and scar on Troutbridge's face as he let go of his howling dogs; then the stern features of Doctor Mountcourt and his attendant pushing him under the swirling waters in a large bath; before the scene gave way to Clifford peering and smiling over his maps and tearing a newspaper into tiny pieces, which he flung into the air; finally, Touchmore nodding his head from side to side, pushing his way through piles of ledgers covered in ancient cobwebs, before thrusting him forwards towards an open grave. As he fell into the grave, he saw again the bloody faces of Pitzer, Sommersby and Gladwyn staring up at him, beckoning him to join them. He struggled to climb out of the grave as they clung onto his legs. He lashed out with his feet as he heard their laughter, until he suddenly broke free. Now he found himself falling into an icy river and his body shaking with the intense cold. He desperately wanted to cry out and let someone come to his aid, but he found himself strangely unable to do so, and he knew then that there was no one there to save him. He seemed to be entering a dark tunnel, which appeared to have no end; his whole body began to burn intensely, and a feeling of helpless rejection came over him as he knew that he was nearing the end. But then a bright light began to shine dimly before him and he saw the dark veil of his lady come into view. Feelings of relief swept over his body, but as he reached out to pull back the veil, the light faded and with it all hope of salvation.

The terrible journey seemed to have no end. Then he saw the smart little cottage in Ledbury and he was overcome with a great longing to enter its door and find there the relief and calm he now so desperately needed, and for which he had always yearned, but before he could make his way up the path, between the rows of flowers, the scene began to fade, and the harder he struggled to reach the door, the further away it slipped from his view. A strange warm glow washed over him and he saw again the intimate, bright room in Crabb's cottage, from where there was food, warmth, and the laughter and joy of children — and he knew that his long journey had come to its end.

'Now then, Mr Ravenscroft, just you take it easy now.'

He looked up at the smiling features of Jennie Crabb.

'Where—'

'It's all right now, sir. You'll be fine,' said the voice of Crabb.

'Have I been ill?' Ravenscroft enquired, in a voice barely audible.

'More than ill, sir, you was quite despaired of,' said Jennie, wiping his brow with a cool flannel.

'How long have I been ill for?' asked Ravenscroft, attempting to raise himself up from the bed.

'Best part of two days, sir. We thought something was up, when you didn't appear yesterday morning, so I persuaded young Stebbins to let me in here,' said Crabb.

'Now just you lie back there, sir,' said Jennie, gently pushing the sick man down onto the bed.

'And you have taken care of me since then?'

Crabb and his wife smiled. 'Least we could do, sir.'

'Then you are good, true friends.'

'Now, sir, don't you go embarrassing me all again,' said Jennie blushing. 'Here's some beef gruel I've prepared for you. Try and drink some of this, Mr Ravenscroft.'

'Have you up on your feet, in no time, will my Jennie's beef gruel,' said Crabb proudly.

Ravenscroft sipped the liquid and then lay back on the bed.

'Now you have a nice quiet sleep Mr Ravenscroft,' said Jennie. 'Sleep will do you a power of good. We'll drop by later and see how you are.'

'Yes. You are quite right. Sleep,' said Ravenscroft, closing his eyes.

Within a minute or two he had fallen asleep, but this time he felt only warmth and reassurance, as his body became relaxed, and his thoughts became at peace with the world.

When he awoke again, he found the room empty, with warm sunlight pouring in through the windows. He eased himself upwards and reached for a glass of water that had been left by his bedside. As the liquid ran down his throat, he felt a strange feeling of contentment come over him, as if he had just been on a long journey and had reached his destination, unscathed and fulfilled.

The door opened and Crabb walked in. 'Glad to see you looking a lot better, sir,' he said in his usual happy, optimistic way.

'I feel a lot better, Crabb. What on earth has happened to me?' he enquired, taking another sip of the water.

'You must have caught a fever or a chill of some kind, being out on those hills, in all those wet clothes for so long. I've had Stebbins dry them all off and had them pressed so they are fit to wear again, sir.'

'Thank you, Crabb, you have thought of everything. I think my condition was probably bought on more by Doctor Mountcourt's prescribed hot and cold baths, rather than being caught out in the rain near the Hollybush! But thank your good wife for looking after me. I will always be in your debt.'

'No problem, sir. To tell you the truth, my Jennie likes caring for those who are sick and less fortunate than herself, and welcomed the opportunity to do so.'

'You are a fortunate man indeed, Crabb, to have such a wife.'

'I know, sir, and I thank the Lord for it.'

'Tell me, what has happened regarding the case during my illness?' asked Ravenscroft.

'Well, sir. Both Doctor Gladwyn and that Penny fellow have been taken to the mortuary. We have received a letter from no less a person than the Superintendent in Worcester, congratulating us on catching the villain who caused all these outrages, even if he is dead, and in fact several prominent people have called into the station to thank us for all our work in catching such a murderous fellow. Sorry, sir, I can see that you are still tired. Why don't I get Stebbins to bring you something to eat, and I'll call by at ten in the morning.'

'As you wish, Crabb,' said Ravenscroft lying down again.

Crabb left the room, leaving Ravenscroft alone with his thoughts. So the case appeared to be over. Everyone seemed to suggest that Old Penny, the blind outcast, had committed the crimes, and who was he to disagree with such a conclusion? He had neither the energy nor the will to pursue the matter further and was relieved the case was now finally closed.

Stebbins entered the room, bearing a tray of welcoming food and liquor.

'Stebbins, you are a good man. I could eat a horse, and that food looks particularly good.'

'Glad to see you is back to your usual form, sir,' said the youth smiling and placing the tray on the bedside table.

'What time is it, Stebbins?'

'Three o'clock in the afternoon, sir.'

'Perhaps I'll venture outside after I've eaten this food. The sunlight and fresh air will do me good.'

'Very good, sir,' grinned the youth.

'And, Stebbins, will you inform Doctor Mountcourt that I will be leaving tomorrow,' said Ravenscroft, knowing that there was little reason for him to stay, and that he would seize the opportunity to be rid of Malvern, the Tudor and all that Raggedstone nonsense for good and all.

'Sorry we'll be losing you, sir,' muttered Stebbins on the way out, before whistling his way down the corridor. Ravenscroft consumed the food and drink that had been bought for him, then rose from his bed and dressed. The sun shining in through the window seemed to offer the prospect of better things to come, and he was determined to take advantage of any fresh situations that would present themselves. He had nearly a week left of his holiday; still time to make it to Brighton.

He made his way slowly down towards the churchyard, gaining in confidence with every step, but having little desire to venture onto the hills. Here he found the seat by the wall, near the Kelly grave he had found previously. He again looked at the headstone and wondered at the tragedy that the words encompassed. Within the space of one year, both the father and the son had been taken, the boy cruelly while still in infancy, leaving the wife and mother to mourn their loss. For a brief moment he saw himself looking down again at the young girl on the cold cobbles of the London alleyway, and wondered whether her past life had yet been mourned by those that had known her? Then his thoughts turned back towards his own childhood, and the sister he had never known, who had died before his own birth, and how each year on the sixth day of November, he and his parents had always made the journey of remembrance up the winding path that led to the tiny churchyard above the village where they had lived. Years later he had buried his parents in that same plot of earth, turned his back on the old life and travelled to London, where he had busied himself with his career in the police force, eventually rising to his present rank of Inspector. In the years that had followed, on bad days, he had often thought of leaving the noisy, dirty, fog bound streets of the capital behind him and returning to his birth village, where he would again take up the threads of that other, earlier life, but always the mood would pass, and he would become reconciled to his usual everyday existence. Had he perhaps always been too eager to accept that world which he had created for himself? Now that he had recovered from the illness, which had threatened to engulf him, there seemed that there was again the possibility of another place — another world — somewhere, which awaited his arrival, where he could be given new opportunities, and where he could be reborn.

He turned away from the headstone and looked up at the church. He sat down, turned his face to the sun, closed his eyes, and felt the gentle warmth beginning to heal his body.

'I think you have been looking for me, Mr Ravenscroft,' said a voice that he had heard briefly before. He opened his eyes, and saw the veiled lady sitting on the seat next to him.

'We met on the train,' he said, without thinking, his thoughts broken by her arrival.

'And you were kind enough to help me with my luggage. I saw you at the Well House that morning on the day after and your face looking out on the churchyard from the window. Then you tried to speak with me here.'

Ravenscroft found her quiet, evenly phrased way of talking slightly unnerving and began to make excuses, but she raised her hand and stopped him almost before he had begun.

'I suppose I must be an item of curiosity to one such as yourself, a police inspector from London.'

'How do you know—'

'You are the talk of the town, Mr Ravenscroft.'

'I see.'

There followed an uneasy silence.

'Now that you have finally caught up with me, Mr Ravenscroft, I see that you are unwilling to satisfy your curiosity.'

'I am sorry. I had not wanted to be so forward.'

'You have come to Malvern to seek something, or perhaps you are escaping from a part of your past?' she enquired, ignoring his last comment.

'I was instructed to take the water cure by my superiors.'

'And have you found what you were seeking?' she said, gently drawing back her veil to reveal a face of fine features and strange determination.

'I am not sure,' he replied looking away, least his gaze should cause offence.

'One day, I am sure, you will find what you are looking for,' she said, smiling gently.

'And you, ma'am, have you found what you are seeking?'

She turned away sharply, but not before Ravenscroft had seen the look of bitterness which had flickered momentarily across her face. 'I'm sorry, I have no desire to cause you any distress,' he added quickly.

'I will never find what I am seeking Mr Ravenscroft,' she said turning to face him. 'You have discovered my husband and child, I see, as I knew you would in time. They lie there together. In years to come the inscription will fade, and when you and I are gone, people will pass by the stone not knowing the joy and grief that they gave in their lifetime. When they died, it was as if my life had ended. So soon, Mr Ravenscroft, it was all so soon. First my husband — then my poor baby. My husband had brought it all upon us, but my son — he was completely blameless. Life is so unfair, Mr Ravenscroft.

Perhaps you could tell me why it is always the innocent who are taken from us?'

'I cannot answer that question, ma'am,' replied Ravenscroft seeking to understand her despair. 'Perhaps in time the pain will pass.'

'Oh, that is what they all say. All those people who think they know what you are going through but who can never hope to understand. Time, I can assure you, does not help to deaden the pain — it merely encompasses all the hurt and anger.' Her voice began to trail away and her eyes to fill with tears, leaving Ravenscroft aware of the futility of his own words.

'Perhaps religion?' was all he could say, but he knew it was only an empty gesture.

'Religion seeks to make grief respectable. It cannot offer me anything.'

'And yet your son and husband are buried here, my good lady, and you visit their grave?'

'There has to be somewhere, where I can sit — and remember them, somewhere where we can be alone, together.'

'Of course, I understand. You spoke of anger just now . . .'

'Yes, there is always anger. Anger that someone you loved has caused all this, through his own stupidity and negligence. Anger that the son, who you loved more than your own life, was taken away from you because of that folly. Anger that grew as you watched them die, slowly and in pain, and knowing all the time that you could do nothing to bring them relief — nothing to make their passing easier. Do you know what all that feels like, Mr Ravenscroft, to know that your own resolve can do so little? And all the time the anger grows, as they slip away from you. No, you cannot, for although I am sure you have loved, Mr Ravenscroft, you have never been witness to that death of love, and there is always the hope, the prospect, that love may re-enter your life some time again in the future, whereas I no longer seek, nor wish to acquire such love ever again. In my situation it is the anger, above all else — the anger that makes my life barely tolerable, until it can be resolved.'

'And do you think that this anger will ever be abated?' asked Ravenscroft, looking into her sad eyes.

'I have spoken too much and too freely, Mr Ravenscroft. You have unfinished business to attend to here in Malvern. In your heart, you know that. When you have completed your mission, we will meet again and I will explain everything,' she said, quickly rising from her seat.

'I am sorry for your loss, Mrs Kelly,' said Ravenscroft, desperately trying to think of other questions he could ask. She smiled briefly, before walking away from the seat. 'You will have no need to seek me out, Mr Ravenscroft. I will know where to find you.'

He watched her walk across the graveyard and down the path that led to the Assembly Rooms, until she turned the corner and was no more. Resuming his seat, he went over their conversation in his mind and began to wonder what terrible events had caused the death of her husband and son. *Through his own stupidity and negligence* — she had said, as if her husband had committed some act of outrage which had caused such loss, such distress. What that act had been, he could only guess.

I will know where to find you — she had said, as if she knew his every move, everything that he was thinking about, and all that was about to happen in the future. The more he considered her words, the more it seemed to him that she knew more about him than he could ever hope to discover about her. Part of him had been satisfied that at last he had spoken with the woman who had occupied his thoughts for so long, but another part of him wanted to know more about this strange woman and her tragic circumstances.

The more he sat there, feeling the warm sun on his face, the more he began to wonder if she had really been there at all, and that perhaps he had imagined the whole encounter? The quiet peace of the graveyard seemed to contrast too deeply with what he had heard and seen.

He rose from his seat and began to make his way back to the Tudor. *You have unfinished business to attend to . . . in your heart you know that* — he heard again those words of reproach and certainty.

As he entered the Tudor he found Stebbins and Doctor Mountcourt conversing together in the entrance hall.

'Mr Ravenscroft. It appears that you are about to leave us,' said Mountcourt in that official formal manner that Ravenscroft had grown used to. 'I'm sorry that we will not be able to affect a full cure, but I fully understand if you wish to depart.'

'I have changed my mind,' replied Ravenscroft. 'I will be staying after all.' Mountcourt looked slightly taken aback by this change of heart. 'There are some matters that need resolving.'

'As you wish, sir, we will, of course, be more than pleased to continue with your course of treatment,' said Mountcourt, recovering his professional composure.

Ravenscroft made his way back to his bedroom, and stood looking out of the window, towards the churchyard and the seat where he had sat some minutes previous. How could a blind man enter a study and place poison in a glass, and also kill two people by hitting them on the head? He, and others, had been too easily swayed by this flawed assumption. Perhaps Old Penny had not been really totally blind at all and had just pretended to be so, but even if this was the case, why would such a poor, wretched, half-blind tramp want to kill three of the town's prominent citizens? There appeared to be no reason behind such an outrage.

No, the case was far from closed. There was still a killer out there, and Ravenscroft now knew that he would find no rest until he had brought the murderer to book.

CHAPTER SEVEN

'Good to see you looking like your old self again,' said Crabb as the two men met outside the Tudor the following morning. 'Rumour has it that you might be leaving us today, sir?'

'Then rumour is incorrect, Crabb. We have a crime to solve, four crimes in fact, and our murderer is still out there,' replied Ravenscourt, a new urgency in his voice.

'Good to hear you say that, sir. I never had that old Penny fellow down for these murders. There would be no purpose for him to have killed them.'

'Exactly! No reason at all. Whoever our murderer is, he used Penny to lure Gladwyn to a remote spot on the hills, so that he could kill him undisturbed and undetected. He was probably there out at Hollybush all the time we were there, watching us from the undergrowth, until he considered it safe to slip quietly away. He had probably arranged to meet up with Old Penny at the cave afterwards, and I would not be surprised if he pushed him over the top of the hill as well!'

'That would have been quite difficult, sir. One of my men could easily have seen him,' suggested Crabb.

'Not if he was making his way along the lower slopes of the hills, hidden in the undergrowth. He would have waited for Penny to return to the cave, killed him, and then disappeared into the wood once more, and made his escape once we had recovered the body and gone back to Malvern.'

'So what next, sir?' asked Crabb.

'We have to find out why these three men were killed. Once we have found the answer to that question, we will have our killer. There is something that links the three men together. Let us consider what they all had in common. They were a closely knit group, having known each other for nearly thirty years. They were all members of the Town Council, with Pitzer due to become mayor in the near future. They were all trustees of Old Lechmere's Almshouses in Colwall. They all dined together, mixed socially and appear to have got on well with each other. Now let's see what they don't have in common, and here we come back to the railway company. Pitzer was not only a director of the new company, he was also one of its major shareholders — and yet the other two had no connections with the new venture at all, so we have no common motive there. No, we are missing something. There has to be something else that binds these men together; something for which an outsider was prepared to kill for. We must discover what that is, Crabb. I think we will begin by going through the late Doctor Gladwyn's personal affects and see what we can discover there, after which I think we have need to pay our Mr Troutbridge another visit. This time, however, we will be prepared. Can you get some of your men to come with us? No news of Armitage, I suppose?' said Ravenscroft, striding away from the Tudor.

'No, sir. I went out to the almshouses yesterday, but he had not returned and no one has seen him for days. I've also asked the Ledbury constabulary to keep an eye on his sister's cottage but there has been no activity there,' replied Crabb, trying to keep up with his superior officer.

'You seemed to have thought of everything, Crabb. On to Gladwyn's! Let us see if we can secure a cab, but no, I see the prospect of a fine day. We should walk. The exercise will do us good and help clear our thoughts!'

'As you wish, sir.'

* * *

Twenty minutes later the two men arrived at Gladwyn's house. Crabb rang the doorbell, which was answered by the maid.

Ravenscroft explained their business and they were shown into Gladwyn's study.

'This is where Doctor Gladwyn keeps all his papers, sir.'

'Thank you. I would be obliged if you would be kind enough to explain to Mrs Gladwyn the nature of our business. We will ring if we require anything,' said Ravenscroft.

The maid left the room and the two men set to work going through Gladwyn's papers.

'Still that awful smell, sir,' sniffed Crabb.

'I've known better physician's rooms,' remarked Ravenscroft.

'What are we looking for, sir?'

'We are looking for anything that can link Gladwyn with Sommersby and Pitzer. Ah, here is the almshouses document appointing Gladwyn as a trustee. It appears to be almost identical to the one we unearthed in Sommersby's rooms, so there is nothing particularly startling there. I'll go through the rest of the drawers of the good doctor's desk, while you have a look in that cabinet.'

Ravenscroft worked his way through the pile of papers. 'These seem to be mainly documents of a medical nature. Here is a copy of Gladwyn's will. Let us have a look at that, see if anyone stood to benefit from his death'. Crabb peered over Ravenscroft's shoulder, as he continued to read the document. 'As we thought, there are no heirs or children — he leaves everything to his wife, except for one or two minor bequests to the town.'

'Nothing there then, sir, meaning old Gladwyn cannot have been killed for his money.'

'Seems you are right, Crabb. Keep on looking, there has to be something here.'

Fifteen minutes later, Ravenscroft slammed the door of the desk. 'There is absolutely nothing; nothing all to suggest why poor Gladwyn was murdered. It seems as though we have drawn a blank, Crabb. There is absolutely nothing in the doctor's papers that might have given us a clue as to why he was murdered. This is all very frustrating. We might as well move on, but before we leave let us have a final look round the room in case we have missed something,' he said, standing up and glancing at the walls. 'Usual photographs of Gladwyn and his wife, taken some years ago by the look of it, medical certificate from Bangor Medical School when he qualified, a faded view of some obscure Welsh mountain scene. There is nothing to interest us here. Come, Crabb, let us be on our way.'

Ravenscroft strode out of the room, and made his way back into the hall, where he found the maid waiting to let them out. As she opened the door, something caught his eye in the hat stand.

'Look, Crabb. This is an almost identical walking stick to the one we found in Sommersby's rooms. See here — the letters M.W.B. in the form of a monogram engraved on the silver handle of the stick. If I am not mistaken these are the same letters that we discovered on Sommersby's walking stick.'

'Interesting, sir,' ventured Crabb.

'Would you take this stick to your mistress and ask Mrs Gladwyn if she can tell us how long her husband has had the item, and if she knows what the letters stand for,' said Ravenscroft, addressing the maid.

The maid took the stick from him and left the hall.

'Is it not interesting, Crabb, that both men should have identical walking sticks with the same letters engraved on the handle?'

'Perhaps they were both members of some club, like say the Oddfellows or a smoking club?' suggested Crabb.

Ravenscroft nodded. 'I wonder what the letters M.W.B. represent?'

Two minutes later the maid returned, still carrying the walking stick. 'Mistress says all she can remember is the master having the stick for as long as she can recall, and that he probably acquired it shortly after they moved to Malvern, she thinks, but she can't be sure. She does not know what the letters stand for. In fact, she was unaware that there were any letters at all on the handle, sir'

Ravenscroft thanked the maid and returned the cane to its resting place, before leaving the house.

'Well, sir, no luck there.'

'It would appear so, but I still think that cane may be of some significance to our investigations. But we will have to put that aside for now, for we have more pressing things to attend to. It is about time we paid our Mr Troutbridge another visit. Let us go back to the station and take some of your men out to the farm. Do you have any guns at the station?'

'There is an old pistol, sir,' replied Crabb.

'Then bring it with us, we may have need of it.'

* * *

Later that morning Ravenscroft and Crabb, accompanied by two other police officers, made their way over the hills in the direction of Troutbridge's farm.

'Do you think we might find Armitage there?' enquired Crabb.

'There remains that possibility, Crabb. He may well have been the face I saw at the window when we drove away last time.'

The police wagon made its way up the rutted track until it arrived at the farm.

'We'll try the shed again first,' suggested Ravenscroft.

The group walked over to the milking shed and entered the building, Crabb calling out Troutbridge's name.

'No sign of him here, sir.'

'Let's try the other buildings. You two men search the buildings on that side of the yard. Crabb, come with me, we'll try that old barn over there.'

They walked over to the building, but as they were about to enter the barn, they were suddenly confronted by Troutbridge, who stepped out abruptly in front of them. The farmer was holding a piece of old rope, the end of which was tied round the collar of a large Alsatian dog.

'What do you want?' he snapped.

'Mr Troutbridge. I would ask you to accompany us to the police station in Malvern for further questioning. I also have permission to search your property,' said Ravenscroft. Crabb looked down nervously at the dog.

'I told you that if you came back, I'd set the dog on you!' snarled Troutbridge.

'Have a care, sir. I would advise you to tie the dog up and come quietly,' said Ravenscroft, eyeing the dog, which had now begun to growl loudly.

'Go to hell!' shouted Troutbridge, seeking to restrain the dog, which was pulling violently on the end of the rope. 'Get off my property, now, or I'll let go of him!'

'Come now, Troutbridge, put up the dog. There is no need for this,' said Ravenscroft, trying to sound as confident as he could.

'I warned you!' shouted Troutbridge.

'Don't you threaten us, my man,' said Crabb.

'Put up the dog, man!' urged Ravenscroft.

Suddenly the dog broke free from its owner, darted across towards the two men, and jumped onto Crabb, throwing him violently to the ground.

'Call off the dog, Troutbridge!' yelled Ravenscroft, taking the pistol from his coat pocket and aiming it at the animal. 'I say, call him off man!' He saw that Crabb had covered his face with his hands and was trying desperately to free himself from the creature. 'For God's sake, sir, shoot!' shouted the constable.

Ravenscroft took steady aim of the gun at the dog and fired.

'You murdering swine,' growled Troutbridge, lunging at Ravenscroft.

'Grab him, men!' Ravenscroft shouted instructions to the other two officers who had run across from the other buildings. 'Put the cuffs on him!'

The constables wrestled Troutbridge to the ground and after a short struggle, secured his wrists with their handcuffs. Ravenscroft walked over to where the dead dog lay on top of Crabb.

'Soon have you out from under there,' he said, pulling the animal away. 'How are you, Crabb?'

'Grief, sir! I thought my number was up! Another few seconds and he would have had his jaws round my throat. 'Tis a good thing we brought the gun,' replied Crabb, lifting himself of the ground.

Ravenscroft placed his hand on the other's shoulder, concerned. 'Are you hurt?'

'It just seems to be my hand, sir, where the beast sank his teeth. Afraid I shall need a new tunic, though,' said Crabb taking out his handkerchief and placing it on his bleeding wrist.

'Here, let me look,' said Ravenscroft, examining his constable's hand. 'We'll go into the house and wash it, and I'll try and find something to bind it with, until we can get a doctor to look at it. Sorry I was a bit late in firing. I didn't want to shoot too soon, until I had a clear view of the dog.'

'That's alright, sir, better late than never,' replied Crabb, holding his wrist.

'He was certainly a vicious creature and no mistake. Dogs like that should not be owned by blaggards like Troutbridge,' said Ravenscroft, staring down at the dead animal.

'Not the animal's fault, sir,' added Crabb.

'You men, put that ruffian in the cart and stay with him while we go into the house,' instructed Ravenscroft. 'Come now, Crabb, let's go and get that hand seen to.'

The two officers dragged the abusive farmer across to the cart, as Ravenscroft lead the way across the yard.

'You won't get away with this Ravenscroft!' shouted Troutbridge as he was being bundled into the cart. 'I'll have the law on you!' Ravenscroft ignored the remarks as he and Crabb opened the door of the farmhouse kitchen.

Ravenscroft surveyed the piles of old papers, rags and jumble, which seemed to clutter every corner of the room. The table was covered with dirty plates and mugs, the remains of a half-eaten meal lying side by side with debris left over from previous meals. Ravenscroft walked over to the bowl and ladled some water into an old cracked bowl.

'Lord, it smells in here!' said Crabb attempting to stem the flow of blood from his injured hand. 'I think I prefer old Gladwyn's surgery to this place.'

'Put your hand in there, Crabb,' instructed Ravenscroft. 'Now let's see if I can find something to bind it with,' he said, searching through the old clothes on the floor.

Crabb placed his hand into the bowl and began to wipe it with his handkerchief. It was not long before the water began to cloud over with the red liquid.

'You've got a nasty gash there,' said Ravenscroft, tearing up an old sheet he had found. 'Give me your wrist and I'll bind it to stop the flow of blood. That should do until we can get it cleaned up better when we return to the station.'

After Crabb's wrist had been attended to, the two men began to look around the room.

'What a dreadful place to live in! I have seen cleaner rooms than this in Whitechapel,' said Ravenscroft. 'How anyone can live in such filth. These plates look as though they have never been cleaned, and this food looks days' old. This bread and cheese appear to have been the last meal eaten but do you notice something, Crabb?'

'There are two plates set?' suggested Crabb.

'Exactly! Troutbridge shared his last meal with someone else.'

'It could be his wife?'

'I don't think so. No woman would put up with this squalor. I think there is someone else in the house.'

'You mean the face you saw at the window?'

The two men looked at one another.

'Upstairs!' said Ravenscroft. 'But quietly. We don't want to frighten him off.'

Ravenscroft crossed over to the staircase and began to make his way up the steps. 'You stay here, Crabb, in case he comes down,' he whispered.

Gaining the landing, Ravenscroft found himself confronted by two closed doors. He paused to listen for a moment, then with his boot, he pushed open the door to one of the rooms but found it empty. Quickly he kicked open the second door.

'So, Mr Armitage, we have caught up with you at last,' he said addressing the lone figure who sat on the side of an old bed, staring up at him with a look of fear, as he entered the room.

'Mr Ravenscroft.'

'You have given us a great deal of trouble, Mr Armitage. You will oblige me by accompanying me to the station, sir,' said Ravenscroft, addressing his quarry.

Armitage stood up slowly and made his way across the room. As he neared Ravenscroft, he suddenly pushed him out of the way, darted from the room, and began to run down the stairs.

'Crabb!' yelled out Ravenscroft.

'I have him, sir,' replied the constable, as Ravenscroft raced down the steps.

'Put the cuffs on him, Crabb. Well, Mr Armitage, that was rather a silly thing to do. We have been looking for you for some days now. You have some questions to answer, sir.'

'I have committed no crime, Inspector. You have no right to arrest me like this,' said the indignant warden.

'I think you will find that we have every right, Mr Armitage. If you are so innocent, what were you doing hiding upstairs, and why did you seek to run away from us?'

'I have a perfect explanation for my presence here.'

'That may be so, sir, but for now you will oblige us by accompanying us to the station.'

Crabb cuffed the bedraggled Armitage and the trio made their way back to the police cart. 'Put him in there with Troutbridge,' instructed Ravenscroft. 'Well, gentlemen, you have both certainly caused us problems this morning. Let us all return to the station and see what we can discover.'

* * *

Ravenscroft and Crabb faced Troutbridge across the table.

'Now then, Mr Troutbridge, what is your relationship to Mr Armitage?' began Ravenscroft.

Troutbridge stared down at the floor and remained silent.

'What was Armitage doing at your farm? We found him hiding in the upstairs bedroom. He had clearly been there for several days. Were you sheltering him? I would advise you to answer, or it will be the worse for you.'

'You shot my dog,' snapped Troutbridge, glaring at his questioner.

'Your dog was attacking Constable Crabb at the time. If I had not shot him, my constable would have been seriously injured, possibly killed, and you would have been facing a murder charge,' said Ravenscroft firmly, knowing that he would be facing an uphill struggle to discover the truth.

'There was no need to have shot him.'

'There was every reason to shoot him. You had ample opportunity to call the dog off, and you chose not to do so. You had no business keeping such a ferocious animal in the first place. Things are looking very black for you, Troutbridge.'

Troutbridge shrugged his shoulders and glowered, as Ravenscroft continued. 'You are facing serious charges — failure to restrain a savage animal, unleashing such an animal, attacking a police officer. The local justices will not take kindly to that kind of behaviour. You already have a bad reputation in the county. Oh yes, we have been checking up on you. You are well known to our colleagues in Ledbury, who inform us that you have been up before the bench on two previous occasions. I would say that things are looking very grim for you, Troutbridge, unless you co-operate with us. Now I want some answers to my questions, or you could find yourself up on a murder charge.'

'You shot my dog,' repeated Troutbridge angrily, but Ravenscroft ignored his last remark.

'How long have you known Armitage?' he asked.

'I've never seen him, before he came to my house.'

'When was that?' asked Crabb.

'Last Monday.'

'What did he want?' asked Ravenscroft, leaning forwards.

'Said he had been driven out of his house and could he stay with me for a few days, until he could go back, like,' replied the farmer grudgingly.

'And you let him stay — a complete stranger who you had never seen before? You let him stay in your house?'

'He paid me to stay. He said he would be gone by the end of the week.'

'You are in the habit of accommodating strangers in your home. I find that very difficult to accept.'

'If they pays. What's wrong with that?'

'Can't think why anyone wouldn't want to stay in your rat-infested hole,' said Crabb, displaying a tougher, sarcastic side that Ravenscroft had not seen before in his colleague.

'Well, I tell you I don't believe a word of it. I think you have known Mr Armitage for at least three years. You will no doubt be surprised to learn that your name appears every month in the accounts of Old Lechmere's Almshouses in Colwall,' said Ravenscroft.

'I don't know nothin' about any old almshouses,' protested Troutbridge, sitting back in his chair and looking up at the ceiling.

'Don't play innocent with me, Troutbridge. You were paid the sum of one pound and ten shillings every month for the past three years. Now I want to know why — and if I don't get the right answer, I'll put you away for so long, your farm will have crumbled down to a pile of old dust by the time you get out of prison, if you ever get out!' said Ravenscroft, raising his voice.

'I've told you, I know nothing about any sums of money,' replied Troutbridge in his usual aggressive tone.

'Have it your own way, Troutbridge. I've tried to help you,' said Ravenscroft leaning back in his chair. Troutbridge glowered at him. 'Let's turn to something else. Why did you poison Mr Pitzer?'

'I ain't poison no one!' protested Troutbridge loudly.

'Why did you hit Mr Sommersby on the back of his head and then topple the bookcase on top of him, so that it looked like an accident?'

'Here, I ain't hit no one on their head. You can't have me for that.'

'Then there was poor Doctor Gladwyn. You killed him by hitting him on the temple, over at Raggedstone,' said Ravenscroft quickly, raising his voice again.

'No! I never did!' shouted Troutbridge.

'And Old Penny,' Ravenscroft banged the table with the palm of his hand. 'Did you push him off the hill by the cave, a poor innocent blind man?'

'No! I ain't killed anyone. You can't pin all these murders on me!'

'We can do whatever we like. My superiors are anxious for a satisfactory conclusion to this affair. They won't mind if we say we have caught you. In fact, they will be more than happy that we have finally caught our man. You will hang, Troutbridge, make no mistake. You will hang very slowly and in great pain, I can assure you. Your days are at an end,' said Ravenscroft, adopting a tone of resignation.

'You can try and hang me if you likes. You can't put anything on me. I never killed anyone,' protested Troutbridge, anxiously looking around the room.

'Do you have a walking stick, Mr Troutbridge?' asked Ravenscroft, suddenly changing tack.

'Walking stick? What use have I got for a bloody walking stick?'

'Here, watch your language, Troutbridge!' interjected Crabb.

'Do the initials M.W.B. mean anything to you?'

The farmer looked puzzled. Ravenscroft went on, 'Have you ever owned a walking stick with the initials M.W.B. engraved on the handle? The question is a simple one to answer.'

'I told you, I never had any walking stick.'

'Have you ever seen a walking stick with those initials on?' asked Ravenscroft quickly.

'No.'

'Perhaps you saw the stick when Mr Pitzer came out to your farm?'

'Don't know any Pitzer. I has no visitors out at my farm.'

'What about Mr Sommersby?' asked Crabb, looking up from his pocket book, where he had been making notes.

'Never heard of Sommersby; don't know anything about him neither.'

'Was Doctor Gladwyn your doctor?' asked Ravenscroft.

'What needs of I for a flaming doctor?' mocked Troutbridge.

'This is your last chance, Troutbridge,' said a frustrated Ravenscroft, realising that his own anger was in danger of rising to the surface. 'If you don't tell us what we want to know, I'm locking you up in our cells until you go up before the Magistrates tomorrow morning. They won't deal with you so lightly. God help you then.'

'Go to blazes! Do what you like,' replied Troutbridge defiantly.

'You've had your chance, Troutbridge. A night in the cells might make you see sense. Lock him up, Crabb!' said Ravenscroft firmly, feigning an air of indifference.

Crabb escorted the farmer from the room, leaving Ravenscroft alone with his thoughts. It did not seem likely that Troutbridge had murdered the three men, not to mention poor Penny, but he was certainly hiding something, and clearly that secret was bound up with Armitage. Perhaps Armitage had killed Pitzer, Sommersby and Gladwyn, and Troutbridge had been his accomplice? Or perhaps the farmer had discovered that Armitage had committed the crimes and was blackmailing him? Troutbridge had to have some hold over Armitage otherwise why would he have been content to have sought sanctuary with the farmer? Then there were the payments. Armitage had been paying Troutbridge a regular sum of money, each month, for the past three years. Why had he paid the farmer the money — or had Armitage invented the payments and kept all the money for himself? But then, if he had done that, why would he have gone to Troutbridge for help? The more he considered these questions, the more unanswered possibilities there remained. He had expected that Troutbridge under his questioning would have been frightened into a confession, and he had been both annoyed and irritated when this had not happened. The farmer was clearly made of stronger stuff. All he could hope for now was that his other prisoner might prove more forthcoming.

Crabb returned to the room. 'Well, sir, we didn't get much out of him.'

'No, our Mr Troutbridge seems very reluctant to tell us what we want. Whatever he is hiding must be of great importance to him. Time we had some words with young Armitage,' said Ravenscroft, trying to put a brave face on it. 'Go and bring him in, Crabb.'

Crabb returned a few moments later with Armitage. Ravenscroft looked across the table at his prisoner, who was still attired in the same clothes he had seen him wearing on his first visit to the almshouses. In fact, the warden's unkempt, bedraggled appearance gave the impression that the man had not changed his clothes for several days. Ravenscroft knew however that his line of questioning with Armitage might even prove more difficult than his interrogation with Troutbridge. The warden might turn out to be a more intelligent, cunning adversary.

'Well, Mr Armitage, this is a right mess you seem to have got yourself into,' began Ravenscroft. 'Let us see where we can begin. Ah, the accounts. When we last spoke, you mentioned that you kept the accounts of the almshouses with your sister in Ledbury. I have to tell you that we have visited your sister—'

'You leave Lucy out of this. She has nothing to do with my situation,' protested Armitage, glaring at his questioner.

'I would hope not. While at your sister's, we went through the accounts and we found that they made interesting reading. Every month you were paying the sum of one pound and ten shillings to Mr Troutbridge — regular payments, every month. What were they for?'

'Mr Troutbridge provided the almshouses with food. I paid him every month. There was nothing wrong with that.'

'He denies knowing anything about such payments. Rather strange I should think, don't you, that he should say that if there was nothing to hide?'

Armitage stared down at the floor and said nothing.

'Why did you leave the almshouses so suddenly after our visit?'

'I had business to transact in Hereford for a few days. On the way back I stopped off at Troutbridge's to discuss our order for next month and as it was so late in the evening, he suggested I stopped the night with him. I had just woken up, when you entered the bedroom. I was still half asleep. I panicked and ran down the stairs,' said the warden, running his hands through his untidy hair.

'I'm afraid I don't believe a word of that, Mr Armitage. Troutbridge says you had been at the farm for several days, and that in fact you paid him to stay there for the week,' said Ravenscroft leaning forwards.

'Troutbridge has a vivid imagination,' mumbled Armitage.

'What do you know about the new Tewkesbury to Leominster Railway Company?' asked Ravenscroft, deciding to change his line of questioning.

'Nothing; I have no interest in railway companies.'

'When we searched your cottage, Mr Armitage, we found an old copy of the *Malvern News*. An article in one of the issues had apparently caught your attention. So much so, that you had even drawn a line all round it.'

'Please continue, Inspector, I am fascinated by all this,' said Armitage, recovering his composure and adopting a more defensive posture.

'The article mentioned that the new railway company intended constructing the line through Colwall. When we made further enquiries, with Mr Clifford the agent at the Malvern Reading Rooms, we discovered that the almshouses would have to be demolished if such a line were to be built.'

'Then this is a serious matter, of which I was not aware.'

'Apparently you and Mr Pitzer had words over the new scheme,' said Crabb.

'I am sorry, gentlemen, you have completely lost me. What does Mr Pitzer have to do with this new railway company?' asked Armitage, appearing to grow in confidence.

'I think Mr Armitage that you know perfectly well—'

'I assure you, I know nothing of what you speak,' interrupted Armitage.

'Mr Pitzer was one of your trustees?'

'Yes.'

'He was also a director and a major shareholder of the Tewkesbury to Leominster Railway Company. He would have stood to gain quite a great deal of money had the scheme gone ahead, whereas you and the residents of the almshouses would have been out in the street.'

'All this has come as a great shock, Inspector. Had I known what Mr Pitzer was involved in, I would certainly have taken it up with him — but as I said before, I knew nothing of his involvement, or indeed anything about this new railway company of which you speak.'

'Then how do you explain the fact, sir, that the article in the newspaper had been so marked?' asked Crabb.

'I don't, Constable. This is the first I have known about it. Ah, of course. The residents often give me their old newspapers to read, after they have finished with them. One of them must have marked the newspaper. Yes, that would explain how that came about,'

Ravenscroft smiled and leaned back in his chair. It was as he thought — the warden had proved himself to be a man of endeavour and deception. 'I must congratulate you, Mr Armitage, on your inventions.'

'What I am telling you is the truth, Inspector. It is not my fault that you choose not to believe it,' replied Armitage, a touch of arrogance creeping into his voice.

'Is that why you killed Pitzer?' asked Ravenscroft leaning forwards again and folding his hands neatly in front of him on the table.

'Oh come, Inspector! You surely cannot think that I killed Pitzer?'

'You wrote Pitzer a letter, making an appointment to see him alone in his study on the night he was killed.'

'This is nonsense,' replied Armitage, turning away.

'It would have been quite easy for you to have gained entry to his study unannounced, from the garden, where you administered the poison.'

'Absolute nonsense! This is all conjecture.'

'And is it also nonsense that you killed Mr Sommersby?' asked Ravenscroft.

'Sommersby? What is this about Sommersby?' Armitage looked shocked.

'Come now, Mr Armitage, I'm sure our friend Troutbridge told you of our visit to his farm, when we mentioned we were investigating the death of Mr Sommersby?'

'He mentioned nothing of this to me. How did Sommersby die?'

'He was hit on the back of the head with a blunt instrument and a heavy bookcase was pulled over on top of him, to make it look like an accident. But I'm sure you know all this, Mr Armitage? Where were you when Sommersby was murdered?' asked Ravenscroft.

'As this is the first I have heard of Sommersby's murder, and as I am therefore completely unaware of what time the schoolmaster was killed, I am unable to say where I was at the time of his death — but as I have told you already Inspector, I have been away in Hereford for a few days. I only returned to Mathon last night.'

'And what precisely were you doing in Hereford?'

Armitage said nothing.

'Well, Mr Armitage, your answer if you please. What was the nature of your business in Hereford?' continued Ravenscroft, wondering what line the warden would come forth with now.

'It is of a delicate nature,' replied Armitage moving uneasily in his seat. 'I was visiting a lady friend.'

'Her name, please, sir?' asked Crabb lifting up his pencil.

'That I am not prepared to disclose. It is a question of honour. The lady is married. If I were to disclose her name, the knowledge would bring disgrace, not only upon her but to all her immediate family as well,' replied Armitage, looking distressed.

'How very convenient, Mr Armitage. If you were to tell us the name of this lady, I am sure that such a lady could confirm your presence in Hereford. You would then be released from all suspicion, but you seem unwilling to do that.'

'I am sorry, I cannot disclose her name. Her husband holds high office.'

'Come now, sir. This is all nonsense, as you well know. You and I both know that you never went to Hereford. I caught sight of you the other day when we visited the farm, looking out of the window. You have been at Troutbridge all the week,' said Ravenscroft, adopting a slight mocking tone.

'You were mistaken, Inspector. It must have been someone else you saw. I have told you I was in Hereford for most of the week,' replied Armitage irritably.

'Did you use Troutbridge to help you kill Sommersby? It was a big bookcase to move on your own.'

'How many more times do I have to tell you — I was in Hereford all week,' replied Armitage.

'Enjoying the pleasures of a lady,' said Crabb.

'For whom we have no name,' added Ravenscroft.

Armitage let out a deep sigh, shook his head and looked out of the window.

'Tell me, Mr Armitage, are you familiar with Raggedstone Hill?' asked Ravenscroft.

'I have been that way one or two times. Why do you ask?'

'Were you there the other day when Doctor Gladwyn was murdered?'

'Gladwyn, murdered! What is this?' asked Armitage anxiously.

'You do not know that Doctor Gladwyn was murdered at a cottage near Raggedstone Hill?'

'No, of course not!'

'Hit on the temple, here, with a stone,' said Crabb, pointing to his forehead.

'This is terrible!'

'Three prominent citizens of Malvern; all trustees of the almshouses; all known to you,' began Ravenscroft.

'Look here, Ravenscroft, you have to believe me when I tell you, that I did not commit any of these murders. I am completely innocent of these crimes,' protested Armitage becoming agitated. 'You have no evidence to link me to any of them.'

'You know Old Penny?' asked Crabb.

'Old Penny? Who in blazes is Old Penny? You are not going to tell me he is dead as well, and accuse me of yet another murder?'

'Tell me, Mr Armitage. Do you own a walking stick?' asked Ravenscroft ignoring the last comment.

'A walking stick? What has my walking stick got to do with all this?'

'Answer the question please, Mr Armitage.'

'Yes, I have a walking stick. I use it when I go out walking on the hills.'

'Describe it to us, if you please,' said Ravenscroft.

'Well, it's just a walking stick. It's made of wood,' replied a bewildered Armitage, becoming more frustrated.

'Does it have a handle, a silver-topped handle?'

'No. It's all wood, as I just told you. What is all this?'

'Do the initials M.W.B. mean anything to you?'

'M.W.B.? No, should they?'

'Those initials appear on the handles of the walking sticks that belong to both Mr Sommersby and Doctor Gladwyn.'

'Well, I don't have a walking stick with an engraved, silver-topped handle, and the initials M.W.B. mean nothing to me,' said Armitage defiantly.

'Mr Armitage, I have to tell you that we are not satisfied with what you have told us this morning,' said Ravenscroft, standing up and pacing the room. 'In fact, I do not believe one word of your story about a lady of honour in Hereford. I think you and Troutbridge are mixed up in something together, and I mean to get to the bottom of it. I believe you have been at Troutbridge's farm for several days now, and furthermore that you know a great deal about the murders of Mr Pitzer, Mr Sommersby, Doctor Gladwyn and Old Penny. You are in very serious trouble. You will shortly be up before the bench on four counts of murder. You can still save yourself, man. I advise you to tell us the truth, Mr Armitage, before it is too late,' pleaded Ravenscroft.

'I have told you all I know,' replied Armitage, looking away in a defiant mood.

'Very well, Armitage. I am detaining you on suspicion of the murders of the said four gentlemen, while we continue with our investigations. Take him away, Crabb, and lock him up in the cells.'

Crabb took a sulking Armitage back to his cell. Frustrated, Ravenscroft stared out of the window. Tired of the warden's theatricalities and his continually changing story, he had encountered one obstacle after another. The truth remained as far away as it had seemed an hour ago.

'That man knows a great deal more than he pretends,' said Ravenscroft, as Crabb returned to the room.

'Neither he nor Troutbridge seem willing to tell us anything. Do you think they committed the murders together?' asked Crabb.

'To tell you the truth, Crabb, I don't honestly know. We seem further away from ever solving these murders. There is one person, however, who could provide us with the answers we require, who could shed a great deal of light on this relationship between Armitage and Troutbridge.'

'And who might that be, sir?'

'A certain young lady in Ledbury; I am convinced that it is she who holds the key to this mystery. It is time I visited Lucy Armitage again.'

CHAPTER EIGHT

Ravenscroft hesitated, looking across at the little black and white cottage in Church Lane, with its neat hanging baskets of early spring flowers. He knew that inside he would in all probability discover the answers to the mystery that bound Armitage and Troutbridge together — and that such knowledge might even lead him to catch the killer of the four men — but he was also aware that such disclosures might cause more pain for its occupier than perhaps he could dare inflict.

Somewhat reluctantly he made his way up the path and rang the doorbell. The maid opened the door to him but before she could speak, Lucy Armitage herself appeared in the hallway. 'Mr Ravenscroft. I hope you have news of my brother. I have been so worried,' she said, anxiously beckoning him inside.

'Your brother is quite safe, Miss Armitage. He is at Malvern Police Station as we speak,' replied Ravenscroft, stepping into the hallway and handing his hat to the maid.

'Oh thank God. I thought that something terrible had happened to him.'

Ravenscroft could see that she had been crying but that her face was now full of relief as she led him into the drawing room.

'Miss Armitage, we discovered your brother hiding at Mr Troutbridge's farm over at Mathon. Do you know why he should have been there?' asked Ravenscroft, sitting beside her on the sofa.

'No. I am not aware of anyone called Troutbridge.' Ravenscroft knew that she was lying, and that he would have to be more forthcoming if he was to obtain the truth.

'Miss Armitage — Lucy — I'm afraid I have to tell you that your brother is in custody on suspicion of murder.'

'Oh no!' she said. 'There must be some mistake. My brother would never hurt anyone. He is a peaceful, considerate man.'

'Your brother tried to escape when we discovered him at Troutbridge's farm. Hardly the behaviour of an innocent man. However, your brother states that he was in Hereford at the time of the second and third murders.'

'Then that must indeed be true,' protested Lucy. 'If my brother maintains he was in Hereford at the time, then why do you not believe him?'

Ravenscroft moved uneasily in his chair, and looked away, knowing that his next remark would cause distress. 'Your brother has told us that he was with a certain lady, a lady with whom he was conducting an affair. The lady in question is apparently married, and your brother is unwilling to disclose her name.'

'No. I do not believe that, Mr Ravenscroft,' replied Lucy becoming upset. 'My brother would never do such a thing!' Ravenscroft noticed that her hands were tightly clutching a handkerchief in her lap and that her eyes were seeking not to be in contact with his own.

'Your brother never spoke of such a lady?'

'No. Never.'

'Do not distress yourself, Lucy,' said Ravenscroft, moving forwards. He reached out and placed a hand upon her clenched wrists. 'If it is any consolation to you, my dear lady, I do not believe that your brother has a mistress in Hereford or that he even went anywhere near the town.'

'But then that would mean—' began Lucy anxiously.

'Yes, it would mean that your brother would not be able to account for his movements at the times of the murders. Did your brother ever talk with you about a railway company that had recently been formed, the Tewkesbury to Leominster Railway Company, to be precise?'

'Yes.'

'Can you remember what he said to you? It may be very important,' said Ravenscroft, removing his hand and resuming a more formal manner.

'James said to me one day that he had learnt that the railway company had been formed, and that the new line would result in the almshouses being demolished. I remember he was very upset about it. The inmates would be evicted from their homes. He said that they would all be put out on the street; they would have no homes. He said that there were people in Malvern who were behind the venture; people who put money and self-interest before philanthropy and consideration. The more he thought about it, the angrier he became. I had never seen him become so angry before.'

'Did your brother ever mention any names of persons, who might be connected to this company?'

'Yes. He mentioned Mr Pitzer, who apparently was also one of the trustees of the almshouses. James could not see how anyone could be both that and yet at the same time a director of the new railway company. He could not understand that. He called it an act of betrayal.'

'Lucy, think carefully before you answer. Did your brother ever issue any threats again Mr Pitzer? Did he ever say, for instance, that he would confront Mr Pitzer or that he would get even with him?'

'No. Never! My brother was angry but he knew there was little he could do. He said the men in Malvern were too powerful; that they all occupied positions of importance and that they could never be touched. He felt powerless against their designs. Oh, Mr Ravenscroft, you cannot believe that

161

my brother is capable of these crimes. Tell me you believe he is innocent?' said Lucy tearfully.

Ravenscroft wanted to reach out to her, to place his hands round her shoulders, to comfort her, to offer her reassurance, to tell her that her brother was innocent, but he knew that he could not, and so remained aloof.

'Lucy, I cannot tell you that, however much I would like to. The fact remains that four men have been murdered in Malvern, and your brother is held on suspicion. He cannot account for his movements. We know that he had found out about the railway company and that he saw the possibility of an end to his work at the almshouses — and he was discovered hiding at Troutbridge's farm,' said Ravenscroft, hating the pain he was causing.

'Then is all lost?' asked Lucy, looking deep into Ravenscroft's eyes.

'My dear Lucy,' he replied, placing his hand on her shoulder. 'I would so like to tell you that your brother is innocent, but I cannot do that until we have caught the murderer. I am sorry.'

'What has my brother said?' asked Lucy, drying her eyes with her handkerchief.

'He adamantly denies that he is responsible for the deaths of the four men, maintaining that he was in Hereford when Sommersby and Gladwyn were both killed. He also declares that he was staying with Troutbridge for one night on his way back from Hereford.'

'And you cannot believe him?' implored Lucy, turning again to face him.

'Lucy, I cannot. I am sure that I saw him at Troutbridge's farm earlier in the week. I believe it was his face I saw at the window, as I drove away.'

'But you cannot be sure it was him?'

'No, I cannot be certain,' replied Ravenscroft. 'Did your brother ever own a walking stick?' he asked, changing the subject abruptly.

'Yes, but why do you ask?' asked Lucy, looking bewildered.

'Did it have a silver engraved handle?'

'No. James would never have been able to afford such things.'

'Do the interlocked initials M.W.B. mean anything to you?'

Lucy thought for a moment, and then said, 'No, they mean nothing to me. What is their significance?'

'At present I do not know. Lucy, your brother is in serious trouble. He is our chief suspect in our murder inquiry and will remain in our cells until either charges are bought against him or if there are future developments in this case that can prove his innocence. At the moment he denies everything. We know that he was involved with Troutbridge but your brother is reluctant to tell us the nature of that involvement. If he refuses to answer our questions truthfully, I cannot do anything for him. Only you can help him,' said Ravenscroft, hoping that his apparent coldness would provoke her into disclosing the truth that he sought.

'How can I help my brother?' asked Lucy.

'By telling me the truth, Lucy,' implored Ravenscroft. 'I think your brother is reluctant to speak out for fear of hurting you. By protecting you, he may end up going to the gallows. I know that you would not want that. I implore you to help save him, my dear lady,' said Ravenscroft.

Lucy Armitage looked at Ravenscroft for a moment, then quickly rising to her feet crossed over to the window. Ravenscroft could see again the tears forming in her eyes as she did so — whatever the secret was that bound Lucy, her brother and Troutbridge together, was not one that could be disclosed easily or without pain.

'Very well, Mr Ravenscroft, I see that I must take you into my confidence, but before I do so, I must swear you to secrecy on this matter. Promise me that?' she asked, looking into his face.

'My dear Lucy, I cannot give you that assurance,' said Ravenscroft rising from his seat and walking over to her. 'What you have to tell me may have some bearing on the murders of three prominent men and one innocent home-less man and as such may have to be made public. However, what you have to say may have little or no relevance to the murders, and if that should prove so, I promise you that I will do everything in my power to guard your secret. I believe that what you have to tell me may help your brother to prove his innocence, and that is why I urge you to this course of action. I think you know that I would never do anything to bring unhappiness to you.'

'Come with me, Mr Ravenscroft,' began Lucy, after a moment's silence.

'I would hope that you would find it possible to call me — Samuel,' interrupted Ravenscroft.

'Mr Ravenscroft — Samuel, I know that I can trust you and that you have the interests of both my brother and I at your heart. After what I have to tell you, however, you may well think differently of me. Come with me, I have some-thing to show you.'

She led the way out of the room and across the hall-way. Ravenscroft followed her up the narrow stairs of the cottage, wondering what was about to be revealed to him, and whether such a disclosure would alter the lives of both he and Lucy.

Lucy paused for a moment on the landing, as if deciding whether she should proceed or yet turn back even at this last minute, but then turning to Ravenscroft, she said in a quiet voice, 'In here. Please do not judge me too harshly.'

She pushed open the door of one of the rooms.

'Thank you, Sally, you can go now,' said Lucy, address-ing her maid. 'Master Richard will be quite alright with us for a while.'

'Very well, ma'am,' replied the maid, leaving the room.

'You see there, Mr Ravenscroft, you have now discov-ered my secret.'

Ravenscroft entered the room. There on the floor was a small child, who was busily engaged in playing with a collection of wooden toys. Lucy walked over to the boy and lifted him up in her arms. Ravenscroft estimated that the boy was probably around three or four years of age.

'And how is my little angel this morning?' asked Lucy, kissing the child on his cheek. 'Have you and Sally been playing with your train?'

The child nodded and smiled — the same smile that Ravenscroft had caught briefly on his hostess's face on his first visit to the house.

'I have bought someone to see you. This is Mr — er — Samuel.'

Unsure of his own reaction, Ravenscroft crossed over to the child and taking one of his small hands said, 'Hallo, Richard, I'm pleased to meet you.'

The boy smiled again. His mother kissed him once more before returning him to his playthings on the floor.

'So you see, Mr Ravenscroft — Richard is my son.'

Ravenscroft said nothing, uncertain of what he should say next. Lucy turned to her boy. 'Mummy and Samuel have a few things to say together. We will leave you with your toys. Will you be a good boy for mamma?'

The child nodded and soon became engrossed once more in his game.

'We will go downstairs, Mr Ravenscroft.'

Ravenscroft followed her down the steps and into the drawing room. Lucy gave instructions for the maid to return upstairs. The two of them sat silently on the sofa.

He felt uneasy, not knowing what to say. He had feared, with mounting anxiety, that the revealing of the secret would not be easy for both of them, but the knowledge that he had now gained was the last thing he had expected. He looked out of the window, at the world outside the small cottage, and wondered whether he should now leave before he caused any further pain.

'I warned you that you would think harshly of me,' she said, after what had seemed like an eternity to him.

'Lucy, I could never sit in judgement upon you,' was all he could say, but he knew the words would sound empty and meaningless.

'That is easy enough to say. Let me tell you my story first, then you will see how foolish I have been and why my brother attempts to protect me. Then you will be in a better position to condemn my stupidity,' began Lucy turning towards him. 'Five years ago, I met and fell in love with a young man, whose name need not concern you. I was just eighteen years old at the time, young, headstrong, and yes, impetuous. The young man promised that he would marry me, and I was foolishly deceived into believing that he meant what he said. We were in love, or so I thought. Then I found myself with child. I knew that the knowledge of this folly would lead to the disgrace of our family, and so it proved. My father had been unwell for some years and once he learned of my plight his illness became more marked and he quickly sank into a decline from which he never recovered.'

She paused for a moment, the tears beginning to form once more in her eyes. Ravenscroft placed his hand on hers, but she quickly drew back and continued with her story.

'I only thank God that my mother had died some years previous. At least she had not been a witness to my disgrace. Worse was to come, however. Once the young man knew of my plight, he had no further need of me. He was more than content to discard me, claiming that the child was not his and that I had slept with another, but I can assure you, Mr Ravenscroft, that I had been entirely faithful to him alone. He left shortly afterwards and went with his regiment to India. Last year I read that he had returned and had married well into London society. I bear him no grudges; the fault had been entirely mine. After my father's death, my brother and I had little to live upon, once my father's debts on the estate had been settled. We were forced to sell our family home, and came here to Ledbury, where James was fortunate enough to find employment as warden of the almshouses in Colwall. I had a little money saved, which enabled me to rent this property and engage a maid. Shortly before we arrived in the area, my darling Richard was born. At first, I'm afraid I was a very bad mother and wanted little to do with the child of my sin, but after a few weeks I found the love between us growing and I realised that my son would be my salvation. I would devote my life to him, see that no harm would ever befall him — and above all else, see that he would never be tainted by the foolish, wanton behaviour of his mother.'

She paused again to wipe the tears from her eyes.

'Lucy, you do not have to continue—' began Ravenscroft.

'Oh, Mr Ravenscroft — Samuel, but I do. When we arrived here, people began to feel sorry for me. I put it about that I was a young widow. My husband had been killed fighting in Africa. Everyone felt sympathy for me, and I was quickly accepted into local society. I did not like lying but I had my son to protect. If my true station should ever have come to light, we would be driven out, my brother would lose his position and my son would grow up cursing the mother who had caused his ruin. You must understand, Samuel — that is why I lied.'

'Of course, Lucy, no other mother could have done more,' said Ravenscroft sympathetically.

'All might then have been well, but for Troutbridge. Troutbridge's brother owned the farm next to our property in Devon. He must have visited his brother and learned of my disgrace. Everyone in the village had known of my folly and both my brother and I had been roundly condemned by local society before we left. One day, shortly after our arrival here, my brother and I were out walking in Ledbury. I remember it was market day, and the local farmers had come to town to buy and sell their animals and produce. One of them was Troutbridge and he recognised both of us. Shortly afterwards he approached my brother and said that unless James paid him a sum of money each month, he would inform everyone as to the true nature of my position. James was forced into taking money from the accounts of the almshouses to pay for Troutbridge's silence. He hated doing it, and I begged him not to do so, but he said that if he did not do it, we would all be ruined. James said it would only be for a while and that one day he would repay all the money to the trustees. Troutbridge was sick and might soon die, or we would eventually go somewhere else, where we were not known, once James had secured a better situation. So now you see it all Mr Ravenscroft — the reasons for James's silence, why he would not tell you of his true relationship to Mr Troutbridge. He was doing it all to protect me, and little Richard, my darling son. Now I am the cause of my brother's downfall. My stupidity and callousness has ruined us all!'

Lucy burst into a new flood of tears. Ravenscroft moved closer and placed an arm round her shoulders. 'Come now, Lucy, all may yet be well.'

'But how can it?' she said, pulling herself away from him. 'You will condemn me as others have done, and as others will do, once they have learnt the details of my sorry foolish story.'

'Lucy, there is no need for anyone to know of your circumstances. I am only thankful that you have sought to confide in me. I will never hurt you. It is not my business to condemn something which happened some years ago, when clearly you were the innocent party, and taken advantage off by another who should have known better.'

'You are very kind, but others will not see it that way,' she protested.

'There is no reason why anyone else should ever know. You can leave Troutbridge to me. I will have words with him, and make sure that the blackmailing stops and that he remains silent. You need have no fears on that score,' said Ravenscroft trying to reassure her. 'Now dry your eyes. Your son will be distressed to see you so upset.'

'You are a good man, Samuel Ravenscroft,' said Lucy drying her eyes, 'and a good honest friend.'

'Perhaps one day you may allow me to be more than that.'

Lucy continued to wipe her eyes on her handkerchief. 'Mr Ravenscroft — Samuel, I must see my brother and explain to him that I have told you everything. He is innocent. I must help him. Can you please take me to Malvern with you now? I must see him,' she said, quickly rising to her feet, a new urgency in her voice.

'Of course,' he replied.

'I will fetch my coat and explain to my maid that we will be away for a while. She is used to attending to my son's needs.'

* * *

Within a few minutes, Ravenscroft had secured a cab for them both and they found themselves on the way to Malvern. The two of them sat in silence as they began the ascent up towards the hills; Ravenscroft running over the morning's events in his mind, attempting to reconcile Lucy's disclosures with the murders he was investigating, his companion anxiously looking at the road, and wishing that they would soon reach their destination. After the events and revelations that had taken place inside the small cottage, Ravenscroft found the bracing air and passing scenery a welcoming relief, affording him a breathing space before the events that would shortly unfold.

'I think you may find your brother somewhat changed,' he began, as they travelled through the Wells. 'When we apprehended him, he was still wearing the same clothes he had taken with him from the almshouses. His appearance is a little dishevelled, to say the least.'

'James was never the tidiest of men,' she replied.

'You must realise, Lucy, that I will have to confront your brother with what you have told me and that I will need to question him further.'

'Can you go any faster?' asked Lucy, passing over Ravenscroft's last remark.

'Old Patch is doing the best he can,' grumbled the cabman.

Arriving at the station, Ravenscroft showed Lucy into one of the small rooms and instructed Crabb to fetch Armitage from his cell. Lucy paced up and down the room, looking down first at the floor, then at the ceiling, and finally at Ravenscroft.

'All will be well; trust me,' he assured her, wanting to place a protective arm around her but realising that the next few minutes would be difficult.

The door opened and Armitage entered, followed by Crabb.

'James!' exclaimed Lucy running towards her brother and drawing him close to her. 'Let me see how you are.'

'Oh, Lucy, but why have they bought you here? You should not have come,' said Armitage, embracing his sister. Ravenscroft and Crabb looked away.

'I have told Inspector Ravenscroft everything, James. Yes, everything. He knows about our situation, about Richard, and why you were paying Troutbridge. There is no need for you to protect me anymore.'

'Lucy, Lucy, why have you been so foolish? There was no need,' he protested.

'There was every need. You could have gone to the gallows. I had no choice. I had to tell him everything. The inspector is a good man, he can help us now.'

Ravenscroft coughed, 'Miss Armitage, I wonder if you would be kind enough to leave the room for a few minutes while I have a few words with your brother. I can assure you that you will be reunited presently.'

Lucy taken aback by the strange formal tone in Ravenscroft's voice, said merely, 'Yes, of course, I understand.'

'Crabb, show Miss Armitage into the other room if you please,' said Ravenscroft. Lucy kissed her brother and after hugging him close and casting an imploring glance at Ravenscroft, left the room with Crabb.

Ravenscroft indicated that Armitage should sit. Now that the truth had been disclosed, he hoped that the warden might be more forthcoming than at his previous interview.

'You should not have involved my sister,' said Armitage declining the seat.

'Sit down, be quiet, and listen to what I have to say, Mr Armitage. If you had told me all about this business with Troutbridge earlier there would have been no reason for me to have visited your sister. You are a foolish man, but you are loyal to your sister and I admire that. I know that you were seeking only to protect her. Now tell me, why did you go to Troutbridge's when we left the almshouses?'

Armitage seated himself on the chair. 'I had nowhere else to go. I knew that it would only be a matter of time before you discovered the discrepancies in the accounts and would seek to arrest me. I panicked. I thought if I saw Troutbridge I could persuade him to let me have the money back and I could replace it in the almshouses accounts, but I realise now that I should have known better. The man was not to be persuaded, of course. I did not know what to do. He seemed content to let me remain there in hiding. I think he gained a great deal of satisfaction from witnessing my plight. One evening I even thought of killing him; that would have put an end to all our misery, but I could not bring myself to do so,' said Armitage running his hands through his hair.

'It is as well that you did not. We already have four murders on our hands.'

'I know I have been incredibly foolish in taking the money, but that is all I have done, Mr Ravenscroft, I swear to you. I did not kill a single one of those four men,' implored the warden.

'What about the newspaper containing the railway article, Mr Armitage?'

'Yes. Of course I read the item, and I did indeed mark it in the paper. I did have words with Pitzer about his being both a trustee and a director of the railway company, but he just assured me that the inmates would be taken care of.'

'Did you believe his assurances? Your sister says you became very angry.'

'No, I just thought that all he was interested in was making money. Money, Mr Ravenscroft, is what makes Malvern run. All that those there are interested in is making money, and whether it is taken from the water-cure patients or made from the building of new houses or railways, it makes no difference. Yes, I became bitter; bitter because a lot of good people were going to be made homeless in this obsession with money.'

Ravenscroft thought hard for a moment or two. Armitage had finally admitted his opposition towards the new railway company in general, and towards Pitzer in particular, but he now began to wonder whether such dislike could have led the warden to have committed the murders he was investigating. Perhaps his own desire to protect Lucy was arguing against such a possibility? But then if Armitage had not murdered Pitzer and his colleagues, then who had? Finally he turned to Armitage and addressed him. 'Mr Armitage, your sister is in great need of you. She has been through a great deal. It was not easy for her to tell me of her situation. You are very close — and it is because of that I have decided to release you, for the present. However I must emphasise that you remain under grave suspicion of the murders of Pitzer, Sommersby, Gladwyn and Old Penny. When new evidence comes to light it may exonerate you from all implication and blame. I will only release you however, if you give me your solemn promise that you will not try to leave the area. You are to remain at either your sister's or at the almshouses. Do I make myself clear?'

'Yes. I thank you — and yes, you have my word, I will not leave the area,' said Armitage, looking directly at Ravenscroft.

'Good — and you and your sister need not concern yourselves anymore with Mr Troutbridge. I will make sure he will be of no further trouble to you. You are not, on any account, to go anywhere near him,' said Ravenscroft standing up.

'You will have my word, Inspector.'

The two men shook hands.

Ravenscroft led Armitage from the room and reunited him with his sister. 'Miss Armitage, I am releasing your brother for the present, on condition that he resides either with you or at the almshouses,' said Ravenscroft.

Lucy embraced her brother.

A few minutes later, Ravenscroft and Crabb escorted the brother and sister outside to the waiting cab.

'Mr Ravenscroft — Samuel — I cannot thank you enough,' said Lucy suddenly embracing Ravenscroft. 'Oh, I am so sorry, I am embarrassing you,' she said conscious that Crabb and her brother were watching, and quickly recovering her composure.

'Take care of your sister, Mr Armitage,' said Ravenscroft, helping Lucy to mount the cab.

'You can be well assured on that point, Inspector,' replied the warden.

As the cab turned onto the roadway, a perplexed Ravenscroft was left wondering if he had done the right thing in releasing Armitage — and whether he would ever see Lucy Armitage again.

CHAPTER NINE

Ravenscroft faced Troutbridge across the table, and the two men looked at one another in silence for some moments.

'Now then, Troutbridge, you are in very serious trouble. We now know that you have been blackmailing Mr Armitage and his sister, and have been receiving regular payments for your silence. A totally reprehensible act, which is only befitting of the lowest dregs of our society,' said Ravenscroft opening a folder of papers before him. 'It is no good denying this — we know everything. Blackmail is a serious offence. The last person I put away for a crime similar to yours was given seven years hard labour. Add on the sentences for keeping a ferocious animal and letting that animal attack a police officer, and we are looking at a minimum sentence of fifteen years penal servitude. Do you know what that means, Troutbridge? Well, I will tell you. You will be on the treadmill for twelve hours a day, or breaking up stones out on the wilds of Dartmoor, or if you are fortunate enough, you may be unpicking hemp for up to fifteen hours a day until your hands are little more than bloody stumps. I have known fit grown men, physically stronger than you, who have been broken within three years; many of them did not survive and died in prison.'

He could see the look of fear spreading across Troutbridge's face. He told himself that it would not be long before he had the farmer where he wanted him. 'I don't think you will ever come out of prison. Your farm will be seized and sold up, your animals slaughtered. Is this what you want?'

'What do you think,' answered the other, still with a note of defiance in his voice. 'If you knows everything, what else do you want?'

'What I am going to do is to offer you a way out from this terrible mess you have got yourself into.'

Ravenscroft could see the look of puzzlement working its way across Troutbridge's face. He looked down at his papers, letting his prisoner sweat for some moments before he continued. 'There is one way in which you can help yourself, and one way only.'

'What? I'll do anything,' replied Troutbridge eagerly. Ravenscroft knew that he had netted his quarry.

'First — you will repay all the money you have taken from Armitage.'

'I don't have it.'

'Then you must find it. You have one week from today to deposit the full sum with my constable at this police station. If the money is not forthcoming, your file will be reopened and you will face trial on the three counts I listed a few moments ago. Secondly, you will swear never to approach either Mr Armitage or his sister ever again, and that you will never utter a word of what you know surrounding the birth of Miss Armitage's son. Again, your file will be kept here, so that if there is any breach in this matter you will find yourself being rearrested and put on trial. Third, you have six months in which to sell your farm and leave the county. You must move at least one hundred miles away from Malvern. After six months I will inform my colleagues in the three counties that if they catch sight of you, you will be apprehended and sent to prison, straight away. These are my conditions. There will be no debate or questions asked. You either accept them now, or you will appear before the magistrates tomorrow morning.'

Ravenscroft closed his file and looked Troutbridge straight in the eye.

'I suppose I don't have a choice,' muttered Troutbridge, turning away, anger still in his eyes.

'That is where you are wrong. There is always a choice. It is up to us individually to see that we make the correct decisions. You have been offered a last chance to start anew, somewhere far away from here. You are a fortunate man. Tell me your answer now, or the offer will be withdrawn. I am a busy man,' said Ravenscroft standing up suddenly, and indicating that the interview was at an end.

'Damn you, Ravenscroft!'

'And we will have less of that as well. So, Troutbridge, which is to be?'

'I will accept your conditions,' muttered a crestfallen Troutbridge.

'Good. I will have Constable Crabb draw up your release papers.'

A few minutes later Ravenscroft and Crabb watched Troutbridge walk away from the station.

'A blacker ruffian never lived on this earth,' muttered Crabb.

Ravenscroft smiled. 'I just took advantage of a situation that arose, and could not resist the temptation to make a great deal of money. Now you have the file under lock and key. In one week Troutbridge should reappear with the money he took from Armitage. That money is to be given back to Armitage, and you must see that it is returned into the account of the trustees of the almshouses.'

'It will be done, sir.'

'And you are also aware of the other conditions?'

'Yes, sir.'

'Good. Then if they are broken, you know what to do with the file. Everything is written down there. At all costs, a lady's honour must be protected in this affair.'

'By a lady, you mean Miss Lucy Armitage?'

'I do. How is that hand of yours now, Crabb?'

'Fine, sir, Jennie put some herbal liniment on it. It should be healed in a day or so.'

'Good.'

'Thank God you shot the animal in time, sir, I reckon he was just about to work his way up to my neck.'

'I'm only sorry I was not quicker in despatching the creature. Now, Crabb, we have both had a long day, and you, in particular, have had an unpleasant experience. Tomorrow we must continue with our investigation. We may have arrived at the truth concerning Armitage and Troutbridge, but our killer is still out there, and we must redouble our efforts to bring him to book. As you live in the Wells, will you go back to Pitzer's house first thing in the morning?'

'Yes, sir. For what purpose?'

'I want you to see if you can find Pitzer's walking stick, and when you have found it, see if it matches the ones belonging to Sommersby and Gladwyn. If it does, ask Mrs Pitzer if she knows anything about the initials on the silver handle. Also bring the stick back with you. Then meet me in the churchyard at Great Malvern at ten o'clock.'

'You still think that the walking sticks and their initials are of some importance?' asked Crabb.

'All through this case, we have been missing something. I am convinced that there are more secrets to be unearthed, and that the key to this mystery lies in the origin of those walking sticks.'

'And if I don't find such a stick, sir?'

'Let us trust that you will — otherwise our investigations may be at an end.'

* * *

After eating a particularly unappetising meal at the Tudor, Ravenscroft was pleased to regain the sanctuary of his room. Lying on his bed, he became aware of how tired he had suddenly become. The events of the day began to run through his mind — the discovery of the walking stick at Gladwyn's, the shooting of the dog at Troutbridge's farm, the long questioning of Troutbridge and Armitage, the visit to Lucy Armitage in Ledbury and the disclosure of her secret. All this activity — and yet he had not yet made an arrest. The last thing he remembered before he fell asleep was the image of Lucy Armitage holding her child, and the face of her son smiling across at him.

'Good morning, sir. It's a beautiful day.'

Ravenscroft woke with a start. Then the awful realisation that he was still at the Tudor swept over him. 'What time is it, Stebbins?' he asked.

'Seven o'clock, sir. It's time for yer bath.'

'No, Stebbins, not that again,' replied Ravenscroft, turning over on his side.

'Cheer up, sir. Look on the bright side.'

'I cannot see one at present, Stebbins.'

'Come now, sir, you will be all the better for it.'

'That I doubt very much.'

Ravenscroft made his way towards the Bath House. He still felt tired, and he had to rub his eyes several times to clear the sleep from them. He could not believe that he was still at the Tudor, and worse still that he was stumbling half blind towards another infernal treatment, which he had little inclination to take. Would that he could solve the case, and so be free to leave the Tudor.

'Good morning, sir. Glad to see you are fully recovered. We have missed you the last few days. Shall we continue, sir?' said the bath attendant in his usual brisk manner.

Not caring anymore, Ravenscroft stepped into the bath and felt the heat burning into his bones. He lay back in the waters and closed his eyes, seeking to extinguish the present world from his thoughts. Just who had murdered Pitzer, Sommersby, Gladwyn and Old Penny — Armitage, Troutbridge, Touchmore, or some other person who at present was unknown to him? Armitage had said that money ruled the town. Was that what the murders had all been about? Money? Then there was the woman in black — *I will know where to find you*, she had said. What part did she play in all this? Were the murders somehow linked to the deaths of her husband and child? Then there were the walking sticks — and the initials M.W.B. What did they mean?

'That will be all now, sir. You can return to your room, sir,' echoed the voice of the attendant breaking into his thoughts.

'No bandages today?' he enquired, hope in his voice.

'We'll start again slowly tomorrow, sir.'

Thank God for that, thought Ravenscroft.

After dressing he decided to make his way up the winding path towards the well house, hoping that he might again see his lady of the black veil, but in that he was disappointed. As he drank the icy spring water, he looked out over the town and realised that this morning he had climbed all the way up to the well without either pausing or coughing. Perhaps the waters were beginning to make their contribution to the betterment of his physical condition, but there again, familiarity with his surroundings may have accounted for his improvement. His fresh vigour was matched by a strange feeling of optimism, which he found difficult to comprehend. Only a few minutes before, as he had lain in the steaming waters of the bath house, he had been plagued by thoughts of his own inadequacy, but now a new, unknown confidence was beginning to take root in his mind. He knew now that he and Crabb would shortly be unravelling the events of the past few days — and that the case would be drawing to its conclusion.

He thanked the attendant and after giving her a coin, made his way back down to the Tudor.

After breakfast, he rested for a while before making his way down to the churchyard. Had he half expected to find the veiled lady there? But she had said she would find him. Here he stood looking down at the grave, with its fresh flowers placed before the headstone.

Sacred to the memory of
Anthony Steward Kelly (1840–1886)
and
Mark Richard Kelly (1885–1887)
Always Remembered.

'Good morning to you, sir.'

He turned to face Crabb.

'Good morning, Crabb. Did you go to Pitzer's?'

'Yes, sir — and I have his stick.'

Ravenscroft took it in his hands and examined the handle. 'Well done, Crabb — and look, the same initials arranged in the same way. Did you ask Mrs Pitzer if she knew anything about them?'

'I did, sir, and like Mrs Gladwyn, she cannot remember when her husband first had the stick, or what the letters stand for. She did say though that she thought her husband had first had the stick a great number of years ago, possibly just after they arrived in the town.'

'That is interesting. If only we knew what these initials stood for — M.W.B. — is it someone's name, or the name of some body, club or society, to which the three men belonged? If only we could find that, we might have our murderer. There is something else that strikes me as being unusual about this case, Crabb. Do you realise that not one of our victims had any children to succeed them? Pitzer and his wife never had any children, Sommersby was unmarried and had no children, as far as we know, and Gladwyn mentions no children in his will. That is something else three of our victims had in common; Old Penny was just, I suspect, in the wrong place at the wrong time. It was almost as though Pitzer, Sommersby and Gladwyn had been killed because they had no one to succeed them, no one to come after them. Don't you find that strange, Crabb?'

'Yes, sir. It is usually the other way round. People sometimes are killed by their relatives so that they can inherit their money.'

'Exactly! I'm sure though there is money behind this. The three men cannot have been killed out of some revenge motive. They seem to have led blameless lives. No, it has to be money. We have just got to find out what these initials stand for.'

'Well, none of them had the initials M., W. or B. for their names, so it can't be anything to do with their families.'

'I think you are correct. M.W.B. What the devil do they stand for? You would think in a town like Malvern . . .' said Ravenscroft, before stopping suddenly. Then: 'Of course! The M. stands for Malvern!'

'Could be, sir? After all, they all lived here for nearly thirty years or more.'

'Good God, Crabb. How could we have been so blind! The answer is literally staring us in the face! It has been here under our noses all this time!'

'I'm sorry, sir. I don't understand you,' said a puzzled Crabb.

'Look along the terrace, up there, at the top of the town. Tell me what you see. The buildings, what can you see, from the left?' said an excited Ravenscroft.

'Well, sir. First there is the boarding establishment, then the wine cellars, the bank, the Oddfellows Hall, the dress shop, the—' recited Crabb.

'Yes. Go back to the bank. What does it say above the bank?'

'The Malvern and Worcestershire Bank.'

'Precisely, the Malvern and Worcestershire Bank — that's what the letters M.W.B. stand for! The B in the centre of the inscription on the stick stands for Bank and the intertwined M and W stand for Malvern and Worcestershire respectively. I remember now on my first morning here, I saw Pitzer going into the bank. It all makes sense. Each of our three victims was associated with the bank in some way.'

'My word, sir, I think you're right. And to think we passed it by every day and not realised,' said Crabb.

'Let us pay a visit to the bank and see what we can dis-cover,' said Ravenscroft, eagerly leading the way out of the churchyard.

The two men walked up the steps and crossed over the road to the bank. Crabb pushed open the heavy doors and the two men entered the building.

'Can I help you, gentlemen?' said a clerk from the other side of the counter.

'We would like to speak with the manager, if you please,' said Crabb.

'Do you have an appointment, sir? Mr Chase is a busy man,' replied the clerk, peering over his spectacles at the constable.

'Would you tell Mr Chase that we are here on police business, and that we must speak with him urgently,' said Ravenscroft.

'Of course, sir, if you will just wait a moment.'

The clerk vacated his position and entered one of the inner rooms.

'Don't like banks, sir,' muttered Crabb.

'Why ever not?' asked Ravenscroft.

'Don't know, sir. It must be the thought of all that money. It makes me feel uneasy.'

Ravenscroft smiled, as the clerk returned.

'Mr Chase will see you now. If you would care to follow me, gentlemen.'

They followed the clerk across the foyer, and along a corridor, until they reached an open door.

'Do come in, gentlemen,' said a voice from inside.

Crabb and Ravenscroft entered the room. They were met by a grey-haired man, of rotund appearance.

'Do please be seated, gentlemen. How may I be of assis-tance to you?'

'I am Inspector Ravenscroft and this is my colleague Constable Crabb. We are investigating the deaths of several prominent citizens of Malvern, and believe you may be able to assist us in our enquiries.'

'Yes, a terrible business, I was at the inquest the other day, but I was under the impression that you had apprehended the murderer, a blind beggar was it not?' replied the manager shaking his head and adopting a mournful disposition.

'We have since then eliminated the beggar from our list of suspects.'

'I see.'

'Mr Chase, we believe that three of our victims were associated with the bank in some way,' said Ravenscroft. 'Each of them possessed one of these walking sticks with the initials M.W.B. on them,' he said, passing over the stick to Chase to inspect.

'I have seen this kind of walking stick before, although I cannot remember the circumstances. Perhaps one of the gentlemen may have shown it to me upon one occasion, but certainly I cannot recall that they did so.'

'Can you tell me whether any, or indeed all, of the deceased men were members of the bank?' asked Ravenscroft.

Chase thought hard for a while.

'Mr Chase, this is a murder inquiry. Anything you tell us concerning the bank and its customers, will I assure you, be treated with the utmost confidence.'

'I believe that both Mr Sommersby and Mr Pitzer were customers of the bank, but I do not recall Doctor Gladwyn being one. Certainly Mr Pitzer conducted a lot of his personal and business interests through the bank,' said Chase, handing the stick back to Ravenscroft.

'You say they were just customers of the bank? So not one of the three gentlemen played any prominent role in the life of the bank?' asked Ravenscroft, feeling somewhat frustrated that his new line of enquiry appeared to be going nowhere.

'No. I'm sorry I cannot help you further.'

Ravenscroft rose from his chair. 'Thank you, Mr Chase. May I ask how long you have been manager of the bank?'

'About twenty years.'

'And when was the bank founded?'

'1857 — thirty years ago. We always remember that because the date is engraved above the front door. You may have noticed it when you entered the building,' replied Chase.

'Do you know who owns the bank — or who the original founders were?'

'That I do not know. All I am aware of is that we have no shareholders, and so no dividends are paid out each year. The money is simply re-invested in the finances of the bank.'

'Does that not strike you as odd, Mr Chase?' asked Ravenscroft.

'It is a little unusual I must admit, but not entirely without precedent. I have known several companies and financial institutions that have what is known as "sleeping partners" on their boards.'

'But surely these so-called "sleeping partners" are used to drawing a dividend? What is unusual in your situation, it seems to me, is that no one claims their dividends. The bank must be in a strong financial position by now, as a consequence, of all this reinvestment?' asked Ravenscroft, warming to his subject.

'You are correct in that assumption, although of course I cannot disclose any figures.'

'Do you have any documents relating to the foundation?' asked Ravenscroft.

'No. I'm afraid not. I do remember, however, someone saying, shortly after my arrival here, that all the material relating to the early days of the bank had recently been removed.'

'Removed? Where to, Mr Chase?'

'I believe they were taken to the Malvern Library and Reading Rooms for safe storage'

'Did that strike you as being somewhat odd, sir?' asked Crabb, writing in his pocket book.

'No, not really. I understand that many of the archives relating to various concerns in the town have been lodged with Mr Clifford for safe custody, should they need to be consulted at any time in the future.'

'Thank you again, Mr Chase, you have been most informative,' said Ravenscroft, shaking the manager's hand.

'I wish you well with your investigations, Inspector. The sooner this man is caught, the better it will be for all of us.'

'Indeed so, Mr Chase.'

The two police officers left the bank and made their way along the Terrace.

'That was most interesting, Crabb,' said Ravenscroft. 'Let us go and see if our Mr Clifford can unearth these papers for us. It will be most interesting to see if we can learn who the founders of the bank were. I feel we may be making progress.'

As they entered the Malvern Library and Reading Rooms, they were greeted by Clifford the librarian in his usual polite, urbane manner. 'Good morning to you, gentlemen. How can I help you today? Perhaps you require more information regarding the railway company?'

'No, thank you, Mr Clifford. It is information about the Malvern and Worcestershire Bank that we require. We understand that some of the papers concerning the bank's foundation were lodged with you about twenty years ago?' asked Ravenscroft.

'Not with me. I only moved to the town about five years ago. The papers may have been lodged with my predecessor, Mr Lamb. I can check should you so wish?'

'If you would be so kind, I would be obliged.'

'I will consult my card index. Just a moment, gentlemen,' said Clifford moving over to a large cabinet at the side of the room, and thumbing through its contents. 'Ah, here we are,' he said. 'Papers relating to the Malvern and Worcestershire Bank, deposited in 1864. I'll just make a note of the reference number.'

'You seem very well organised here, Mr Clifford,' said Ravenscroft.

'We try to be. I say "we" as the system was instigated by my predecessor. I have merely continued his good work, with a few modifications of my own. I'll just go to the storage room, down below, and retrieve the papers you require. I won't keep you too long, gentlemen.'

Clifford disappeared down a staircase, leaving Ravenscroft and Crabb to look round the shelves of the room.

'Let us hope he can retrieve the papers. It would be interesting to see what they can tell us. I feel we are not far away from uncovering our mystery,' said Ravenscroft.

The librarian returned presently, clutching a file in his hands, a worried expression on his face. 'Gentlemen, I'm afraid there is a problem. You will see here, on the outside of the folder it itemises a list of contents. The first item is a document stating the terms of the foundation of the bank. Unfortunately it seems to be missing. The other papers appear to be relating to the annual accounts in the early years of the bank. They all seem to be present.'

Ravenscroft searched through the remaining papers. 'You are correct, Mr Clifford. The paper is indeed missing. Someone has clearly removed it.'

'Dear me! This is most irregular. I can only apologise, gentlemen,' said Clifford, looking downcast.

'Mr Clifford. How easy would it have been for someone to have removed this item without your knowledge?' asked Ravenscroft, closing the file.

'We have people in here all the time, asking to look at the documents. I do not usually stand over them while they are engaged in their research.'

'So it would have been comparatively easy for someone to have removed this document, without your knowledge?' said Ravenscroft, annoyed that they had come so far, only to be denied access to the one paper they required.

'Yes. I suppose so. Dear me, this has not happened before,' said an apologetic Clifford.

'As far as you know,' smiled Ravenscroft grimly. 'Do you recall anyone recently asking to see these papers?'

'No, not that I recall.'

'You don't keep a record of who asks to see certain papers?'

'I'm afraid not. It is impossible to record all details like that.'

'Thank you, Mr Clifford. Would you please inform us straight away should such a paper come to light?' asked Ravenscroft.

'Certainly, I will make a further search in the storage room. There is always the possibility that the item may have been filed in another place.'

Ravenscroft shook hands with Clifford and the two men left the Reading Rooms.

'This is most frustrating, Crabb. We were so close to discovering the truth. Quite clearly someone has removed the document relating to the foundation of the bank, so that the information could not be made available to people such as ourselves. I have a deep suspicion that all our three targeted victims were founders of the bank — hence the reason for the walking sticks — and that there must therefore be others whose names would have been on the foundation document.'

'Now we will never know who they were, sir,' said Crabb, dejected.

'Would you not say that our Mr Clifford is usually a most methodical, careful man?' asked Ravenscroft suddenly stopping.

'Yes, sir. He seems to know what is going on in the town,' answered Crabb.

'Precisely, and yet he keeps no records of those who view his documents, and appears not to check for any missing papers once they have been viewed. That would seem to be behaviour which is completely contrary to his normal approach to things.'

'You don't think that it was Clifford himself who removed the document?' asked Crabb.

'There is that possibility. We have no way of telling when the document was taken. It was clearly deposited with the library in 1864. Clifford arrived five years ago. It could have been taken years ago before his arrival, hence the discovery of its loss not being evident until today. On the other hand, as our murders have all taken place recently, one would suppose that the document was also removed sometime in the last few weeks. But had that been the case, Mr Clifford would surely have remembered someone viewing the papers. Unfortunately we have no way of telling which is the case,' said Ravenscroft deep in thought.

'Our Mr Clifford does not look like a murderer. He may appear to be rather too smart for his own suit, but he don't look the killing type,' suggested Crabb.

'In my experience, Crabb, crimes are committed by two types of people. The first are perpetrated by hot-blooded, emotional people who often kill on the spur of the moment or out of desperation of some kind. The second group are those quiet, unassuming people who calculate precisely what they are going to do and when they are going to do it, and who then fully justify their actions to themselves. I would say that our murderer here would be of the second kind, and in that case Mr Clifford could fit into that group. However, we have no evidence to link him to the crimes at present; we cannot condemn a man by his looks and manner alone, or because of his apparent negligence. We must always keep an open mind.'

'You think our murderer also took the papers, sir?'

'In all probability, but we still don't know who that person was.'

'So what do we do now, sir? What else can we do?' asked Crabb, looking to guidance from his superior officer.

'Very little it would seem, until we have established the names of the other founders of the bank,' replied Ravenscroft.

'The only thing we could do, sir, is examine everyone's walking stick,' suggested Crabb half-heartedly.

'Of course, Crabb!' exclaimed Ravenscroft looking across the churchyard of the Priory Church. 'That's what we must do. There are others, with similar sticks, who must have some connection with the foundation of the bank. I remember now. On the day we visited Touchmore in his office over there, he removed a pile of papers from a chair so that I could sit down. He asked me to hand him his cane, which was also on the chair, saying he had been looking for it all morning. I'm sure the cane had a silver handle,' said Ravenscroft excitedly.

'Then you think our Reverend is another of the founders of the bank?'

'There is only one way to find out. Let's go and see if the Reverend Touchmore is still in residence.'

The two officers walked along the path across the churchyard until they reached the old buildings that housed the church offices. Opening the door, they made their way up the stairs. Touchmore's door was open, and the cleric himself was sitting at his desk busily writing with one hand, while using the other to mop his brow with a large handkerchief. 'Ah, gentlemen, do please come in,' he said without looking up. 'I won't keep you a moment. I have to complete these returns for the bishop. Should have been sent to the deanery yesterday, but one has been so busy. There never seems enough hours in the day, never enough hours.'

'Indeed, Reverend,' sympathised Ravenscroft.

'Do please take a seat. Just throw those papers in the corner, will you.'

Crabb picked up the papers and added them to one of the piles.

'Mr Touchmore. We are still making enquiries into the deaths of Mr Pitzer, Mr Sommersby and Doctor Gladwyn, and think you may be able to assist us,' said Ravenscroft sitting down on the dusty chair.

'I was under the impression, Inspector, that you had solved the case. I believe some old half-blind beggar had committed the atrocities, before falling to his death on the hills,' said Touchmore, laying down his pen and replacing his handkerchief in his coat pocket.

'We don't think the beggar committed the crimes, so our enquiries are continuing.'

'Dear me, what a terrible business all this has been. I have lost three of my dearest friends, all gone in such a short time. We offer up prayers for their souls of course, but that will not bring them back. That which is lost, can never be regained.'

'Can I ask whether you own a walking stick similar to this one?' asked Ravenscroft showing Touchmore the stick. 'I would be obliged if you would pay particular attention to the silver handle, sir.'

'I do indeed, but where did you get—?'

'It belongs to Mr Pitzer. Both Doctor Sommersby and Doctor Gladwyn had similar sticks. I believe the initials M., B. and W. stand for the Malvern and Worcestershire Bank if I am not mistaken?'

'That is correct, Inspector.'

'I believe that these sticks were made for the founders of the bank, Reverend.'

'You are correct again, Mr Ravenscroft. When we founded the bank in 1857, we each decided to commemorate the event by having a walking stick made for each of the six founders, so that we would each have a reminder of our commitment.'

'You say there were six founders?' asked Ravenscroft leaning forwards eagerly in his chair. 'Who were they?'

'There were six of us, as I said. Pitzer, Sommersby, Gladwyn, myself — and the other two were Gastrux and Lambert, I believe.' replied Touchmore, deep in thought.

'You say, you believe. That would seem to suggest that you have not seen the other two members for a while?'

'Why, yes, I suppose so. Poor Gastrux — he was of French origin I believe — was killed shortly after the foundation. He died in a hunting accident, while out riding with the Ledbury Hunt. I remember it was a terrible business; broke his neck in the fall, there was nothing anyone could do for the poor man,' replied the cleric, shaking his head.

'And Lambert, what happened to him, sir?' asked Crabb, impatiently breaking into the clergyman's flow of words.

'Lambert? Let me see. What did happen to him? He was a doctor, I believe. Ah yes, he left a year or so after the foundation. I think he went to take on a practice somewhere up north.'

'Can you remember where exactly? It may have considerable bearing on this case,' urged Ravenscroft.

'Let me see. I should remember. Somewhere near the Lake District — something "Over Sands". Yes, that's it — Grange-Over-Sands — funny name, that's why I remember it. Grange-Over-Sands; a fashionable resort I believe. Not that I have ever been there of course. Not so fashionable or as important as Malvern obviously.'

'Have you ever heard from this Doctor Lambert since his departure?'

'No. Not a word, Inspector, in all these years. Interesting how one fails to keep in touch with people once they have left. I suppose that is where that saying comes from — "out of sight, out of mind".'

'So let me see, Reverend. There were six founders to the bank. Mr Chase has informed us that not one of the founders has ever drawn any kind of dividend. Why was that, sir?'

'I can see that you have been doing your homework, Inspector. When we founded the bank it was decided amongst ourselves that the profits would always be reinvested. We were a tontine you see.'

'A tontine. What's that?' asked Crabb, looking up from his notebook, a puzzled expression of his face.

'It's a financial agreement drawn up by a number of parties, the chief clause of which is that all the investment or funds, will all eventually go to the surviving member,' explained Ravenscroft. 'I know of one or two places in London, where properties have been built by the members of the tontine, and the ownership eventually falls to which ever member of the foundation outlives the others,' said Ravenscroft, leaning back in his chair.

'That is quite correct, Inspector. Each of the six of us put in an equal sum of money into the foundation, with the stipulation that whoever was the last to survive would inherit the bank.'

'Would it be correct to say, that in the days of the foundation, such investment was then of a modest sum, but that over the years the initial investment has grown considerably?' asked Ravenscroft.

'Yes, I suppose, it would be fair to say that,' replied Touchmore.

'And were you all of a similar age when the foundation was made?'

Touchmore thought for a moment or two, then replied, 'Yes, I suppose we were. One or two of us may have been a year or two older, or younger, whichever way you look at it, but generally speaking, yes, I believe we were all in our thirties.'

'So you each had an equal chance of surviving?' asked Crabb.

'That is rather an insensitive way of putting it, Constable,' reprimanded Touchmore.

'Then you and Doctor Lambert are the only two founders still alive?' asked Ravenscroft. 'Whichever one of you outlives the other, will inherit the bank?'

'Well, yes, I suppose we are the only two left, although I cannot say whether Doctor Lambert is still alive or not. I should perhaps say, Inspector, that our foundation was not quite so straightforward as you have suggested,' said Touchmore leaning forwards in his chair.

'Please explain, sir?' asked Ravenscroft.

'The tontine stipulated that the legacy, for want of a better word, could also be claimed by any surviving children of the six partners. That may sound a little involved I know, but we wanted to make sure that if any of us had children, and they survived, then they could inherit the bank.'

'Let me see if I have this correct, sir. If all of the six original members are dead, then the legacy can be claimed by any of their surviving children. But surely that would cause immense problems?' asked Ravenscroft somewhat bewildered.

'We saw the possibilities of that situation arising, so we stated that only the eldest surviving child of each of the

original six members could claim, — and not their descend-
ants or siblings — and that it would only go to whichever
child who survived above all others. That way the legacy
would grow for perhaps seventy or eighty years or more.'

'Thank you, Reverend, it is all becoming clear now,'
said Ravenscroft.

'It's as cloudy as a Malvern fog to me,' said Crabb.

'Pitzer died because he had no children to inherit.
Sommersby was killed because he had no children — and
Gladwyn, also because there were no children to come after
him. Whoever killed these three gentlemen must have been
more than aware of these facts,' said Ravenscroft.

'And, alas, in my case, although my son was alive at
the foundation, he died of a fever shortly afterwards, as I
previously explained to you,' offered Touchmore, a note of
sadness creeping into his voice.

'So after your own death, Reverend, that would leave
just Gastrux and Lambert?' said Ravenscroft.

'I suppose so, Inspector, although Gastrux was a bache-
lor at the time of his hunting accident.'

'So that just leaves Lambert,' said Crabb.

'That would seem to be the case,' replied Touchmore.

'Do you know whether Lambert had any children?'
asked Ravenscroft.

'I believe not. Certainly he was married at the time of
the foundation. Yes, come to think of it, when he left for
Grange his wife was heavily pregnant. I remember remarking
to him at the time that he should take good care of her on
the long journey.'

'So Lambert had a child, which means that there is only
yourself, and either Lambert or his heir, who are now the
surviving members of the tontine,' said Ravenscroft.

'Oh dear me, I had never thought of it, like that. Money
is such an unsettling thing.'

'Reverend, you have been more than helpful to us in
our investigations. I must warn you however that you could
be in grave danger. Whoever killed Pitzer, Sommersby and

Gladwyn, could also seek to kill you. We must take precautions. I will send a uniformed officer round shortly to accompany you at all times. Until then I would advise you not to be alone,' said Ravenscroft, adopting an urgent tone.

'Is that really necessary, Inspector?' asked Touchmore.

'I'm afraid so, sir, but rest assured it will only be a day or so. I am confident, that given the information you have just given us, we may shortly be able to make an arrest. Now, sir, I fancy that we have taken up too much of your time. Is there somewhere that you can go now, for the next hour or so, where you will not be alone, until my man can be with you?'

'I am due to take a service in the church in a few minutes,' said Touchmore.

'Good. We'll send the constable there. Shall we go together?'

'I need to finish these returns first, Inspector.'

'Nevertheless, sir, we would be a lot happier if you were to accompany us to the church. I cannot take the risk of leaving you here, sir, on your own,' said Ravenscroft, trying to sound as serious as he could.

'Very well, Inspector,' Touchmore sighed. 'I suppose the returns can wait a day longer.'

The three men made their way out of Touchmore's office and down the steps, where the cleric bade them farewell. The two policemen watched him cross over to the church.

'I believe now we have the reason for our murders. All three men were killed because they were members of the tontine, and because they had no one to follow on after them. Our killer clearly has his eyes on the vast fortunes of the Malvern and Worcestershire Bank,' said Ravenscroft.

'The Reverend Touchmore could be our killer. He would have a lot to gain if all the others were dead,' suggested Crabb.

'There is that possibility, but it is this Lambert that interests me. Touchmore stated that when Doctor Lambert left Malvern to take up a practice in Grange-Over-Sands, his wife was expecting a child. I wonder whether that child survived?' said Ravenscroft deep in thought. 'I think, Crabb, it is time that we laid a trap for our killer. Put it about the town that I am on the point of making an arrest, and that our killer has connections with the bank. Meanwhile I intend visiting many parts of the town making myself conspicuous with Pitzer's stick.'

'Yes, sir. I'll see to that straight away, and I'll arrange for that constable to be sent along to keep an eye Touchmore,' replied Crabb.

'Good. I think we shall have our killer by tomorrow evening.'

'How can you be so certain of that, sir?' asked Crabb, somewhat taken aback by this new certainty in his superior's manner.

'Because I know that Lambert's child is in Malvern — and that he has been here for some years now!'

CHAPTER TEN

After visiting the Telegraph Station and despatching a number of messages, Ravenscroft walked around the town, before returning yet again to the Malvern Library and Reading Rooms where he was greeted by the urbane Clifford.

'Twice in one day, Inspector,' remarked the librarian.

'I am in need of some of your excellent coffee, Mr Clifford,' said Ravenscroft.

'Of course, sir, if you would care to take a seat.'

Ravenscroft walked into the main room and busied himself examining a large map of the hills, which was hanging on one of the walls. With his finger, he traced the route that led from St Ann's Well, upwards higher onto the hills, making a mental remembrance of the many variations such a journey entailed. He wondered whether the librarian had discovered the whereabouts of the missing document, but somehow he doubted it. It was evident that whoever had murdered Pitzer, Sommersby and Gladwyn, had also managed to remove the foundation document, in order to cover his tracks. It was a pity that Clifford could not remember who might have taken the missing papers.

A few minutes later the librarian returned with the coffee. 'I see you have been studying the plan of the hills, Mr Ravenscroft.'

'There seem quite a number of paths on the hills.'

'That is so. The town has been fortunate, over the years, in having a number of benefactors who have created a number of new pathways along the sides of the hills.'

'I imagine there would be splendid views from the top of the highest hill.'

'There are indeed, exceedingly fine views. I have been fortunate, since my arrival here, to have climbed up to the summit on a number of occasions. You should do the same before you leave Mr Ravenscroft. You will not be disappointed.'

'I am sure I would not be.'

'I have made a further search of the storage room, but unfortunately I have not been able to locate the document. I can only apologise for such carelessness. I can only conclude that the document for which you were looking was removed during the time of my predecessor.'

'That is no longer a problem, Mr Clifford. I have spoken with the Reverend Touchmore who was one of the founders of the bank, and he was able to provide me with full details of the foundation in regard to the six partners,' said Ravenscroft, sipping his coffee.

'Most fortunate,' replied Clifford, giving a half smile.

'Yes, I must say that our investigations are going remarkably well. I am awaiting replies to several telegrams that I have just despatched, after which I am confident we will be able to make an arrest.'

'That is good news, Inspector. This has all been a terrible business for the town.'

'No one, Mr Clifford, can escape the law for ever,' remarked Ravenscroft.

'Indeed not. I wish you success with your endeavour.'

After finishing his coffee, Ravenscroft made his way back to the Tudor, where he was met by an anxious Stebbins in the entrance hall.

'Ah, there you are, Mr Ravenscroft. May I remind you that it will shortly be time for yer bath, sir.'

'I have no time, nor any need, of your bath today, Stebbins. In fact I do believe that I shall never have need of your bath ever again,' said Ravenscroft cheerfully.

'Does that mean you will soon be leaving us, Mr Ravenscroft?' came a voice from out of the inner office.

'It does indeed, Doctor Mountcourt.'

'I hear in the town that you intend shortly to make an arrest?' said Mountcourt, emerging from the office, carrying a large folder of medical notes.

'I do indeed, sir. I am just awaiting the replies to several of my telegraph enquiries,' replied Ravenscroft.

'I cannot recommend that you should leave us so soon, Mr Ravenscroft. You have not yet undergone the rest of your treatment,' said Mountcourt in his usual efficient dry manner.

'Duty calls on me in London, sir, once this case is concluded. I can assure you that your treatment has led to a great improvement in my condition, and that one day I will undoubtedly return to undergo further attention,' lied Ravenscroft, who had no intention of ever doing such a thing in the future, if it could be avoided.

'As you wish, sir, obviously we cannot compel our patients to remain with us to see out their courses of treatment. I will have your bill drawn up tomorrow,' said Mountcourt disappearing from view. Ravenscourt knew that he had lied unconvincingly, and that Mountcourt had known that he had no intention of ever returning to the Tudor to undergo the terrors of the Water Cure.

'Stebbins. I cannot quite face the rigours of the Tudor lunch today. Do you think you could find me something more appealing?' whispered Ravenscroft, lest Mountcourt should still be within hearing distance.

'Say no more, sir. I'll see what I can find in the kitchens. I believe there was a nice leg of mutton left over from last night's supper. I'll bring it to yer room, sir.'

'Good man, Stebbins. Here's a brand new sixpence for you.'

'Thank you, sir,' grinned the youth, accepting the coin, before whistling his way down to the kitchens.

Ravenscroft made his way back to his room and lay down on his bed until a knock at the door indicated that Stebbins had returned with his food.

After lunch Ravenscroft made his way down to the Priory churchyard. The grounds were empty of people, and he reclaimed the seat by the grave where he had spoken with the veiled lady. As he looked up at the exterior of the Malvern and Worcestershire Bank, his thoughts turned again to Whitechapel and he saw once more the black cloak running ahead of him down the narrow alleyway. Shortly he would be returning to that world. Such a lot had happened since his arrival in Malvern, and when he had first set foot in the town he could not have dreamt that such a tranquil and refined place would have involved him in the hunt for the murderer of three of its most prominent inhabitants. And it had all been caused by the foundation of the bank thirty years previous, and the desire of one person to stop at nothing until he or she had achieved complete control of the tontine.

The two worlds of Malvern and Whitechapel seemed so far apart that they appeared at first to have little in common, but the more he considered the matter the more he became aware of the similarities between the two places. It was money that lay beneath the surface. In Whitechapel it had been the lack of money that had caused many of its inhabitants to turn to crime: to steal, to sell their bodies, and even occasionally to kill, in order to acquire a few coins so that they might live. Whereas in Malvern, money ruled the town through its prosperous business men, with dark deeds done in closed rooms and near lonely hill tops in the quest for its acquisition.

'I find you alone with your thoughts, Mr Ravenscroft.'

She had slipped so quietly into the seat beside him, so much so, that he had not until then been aware of her presence in the church yard. He was surprised to discover that her face was not covered by her usual veil.

'I should leave,' he said, without thinking. 'You wish to be alone with your husband and son.'

'I knew that you would be here,' she replied placing her hand on his arm and indicating that he should stay. 'I believe that you will shortly be leaving the town Mr Ravenscroft.'

'That is correct, my dear lady.'

'So you have caught your murderer?'

'I hope to be making an arrest shortly.'

They sat in silence for some moments, looking out across the churchyard.

'It is so calm here, so peaceful. It will be almost a shame to leave it,' she said presently.

'You are leaving the town?' asked Ravenscroft.

'There comes a time when one must move on. There is unfinished business that must be resolved,' she said, looking sadly at the gravestone.

'Business that concerns your late husband and son?' asked Ravenscroft, before correcting himself. 'I'm sorry, I should not intrude on your personal family affairs.'

'Your veil of politeness seeks only to mask your inquisitive nature, Mr Ravenscroft,' she replied, allowing herself a brief smile.

'I suppose that is what comes of being a policeman.'

'And as such you must always be looking out for that which is corrupt in people?'

'Not at all, there are many good people out there. I also believe that there is some goodness in all of us,' said Ravenscroft.

'I do not think so, Inspector. There are some evil people who seek to condemn others to a hell which was not of their own making,' she replied, a touch of bitterness creeping into her voice.

'You have suffered such torments because of the deaths of your husband and son?' enquired Ravenscroft.

'I see your curiosity will not be satisfied. Very well then Mr Ravenscroft, you shall hear my story. I married my husband, here in Malvern, some six years ago. At first we were gloriously happy and content with one another, and I believed that life could be no better than that. Then my husband started to visit London for two or three days each month, always on business he said. At first I was content to accept the necessity of his absences from home, but after a year I came to resent the time we were apart from one another. Then I began to notice small changes in his behaviour. He became irritable and bad tempered; he developed a bad cough and would often pay visits to our doctors. I knew that something was amiss and encouraged him to tell me the cause of his ill humour and his sickness, but always he resisted. We drew apart and I began to fear for my marriage. My husband continued to visit London each month, and I noticed he was often ill upon his return. Then I found myself with child and hoped that the birth of our son would bring us closer together, that we could somehow repair the damage of our broken marriage, but in this I was mistaken. Even when my darling Mark was born three years ago, my husband made no attempt to take an interest in him. It was as though he was hiding some terrible secret, which he could not impart to me. In the year that followed my husband became seriously ill. I felt powerless to arrest his decline. I knew shortly that he would die. Then one night, two weeks before he died, he confessed everything. On his visits to London he had frequented the dens and alleyways of Whitechapel, where he had satisfied his manly urges with the women who plied their trade there. So strong had their allure been that he had returned there time and time again. It had become like a drug to him. The women had entrapped him. Then he had caught some dreadful disease from one of them. At first he had sought to hide it from me, and this had explained his difficult moods and his increasing coldness towards me. He had tried to break free from his temptation, Mr Ravenscroft, but he had found that he could not. He had hoped that by having a child he might be redeemed, but of course he was not. Shortly after he had told me all this my husband died, leaving my son and me alone in this world. At first I accepted his death and blamed his folly and his lust for his own down-fall — but then I learnt a harsher truth. My husband had already contracted the fatal illness before the conception of our child!'

She paused to turn away, leaving Ravenscroft feeling disturbed and uneasy, not knowing whether to issue words of comfort or condemnation.

'Shortly after the death of my husband, my child fell grievously ill and I knew then that he had inherited the illness that my husband had contracted in London. During the next few months I watched my boy, my darling sweet boy, die slowly and in agony — and I could do nothing to save him, nothing to relieve his pain and suffering. To watch a son slowly slip away from you, like that, is a terrible thing. So now you know my story, Mr Ravenscroft — and there they lie, side by side, my weak, foolish husband who had fallen under the spell of those terrible evil women and who had been unable to resist them, and my poor innocent child who died as a result of that evil.'

Ravenscroft had become aware of the increasing bitter-ness in her voice, and felt helpless in her presence, saying only, 'I am sorry' and knowing that it would not be enough. Suddenly she turned on him, a new anger replacing the agony in her voice.

'Sorry! That is all you can say, after all those whores have done to my family. I tell you, Mr Ravenscroft, that I will not rest until I have tracked them all down, every one of those evil women, and made them pay for the pain and suffering they have inflicted on my son!'

'My dear Mrs Kelly, I must urge restraint. I appreciate the way you feel now, but you cannot take the law into your own hands. I know that you have suffered this terrible loss, but whatever you do now will not bring your son back to life.'

'So you would have me forget?'

'No, my dear lady, you must never forget. I would ask only restraint, and to allow the passage of time to heal the pain,' he urged.

'We have spoken enough. I have said too much,' she announced, suddenly standing up. 'I wish you well in the apprehension of your killer.'

'Please. I . . . er . . . please, we should talk some more,' said Ravenscroft, taken aback by the abrupt termination of their conversation.

'The time for talking is past, Mr Ravenscroft. Good day to you,' she said beginning to walk away.

'But — will we ever meet again, Mrs Kelly?'

'I think so, Mr Ravenscroft, I believe so.'

'Then good day to you, Mrs Kelly,' called out Ravenscroft, as he watched the lone figure walk out of the churchyard. He felt drained and moved by the words he had just heard, and cursed the feeble responses he had uttered, as her story had unfolded. Since their first encounters on the train journey to Malvern and at the Well House, his desire to know more about the mysterious veiled widow had grown, but now that curiosity had finally been fulfilled, he felt no personal satisfaction at its outcome, but rather ashamed that he had intruded on another's grief.

He walked over to the grave and looked down once more at the inscription on the stone. Anthony Kelly and his young son were both now at peace but for their mother, the grief and bitterness continued. He wondered whether the anger she so keenly felt would ever be lessened with the passing of the years; and whether she would ever gain the peace and acceptance that had eluded her for so long.

* * *

Later that afternoon he met up with Crabb outside the Assembly Rooms.

'There you are, sir. I'm afraid we have a slight problem,' said Crabb, clearly agitated.

'Speak on Crabb.'

'Jenkins, the constable we assigned to keep an eye on Touchmore, has just returned to the station to report that the reverend gentleman seems to have given him the slip. Apparently Touchmore was conducting a service in the church and went into the vestry at the end. When he did not reappear after fifteen minutes Jenkins went to investigate and found that there was no one in there. Apparently there was another door that led outside, and so Touchmore must have decided to leave that way without telling anyone. I've asked Jenkins to check the usual places where the reverend might be.'

'Let us trust that no danger befalls him,' replied Ravenscroft.

'He could have gone into hiding, sir. If he were our killer, he may have decided to fly the nest before he was discovered, if you see what I mean, sir,' said Crabb. 'As the only surviving member of the original six members of your tontine, he stands to inherit a great deal of money.'

'We do not know that he is the last. There also remains Lambert, or at least the possibility of Lambert's child.'

'You said you believed that the child was here in Malvern, sir?'

'I am convinced of it. The child would now of course be in its late twenties.'

'Armitage and Clifford would both be of that age,' suggested Crabb.

'Indeed. But we must also consider the possibility that he or she may have aged their appearance, in order to mask their true identity,' replied Ravenscroft.

'That could suggest Troutbridge, sir.'

'Or even that old Lambert himself has made a return.'

'Surely someone would have recognised him?'

'Not after nearly thirty years, if he had changed his appearance,' said Ravenscroft.

'Then our killer could be practically anyone. You said a moment ago, sir, that the murderer could have been a woman?'

'Yes, Lambert's child could have been a girl.'

'Miss Armitage? She and her brother could both be children of Lambert?' suggested Crabb.

'I think not.'

'Then there is your veiled lady in black? You mentioned her the other day. Have you met with her again, sir?'

'I have indeed Crabb, but the information that she gave me was of a personal nature, and appears not to be related to this case.'

'Well then, we seem no further forward, if you don't mind me saying so, sir. Half the town could be included in our list of suspects.'

'No, I believe our killer is already well known to us. You have put it about the town that I am shortly to make an arrest?' asked Ravenscroft.

'Indeed, sir.'

'I have also let it be known that I am awaiting the replies from certain communications, before we close the case. It will not be long now Crabb before our murderer shows his, or her, final hand. Until then I suggest you go home to that charming wife of yours. I have taken you away from her for far too long.'

* * *

It was later that afternoon when Ravenscroft began to make his final ascent up the winding path to the well house of St Ann.

'Going out again, is we?' Stebbins had asked him as he had walked through the entrance hall of the Tudor.

'Indeed so, Stebbins, it's a grand afternoon for a walk up to the Beacon.'

'You wants to be careful up there, Mr Ravenscroft. We had a gent staying with us last year, who broke his leg and had to be carried down in the dark.'

'I assure you, Stebbins, that I have no intention of breaking a leg or falling over the edge in the darkness.'

As he had walked across the road, he had encountered Clifford. 'Good afternoon to you, Mr Ravenscroft.'

'Good afternoon to you, Mr Clifford.'

'Have you apprehended your murderer yet, Inspector?' the librarian had asked.

'Not yet, Mr Clifford, but we are expecting to make an arrest very soon.'

The librarian had given a polite nod, before making his way along the terrace.

Now pausing halfway up the path, Ravenscroft turned slightly to see whether another was following him, but could see no one and continued on his way.

Upon reaching the well house he found the attendant still in residence, but locking up the premises for the night. He exchanged a few words of greeting with the old woman, before seeking out the path at the rear of the property, which he knew would take him further up onto the higher reaches of the hills.

Fifteen minutes later he reached the upper path, which circled a large hill on the northern edge of the range and looked down to where the well house nestled in the cleft of the lower hills. It seemed so small and insignificant in the distance, sheltering from the elements and already in shadow. Ravenscroft wiped his brow, and wondered at his own agility and stamina in climbing so far in such a short time. Below him the tower of the Priory stood tall and firm, dominating the rest of the town. He saw the roads and the fields stretching out into the distance and thought he saw the edges of the town of Worcester at the horizon's edge to the north, and the meandering river on the plain on its way to Upton and Tewkesbury. The sun was beginning to set over the western side of the hills behind him, leaving vast areas of the near landscape in shadow as he looked down.

But he told himself that he had not climbed the hill, alone, and at this late hour of the afternoon, to marvel at the ancient lands before him. His eyes strained to see if he could see another following in his footsteps, but however hard he looked he could see no one. Ravenscroft sighed. Perhaps this had been a foolish venture after all, and he should retrace his steps back to the well house and the town, before that side of the hill was completely in shadow?

Then he looked along the path to his right, to where the great hill seemed to stare down on them all — and there in the distance he saw the small outline of a figure, and he knew that his quest would shortly be rewarded.

He walked for another minute, then paused, and thought he saw the other beginning to walk along the path in his direction.

Ravenscroft continued his walk, away from the figure, towards the slopes of the northern hill, not wishing to turn around, should his follower consider that he had been observed in so doing. As he quickened his pace he felt the beat of his heart becoming louder. He paused once more, and under the pretext of removing one item of his footwear to free an imaginary stone from its inside, he glanced over his shoulder quickly and saw that the figure had closed the distance between the two of them.

Swiftly replacing his boot, he continued with his journey. At this time of the early evening, when the paths were free from walkers, and the sun was setting, he began to feel that the quiet, eerie peace of the hills above him would suddenly overwhelm and engulf him. A man could fall to his death out here, he thought, or lie injured all night beneath the stars and no one would ever know of his plight and his loss. He drew his coat closer to him as he felt a cold shiver run down his back.

He walked faster now, knowing all the time that the other would be gaining upon him and that their meeting would be inevitable.

In the distance he could see the rock of the Ivy Scar coming into view. He increased his pace so that he might reach the seat near its summit in good time. He looked behind him and saw that the figure had stopped also, and was looking in his direction. Dressed entirely in black from head to toe, Ravenscroft was unable, however, to make out the features of his pursuer.

He gained the seat, near the edge of the rock, where the land fell away sharply, and stared out at the landscape below him, waiting for the other to join him — knowing that shortly he would be able to confirm everything he had suspected.

'Good evening to you, Mr Ravenscroft,' said the figure in the black cloak sitting down beside him.

Ravenscroft said nothing, as the other continued. 'A fine view up here, I think you would agree? So isolated, yet you feel you have the world at your feet. So much so, you feel you could achieve almost anything. You have done well, Mr Ravenscroft. I gather you have received the replies to your telegrams?'

'I did indeed receive these, late this afternoon' said Ravenscroft, reaching deep into his coat pocket, and taking out some sheets of folded paper.

'The first reply confirms that Charles Lambert was a medical practitioner in Grange-Over-Sands, for many years, until his death five years ago. The second confirms the birth of his child, a child who joined his father in the medical practice when it grew up, becoming in fact a partner in that same concern. When Charles Lambert died, the practice was sold, and his son who also went by the name of Charles Lambert, moved to Malvern where he changed his name — becoming the proprietor and chief medical officer of the Tudor Hydropathic Establishment! You did well Doctor Mountcourt — or should I say Doctor Lambert? — to conceal your identity, but not well enough.'

'I really must congratulate you on your fine detective work,' said Mountcourt, smiling. 'May I ask when it was you first suspected me?'

'As soon as I discovered the true significance of the walking sticks this morning, I recalled that other morning when we encountered each other outside St Ann's well. Your stick made a tapping sound on the path and I remember looking up and seeing the silver handle.'

'Yes, that was rather foolish and vain of me. I inherited the stick from my father, and as it was so fine, I could not resist using it.'

'Then there was the morning after my illness, when you were quite put out when you learnt that I was staying on at the Tudor, and in Malvern, to continue with my investigations into the case. You had hoped that there had been enough suspicion put on Old Penny to warrant an end to the matter. You were not very good at disguising your feelings, Doctor Lambert.'

'I see I have underestimated you, Inspector.'

'From my first-hand observations, I could also see that the Tudor had seen better days,' continued Ravenscroft. 'The premises must have been costing you a lot to run and maintain, and yet the half empty dining room and treatment rooms suggested that you had not been successful in attracting a sufficient wealthy clientele.'

'You are correct in your observations,' replied Mountcourt calmly.

'Tell me one thing. Did you come back to Malvern with the intention of removing the other members of the tontine or did the idea take root only once you had arrived here?' asked Ravenscroft.

'My father told me about the legacy of the tontine shortly before he died, and urged me to seek out my claim. When I heard that the Tudor was up for sale, I decided to return to Malvern and purchase the establishment, a rash act that was to prove costly for me. The first thing I did upon my arrival here was to visit the bank to see if I could find out more about the surviving founders of the tontine, but of course they knew nothing. Then I thought that perhaps the original papers had been lodged at the Library and Reading Rooms, so one day I went there to view them. It was an easy act to remove the original foundation document from the file while Clifford was attending to another client. Now that I knew who the other members of the tontine were, I was prepared at first to wait for each of them to die — they were after all quite elderly, and would be sure to die in the coming years. I also learnt that none of them had any surviving heirs, which made my own claim all the stronger.'

'But you found after a while that you could not wait?' interjected Ravenscroft.

'My debts at the Tudor were mounting. I had little funds available to improve the facilities and the clientele began to go elsewhere to the more fashionable establishments in the town. I was heavily mortgaged and knew that another few months would have seen the end of all my hopes,' continued Mountcourt in a dry matter-of-fact tone of voice. 'So I decided to kill Pitzer. I wrote him a letter saying that I had some important confidential news concerning the railway company, which might be of some financial benefit to him, but that I could not be seen conversing with him as I had interests in a rival concern. I knew that he could not resist such a meeting, being the greedy man that he was. I arranged for a boy from the town to deliver the letter, and then kept my rendezvous with Pitzer in his study. It was easy to pour the poison into his glass when he was not looking, but as he fell forwards, he dropped the glass on the floor and the maid called out. I was fearful that she might enter at any moment, so I only had time to pick up the glass and remove my letter before hastily leaving the room.'

'Leaving the door slightly ajar behind you, and not having time to rinse out the glass,' added Ravenscroft.

'I suppose you would have noticed that. If you had not been there that night, Ravenscroft, I would have succeeded in my plans. I knew that stupid man Gladwyn would have declared that Pitzer had died of a stroke, or some such like, and no one would have guessed that he had been poisoned — but then you had to interfere,' said Mountcourt, a note of annoyance creeping into his voice.

'Then you killed Sommersby,' said Ravenscroft.

'That was easy. All I had to do was to wait until all the pupils were engaged elsewhere and slip into the library from the quadrangle when he was alone. Yes, Inspector, I hit him on the head, and then pulled the bookcase over on top of him to make it look like an accident — but again, of course you were there on the scene to prove the case. You were in danger of becoming a nuisance, Inspector Ravenscroft! I resolved to lie low for a while and hope that Gladwyn and Touchmore would soon die — and that you would eventually become frustrated trying to solve the case and leave for London.'

'But then Gladwyn guessed the terrible truth and recognised you as the son of his former colleague,' suggested Ravenscroft.

'Right again, Inspector! I had become friendly with the old tramp, Penny, and could see how he could be useful to me. I instructed him to watch Gladwyn's house — yes, his eyesight was not as bad as everyone had supposed — and that was where he saw you and your assistant. I knew I had to act quickly before Gladwyn worked out who had killed Pitzer and Sommersby. I gave Old Penny instructions about how to make up a story about his dying wife, and how he was to lure Gladwyn out to the Raggedstone, where I could confront and kill him without others seeing — but then you arrived shortly on the scene and I had to hide in the undergrowth. I was so close to you I could hear every word you said. Is that not frustrating to learn now, Inspector? That you were within yards of catching your quarry! I had told Penny that he was to make his way back with all haste, to the old cave, where he was to hide until I could join him later. As you and your constable set off in pursuit of the old tramp, I was given enough time to make my way along the lower slopes of the hills, until I saw my opportunity to meet up with him.'

'Where you pushed him off the cliff top,' added Ravenscroft.

'Oh don't be so dramatic, Inspector! The man was a useless parasite anyway, a drain on society,' replied Mountcourt with a sneer. 'Then you fell ill and everyone thought that Penny had killed the three men. I knew I was safe — and that only Touchmore now stood between the tontine legacy and me. All I had to do then was to wait for you to leave, and dispose of Touchmore later in my own time. But then you changed your mind and decided to stay — damn you, Ravenscroft! But then my luck changed again, with the arrests of Armitage and Troutbridge. Perhaps you would be stupid enough to think that they had committed the murders! I should have known better. When I heard this morning that you had gone to the bank and were parading round with that stupid stick, I knew that it would only be a matter of time before you discovered the truth.'

'You could not expect that you could hide for ever? Everyone is answerable to the law,' said Ravenscroft.

'The law, my dear Inspector, what use is the law to us out here?' laughed Mountcourt. 'Why do you think I have confessed all this to you? You must have realised by now that I cannot possibly let you arrest me,' he said, standing up. 'No, the townsfolk of Malvern will wake up tomorrow morning to learn of yet another tragic accident. How the poor unfortunate police inspector had fallen to his death from the Ivy Scar Rock. The poor man was under a great deal of pressure to bring the murderer to book, they will say, and they will surmise that perhaps you really committed suicide rather than face the terrible truth that you were a pathetic failure.'

'You seem to have it all worked out,' answered Ravenscroft.

'Then in a month or two's time that idiot Touchmore will meet with a fatal accident. I haven't quite decided how he will meet his end. Something religious, I think. Maybe a loose step on the way up to the church tower, a piece of falling masonry — that would be poetic justice indeed. Then I will claim the tontine inheritance, and nothing will stand in my way!' said Mountcourt, becoming increasingly agitated, as he paced up and down.

'You are quite mad, Lambert!' said Ravenscroft.

'Mad!' snarled Mountcourt. 'You dare to call me mad! What I have done requires sheer genius. It is such a shame you won't be able to tell the world about your little adventure up here,' he said pulling on the handle of the walking stick. 'Quite a neat little addition I think you would agree. When my father had this stick made, he decided to have this fine blade fitted inside. I am so sorry Ravenscroft. You were such a worthy opponent, but you must know that after all that I have told you, that I cannot let you go,' he said brandishing the blade and advancing towards him.

'And you do not think, that I would have been so stupid as to have come up here alone,' said Ravenscroft, standing up and facing his opponent.

'Oh, my dear Inspector, it is futile for you to pretend. At this time of the evening the hills are quite deserted. You forget that I followed you up here from the well house up another path. There was no one behind either of us. There is no one that can come to you aid. It is all over with you, Ravenscroft.'

Ravenscroft took out a whistle from his pocket and gave three short blasts.

'You silly man,' laughed Mountcourt. 'No one will hear that down in the town. I'm sorry, but it really is the end for you!'

'Put down that blade or I will fire!' shouted the voice of Crabb.

Mountcourt paused, a look of anger enveloping his face.

'I knew, Mountcourt, that you would not resist the temptation to follow me. At this moment my constable has a loaded revolver pointing at your back. I also have three other police officers waiting behind the other side of the rock. I would advise you to lay down your blade as my constable instructs. It is all over now, Lambert, you have nowhere to go,' said Ravenscroft, drawing himself up to his full height.

'Damn you, Ravenscroft!' yelled Mountcourt, rushing towards Ravenscroft with a look of intense loathing. 'Damn you!'

'Crabb!' shouted Ravenscroft.

The shot rang out.

Mountcourt staggered forwards, clutching his chest and dropping the blade at Ravenscroft's feet.

'Quickly, grab him, men, before he goes over the edge,' yelled Crabb.

But it was too late, for as he fell, Mountcourt's feet slipped and with one last cry, he disappeared from view over the side of the rock.

'Are you alright, sir?' enquired Crabb as the men rushed forwards.

'I'm fine, thank you, Crabb. Quickly, grab Mountcourt!'

Ravenscroft and the men rushed to the edge of the rock and peered over the side. The body of Mountcourt could be seen dropping down the long slope of the hill, until a clump of trees in the distance appeared to halt its descent, finally hiding it from view.

'I don't think he will be bothering us again, sir,' said Crabb.

'I tell you one thing, Crabb. You're a damn fine shot! Thank God!'

CHAPTER ELEVEN

The following morning found Crabb and Ravenscroft standing on the crowded platform of Great Malvern station.

'Well, sir. I will be sorry to see you leave,' said Crabb, looking a little downhearted.

'Unfortunately, I have to report back for duty tomorrow, Crabb.'

'I guess you never did get to Brighton, sir. There is always next year. Thought you might like to know, the men recovered Mountcourt's body from the valley this morning.'

'He managed to escape the gallows in the end. That leaves the Reverend Touchmore as the only surviving member of the tontine,' said Ravenscroft. 'I wonder what he will do with all his inheritance.'

'Rumour has it that he will give some of it towards the restoration of the church.'

'Then at least some good may come out of all this. No doubt another buyer will come forward to purchase the Tudor and who knows? One day it may be restored to its former splendour. Well, it is time I boarded the train. It has been a pleasure working with you, Crabb. Should you ever decide that you would like to work in London, I would be more than happy to put in a good word for you,' said Ravenscroft shaking hands with his constable.

'That is uncommonly good of you, sir, but to tell you the truth, me and my Jennie quite like it here in Malvern. We reckon there could be nowhere finer, sir, to bring up children,' said Crabb opening the carriage door.

'Perhaps one day, we may have the opportunity to work together again, on some particularly baffling case, or other.'

'I would look forward to that, sir,' beamed Crabb.

'Give my best wishes to your wife.'

'I will, sir. Oh, that reminds me. Jennie and I were talking together last night, and we thought we would ask you, if you would kindly see your way, to being a godparent to our child, when it's born, like,' said Crabb somewhat awkwardly.

'My dear Tom, you do me a great honour! I will be more than delighted,' said Ravenscroft shaking the other's hand vigorously.

'That is uncommonly good of you, sir. Jennie will be well pleased. And what will you do on your return to London, sir?'

'Oh, I will go back to the dark alleyways of Whitechapel, where no doubt I will endeavour to apprehend a few more criminals, while attempting to keep as far away as possible from my superiors,' laughed Ravenscroft, boarding the train.

'Well, sir, if you should ever find yourself in Malvern again, you will always find a warm welcome awaits you in Westminster Road,' said Crabb slamming the door of the compartment to, as the guard blew his whistle.

'Thank you, Tom. I will certainly remember,' said Ravenscroft leaning out of the carriage window, as the train started to move forwards.

'And don't forget, sir, there is always a certain young lady in Ledbury, who would no doubt be more than pleased to see you, should you find yourself in the neighbourhood,' shouted Crabb.

'I won't forget,' smiled Ravenscroft, waving his hand at the decreasing figure of Crabb, as the train drew away from Great Malvern Station.

EPILOGUE

LONDON 1887

'London! Paddington! All Change!'

Ravenscroft awoke with a start — and realised that he had been asleep since the train had left Oxford.

His journey back to the capital had been uneventful, and as he had sat back in his seat, he had been surprised by how tired he had now become. Malvern had already become like a distant dream to him, so much so, that for a moment he had begun to wonder whether he had really been there at all. Perhaps Pitzer, Sommersby, Gladwyn and the old beggar were still alive, and Lambert still practicing in Grange-Over-Sands? Perhaps Lucy Armitage still sat in the tiny cottage in Ledbury, and her brother continued to look after the welfare of the inmates of Old Lechmere's Almshouses? Perhaps the events of the previous two weeks were still waiting to unfold, and he had yet to encounter the mysterious woman in black? But now, as people began to leave the train, he knew that the great City of London would be seeking to encompass him once more.

He stepped out onto the platform. After the peace and quiet of Malvern, the noise and bustle of the crowded terminus came as a rude shock to his system.

Carrying his suitcase in one hand, and his newspaper in the other, he made his way along the platform, rubbing shoulders with the other passengers, who were all busily engaged in going in the same direction. The reality of his present situation began to break suddenly over him, and he felt a sickly emptiness in the pit of his stomach. He knew he would now attempt to secure a cab from outside the station; a cab which would take him back to the grey dismal lodgings where he resided, overlooking the tree lined square in an unfashionable suburb of the capital. He knew that in the morning he would climb the stairs at the Yard, where he would report for duty. No doubt his superior would again reprimand him, before sending him back onto the streets — they were too short of officers to dismiss him from the force! Then the pattern of his life would be resumed, as it had before, and he would again seek out the vagrants, pickpockets and thieves from the darkened alleyways and dens of Whitechapel.

He made his way out of the station and onto the forecourt, where a large number of cabs stood waiting in the rain to transport the new arrivals to all four corners of the metropolis. He joined the line of prospective customers, as it shuffled forwards.

'Where to, Madam?' shouted out one of cabmen.

'Whitechapel!' came back the reply.

The sound of the woman's voice bought Ravenscroft to a sudden standstill, and he felt a cold shiver run down his spine.

Surely not? It could not be possible?

He looked upwards and saw a familiar, black veiled, figure climbing into the cab.

He pushed forwards, crying out, 'Mrs Kelly!' — but before he could reach the rank, the driver had cracked his whip, and the vehicle had driven away at high speed.

Ravenscroft stood watching the cab as it reached the end of the road — and for a brief moment thought its occupant had turned in his direction, and had raised her hand in a form of recognition — before it turned the corner and disappeared from view.

The events of the past few days seemed suddenly to crowd in on him. As the line of waiting customers surged forwards, he could feel his lungs tightening and his brow becoming wet with perspiration.

'Where to, guv'nor?'

'I'm sorry—' he mumbled, in a voice that seemed not like his own.

'Where do you want to go to?' shouted the cab driver again, in an irritable manner.

'Nowhere,' replied Ravenscroft.

'Then why are you wasting my time governor?'

'I don't know. I'm sorry,' he said walking away, hearing the driver cursing him from behind.

Ravenscroft made his way back into the station, and after a moment's thought, strode toward the ticket office.

'Can I help you, sir?' asked the clerk.

'When is the next train to Ledbury?' asked Ravenscroft.

'In about fifteen minutes, sir. Would you like a single, or a return?'

Ravenscroft thought for a moment.

'A single, please. That will be fine. A single to Ledbury.'

THE END

ALSO BY KERRY TOMBS

**INSPECTOR RAVENSCROFT DETECTIVE
MYSTERIES**
Book 1: THE MALVERN MURDERS
Book 2: THE WORCESTER WHISPERERS
Book 3: THE LEDBURY LAMPLIGHTERS

More from the Inspector Ravenscroft Detective Mysteries
series coming soon!

FREE KINDLE BOOKS